The Rise of Ferryn

—

Jessica Gadziala

Dedication

This one goes out to every reader and blogger
who spread the word and helped me get to where I am now.
You're my heroes.
You have my eternal gratitude.

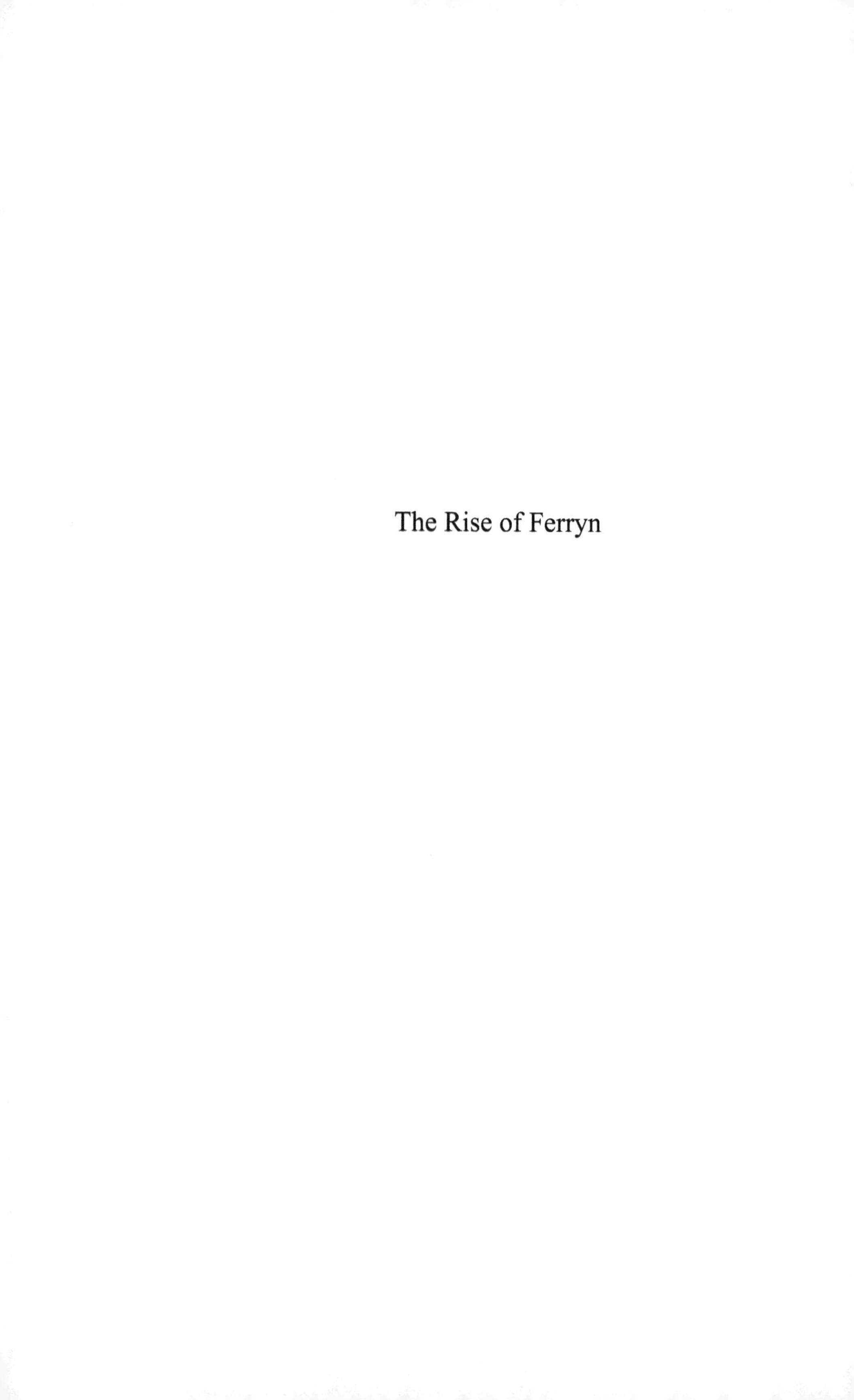

The Rise of Ferryn

One

Ferryn - Present Day

I could feel the little bones cracking in my hand.
Distal phalanx.
Middle phalanx.
Proximal phalanx.
There should have been pain.
Once upon a time, there had been. The searing, throbbing pain telling me one part of me was no longer attached to what it once had been connected to.
I remembered that sensation all too well. The way I would cradle my hand to my chest, my uninjured hand holding the wrist, trying to keep it still to prevent hurting it more.
Leaving my face open, unprotected. Inviting more pain.
The zygomatic.
Mandible.
Temporal.
I quickly learned to fight through it, to keep my guards up.

And my body slowly did what bodies do.
Hardened.
Strengthened.
Built a tolerance.
So that, eventually, the telltale crunch of my distal phalanx—fingertip—was met only with a twinge followed by welcome numbness.

I was going to be cripplingly arthritic by the time I hit forty. But there were some things in life worth doing, regardless of the consequence.

"Stop worrying about your goddamn manicure, and fight back."

Those were familiar words, old taunts, meant to strip away the girl I had once been. They no longer had the bite they once did. For years, my nails had been kept military short, prone to splitting, breaking, haloed over by often bloody cuticles thanks to a newfound bad habit of chewing them in tense moments alone.

Well, let's face it, all moments alone were tense moments. Silence was filled with the swirling abyss inside my head.

Nothing, nothing could drown out the screaming.
Or the memories.

I shook my hand once, throwing off the sting, before curling my fingers into a fist and lunging once again.

Manicures were something I left in the past.
In another time.
Another life.

Along with family, friends, a comfortable bed, bones that didn't crack, and muscles that didn't scream first thing in the morning.
Birthdays.
Christmases.
Love.
Light.
Warmth.

This world was one of inky darkness, an atmospheric gloom reminiscent of gothic fiction, something you would never think could exist in modern times.

Exist it did, though. And it was the place I had learned to call, if not home, then some sort of headquarters. A place I could find a small bit of comfort in, where I could rest my head, train my body, steel my mind, and slough off all the layers of the girl I used to be—someone I no longer recognized, a too-soft soul that could never survive in this environment.

That said, not much could or did.

Survive here.

The two of us did, but just barely.

Hidden away deep in the woods under trees half-heartedly holding onto their lives, gray bark and leafless limbs, maybe losing their will to grow where there was no sun to feel warming their appendages, no wind to feel blowing through them.

Everything was dark. The sun dared not shine here for too long, always chased away by storm clouds and violent rains. The kind that made small lakes all around, that sank in through your layers of clothes if you had to walk out in it for more than a moment or two, that made the walls and floors and fabrics inside constantly feel damp. I swear I hadn't felt utterly dry in eight years. I was sure I no longer fully grasped the concept.

It wasn't even all that far from where I had grown up—just an eight-hour drive—one state away, really.

It may as well have been on another planet.

This land was foreign to me, so different than the populated area I had been raised in, full of familiar places, comforting sights, bright sun, oppressively cheerful summers, and moody only for a few weeks in the fall.

But it was okay.

I only missed it in a nostalgic sort of way, knowing it was a place for the old Ferryn—young and rebellious, a little self-centered, a little vain, a lot more naive than she really should have been. Made that way, thanks to being raised in the protective embrace of a biker gang and all the badass men and women who flocked around it.

It wasn't, though, a place where I could picture this newer version of myself. Many times, I tried. There were more nights than I cared to think of where grief and defeat and hopelessness wrapped me up in their spindly arms, squeezing a bit too tight, making almost everything within me beg to flee, to get away from it all, to say fuck it to my plans, to my mission. To run, go back to that old life, those old people, fall at their feet, beg them to forgive me for what I had done to them. *All for nothing.*

It would be for nothing if I gave up.

Even when what was left of my soul cried desperately to head back there, I simply couldn't picture it. This version of me—older, harder, colder—walking down the streets of Navesink Bank, a black cloud following me around.. yeah, no. I couldn't see it. Even though I always knew it was going to happen.

How could someone even do it? I wouldn't be the first person to have to go back to my old life as a new person, who would need to reintroduce myself to people who had once known me so well, have to watch the confusion—and, let's face it, disappointment—at this new version of me, so wholly different from the image of me they had in their minds.

A sharp whack to the backs of my legs jarred me back to the present just in time to brace my fall, prevent me from whacking my face against the merciless concrete. There was a laughably thin mat covering it, deep charcoal stained deeper in spots by old blood. Mostly my own. Though I did occasionally manage to get a lucky shot or two in.

Sucking in a breath, I threw my weight, rolling onto my back, and staring up at my attacker.

"You're not focusing. Stop daydreaming about makeup and party dresses, and fucking fight back."

His voice was one that boomed even if he didn't necessarily raise it, the kind that managed to bounce off the walls and reverberate into your chest, vibrating through your ribcage. Even after all these years, it didn't lose the edge it always had for me. I still often had to fight the urge to do his bidding the instant he spoke to me simply because everything about his voice demanded compliance. *Immediate* compliance.

A snort bubbled up and burst out—a low, sarcastic sound.

Makeup and party dresses.

I hadn't even seen a tube of lipstick in the better part of a decade. The thought of a party dress made my lip curl.

"I think you know more about makeup than I do at this point," I told him, curling upward, hugging my knees to my chest for a moment, finger poking through a hole in the knee of my black yoga pants, running a fingertip over a crisscross of scars found on the skin peeking through. I didn't even remember what caused them. Or when I had gotten them. Though, judging by the amount of color fade, they were old ones. Hell, they may have even been from my old life, from my reckless days of climbing and falling out of trees, giving my mother a mild heart attack.

"We've only been at this an hour, kid. You have only landed two punches," he reminded me, turning on his heel, stalking over to the side of the room, grabbing a bottle of water, leaving his broad back to me.

Once upon a time, that would be all that I would see. A man's back. A tall, wide, strong man's back.

Now, though, I saw the half a dozen ways I could attack from behind. I saw the slight lean to the right that said he favored his left knee when it was cold and wet. Which meant most of the time. I saw the rise and fall of his breath, annoyingly not winded while my chest rose and fell much more dramatically, despite being slimmer.

Though that was likely because this beast of a man took a two and a half hour run every single morning while I grumbled at my pillow, asking it to be softer and more supportive, and all the while it rolled its eyes at my neediness.

What can I say, cardio had never been my favorite thing. Even if I understood how important stamina was in a fight. I cursed through the run he dragged me on with him twice a week. At half his speed. For half the time.

"You're leaving," he said, turning back, dark eyes pinning me, daring me to try to lie to him. I'd never even tried. But everything about him said that you shouldn't even think about doing so.

"What?" I asked, head jerking back, brows drawing together.

"You're leaving."

He was not a man of many words. To him, the fewer the better. Luckily, I was raised around someone else much like him. I was used to short, clipped sentences and long looks that often said more than words could.

"I never said I was leaving."

"You're growing your hair out," he observed, jerking his chin toward my head.

My hand rose instinctively, feeling the still somewhat foreign feel of short-cropped hair up the sides of my head to where it grew longer on top.

When I had shown up here, it had been with a newly buzzed head. Gone were the long, shiny, midnight locks I had all my life. I wanted to look like a woman on a mission. Because that was exactly what I was. Over the years, it made the most sense to simply keep buzzing it. Long hair got in the way. It was a hindrance in a fight. It could be used against you.

I wasn't even sure how long ago it was that I stopped buzzing the whole head, leaving it long on top, raising the blade a bit down the sides and back.

It hadn't been a conscious decision as far as I could tell. It was something I did on autopilot. Like brushing my teeth. Like taking inventory of my new cuts and bruises when I got changed for the day.

For a while, I had started to inwardly praise my powerful observation abilities. Clearly, that had been premature if I missed something so big in my own daily life.

He noticed.

Of course he did.

He noticed everything.

It was part of what made him so dangerous.

"Don't look like a prepubescent boy anymore," he added, making me shoot small eyes at him.

"Gee, thanks."

Sixteen-year-old me would have been very disappointed in how I turned out. She'd always been secretly—or not so secretly—hoping her boobs would show up one day. They never did. I was almost board-flat. Actually, probably even smaller than I had been eight years before. Constant workouts could do that to a woman. And, well, being utterly devoid of womanly softness worked in my favor in more ways than one.

"So, you're leaving."

"I..." I couldn't seem to find the words to deny it. Or confirm. For the first time in a long time, there was no certainty to be found, no clearly defined routine, no endless schedule of grueling workouts, and snatches of uneasy sleep. "I don't know," I admitted.

"What is there to go back to?"

On the surface, that was a stupid question. While he and I, well, we had spent many years side-by-side, we had never sat around and had heart-to-hearts. Neither of us were even entirely sure we had such things anymore. We didn't bare our souls, knowing they were full of ghosts and demons and the kind of rage that boiled, threatened to sear straight through vein, tendon, muscle, fat, and bone, that could burn you up entirely.

We weren't the sharing sort.

But he knew me before I even showed up.

He was aware of where I came from.

What I left behind.

An outlaw biker dad, the best mom in the world, two little brothers who likely weren't so little anymore, aunts, uncles, friends, my crush, a life.

He knew they were there to go back to.

But I knew *him* well enough to understand that he wasn't asking about that. He was asking me if there was enough of me, of the daughter, the sister, the niece, the friend left. If they would even recognize me. If they would want to.

Because, many many years ago, he had stood where I was standing; he needed to ask himself the same thing.

The answer, for him, was no.

No.

There was not enough of the old him left anymore. And, what's more, what was left was something he knew they could never accept, that he would not be so selfish as to expect them to even try, to pretend, to lie to his face.

He'd walked away.

And when he had walked away, he stayed away.

Maybe he had expected me to do the same.

Maybe a part of me wondered if I would follow in his footsteps.

It had been easy in those first few, hard years to picture myself going back, throwing my arms around all of them, apologizing, asking them to understand, to take me back.

But as things changed, as I changed, as this mission of mine became bigger than myself, it got harder to imagine them wanting to embrace me. And that I could even accept that from them anymore.

I cut people when they got too close.

That's what I did.

And the thought of cutting any of them, well, that was the kind of shit that kept me awake at night, staring at the cracks on the ceiling, feeling the spider web effect of them in my soul as well.

No matter which way you looked at it, the decision would be selfish, wouldn't it?

To stay away, to keep them wondering, to leave them always feeling like something was missing.

Or to go back, and to *prove* to them that something was missing. The girl they had loved and raised. She was gone. Long, long gone. I wore her shell, but had been hollowed out, filled with things I never wanted them to know existed, never wanted them to see. And then, what? Ask them to try to accept this person?

It was selfish to stay gone.

But it was just as selfish to go back.

In the end, it came down to one truth.

"I promised my mother I would be back one day," I confessed.

I wrote her letters. Every single week, I sat down, found something to write about, took a trip out of our little wooded compound, traveled far and wide to mail it out because I knew that my family had the power of tracking me down if I simply dropped it in the closest mailbox. Once, in a really low moment, in a really sad place in my heart and mind, I had signed off promising that I would be home one day.

Long before that girl broke and shattered and had to be rebuilt.

But if there was one thing my father drilled into me as a kid, it was to be impeccable with my word, to stand behind my promises, to be trustworthy.

I had to go back.

No matter what I went back to.

No matter the anger, the grief, the resentment, the confusion.

I had to go back.

The question was simply when.

A week, a year, five? I had no idea.

"What about the mission?" he asked, making my head snap up.

"The mission is the mission. It has nothing to do with my family."

"You go back, they become your focus."

"No," I told him, gaining my feet, rolling my neck, feeling the satisfying crack. "Nothing will ever change the mission," I told him.

Then I lunged.

If he was looking for a fight, if he wanted to get me to focus, he knew my trigger, and he knew it was set to hair.

The mission.

It was all there was for me.

Eight years.

Eight years of my life dedicated to it.

I ripped the girl I had been apart at the seams, rebuilt her with stronger materials, set fire to her burning rage, showed her that as ugly as she may have once thought it was, it was infinitely worse. That demons wore the faces of men in this world. And that someone needed to send them on back to hell.

I killed myself to be reborn into the body and mind and soul of someone who could do what needed to be done.

I didn't do all of that just to shrug it off like a sweater that no longer fit right, to go back to my old life, and be that old person.

It wasn't possible.

I was too far gone.

Even if I wanted to, it wasn't an option anymore.

This was who I was.

As ugly as it was.

And this was what I did.

Righteous, but wicked in its own way.

I had finally succeeded in becoming what I told myself I needed to be over eight years before.

A weapon.

I was a weapon.

And the mission was to cut down anyone who dared believe they could get away with their evil, who thought there was nothing to fear.

There was.

Me.

I wanted to show them all that they should be piss-themselves fucking scared of me.

That was the mission.

And I took it very, very seriously.

Nothing and no one would take it away from me.

Not even those who wore the faces of family and had the best of intentions.

—

Two weeks later, it happened.

Something I—and he—had previously thought impossible.

I beat him.

I bested my teacher.

We both sat there in strained silence, sweat soaking through our clothes, breathing ragged, bodies exhausted, aching, minds completely shocked.

"Now," he said, nodding at me.

"Now what?" I asked, sucking in a greedy breath.

"Now you go home."

If there was any emotion in him about me leaving, he showed none as he pushed up off the floor, swiping the blood from under his nose with the back of his arm, walking out of the building into the steadily falling rain.

Even as nerves swarmed my system, I knew he was right.

It was time.

I was going back to Navesink Bank.

I was going home.
To what, I had no idea.
But I was about to find out.

Two

- Eight Years Before -

What was she doing?

Girls like her—privileged, loved, happy girls—didn't run away from home.

That said, girls like her—raised under the watchful eye of an entire outlaw biker gang and having aunts that owned martial arts studios and ran a sort of paramilitary camp—didn't often find themselves kidnapped, tormented, left to save themselves, leaving them a raw, open wound.

Girls like her didn't get shown the ugliness of the world at such a young age, get thrown into a situation that forced them to use the self-defense they'd learned growing up in a real life-or-death situation, trying to save another sixteen-year-old girl so traumatized that she couldn't even fight back if she wanted to.

Girls like her weren't locked in basements by human traffickers. Girls like her weren't forced to live with the promise of rape and torture. Girls like her weren't made to watch the aftermath of other girls like her being tossed down on the floor, body and mind broken from such abuse.

And girls like her definitely didn't find out that it was all part of some twisted power play amongst a family that they had known and loved, and the woman who turned out to be her grandmother. A woman so wicked, so evil, so vile that she could even imagine kidnapping and traumatizing their only granddaughter. Someone with such a black soul that she could gleefully traffick *other* women just for profit.

Girls like her didn't fight grown men full of bad intentions with the tops of toilet tanks.

Girls like her didn't raise a gun, aim, and shoot.

Girls like her didn't take lives.

Girls like her didn't kill their own grandmothers.

But, well, Ferryn wasn't even sure what a *girl like her* was anymore.

All she knew as she made her way out of Navesink Bank was that she wasn't the girl she was when she had been thrown in a trunk and ripped away from the life she had always known.

Everything had changed.

Not just because of the days of fear and hunger and cold and uncertainty, but because of the things she had discovered about the world. About the ugliness to be found there. About how many girls and women were defenseless. About how many men—and women—decided to take advantage of that.

As she ran off, the only thing that seemed to permeate through the swirling thoughts in her head was that something had to be done. Someone had to help.

She knew, also, even as the brambles bit at her feet, ripping them open across the forest floor, that everyone says something should be done. And no one ever does anything.

The law had its limits.

The criminals knew that.

It just made them better at it.

It made it harder to find them, to stop them.

So many news stories that had been background noise to the seemingly pressing concerns of teenage life suddenly came rushing back to her, the memory of them blocking out the wind through the trees, the sounds of her loved ones calling her name.

News stories about how rape victims end up in jail for killing their attackers. About how rapists get a few months in jail or simply probation and a stern, "Bad boy, don't do that again!" from the judge. About girls—especially girls from inner cities, children of illegal immigrants, or ones from foster care—going missing, never to be heard from again. Likely thrown on ships, taken overseas, drugged, used by men for money over and over and over again for years. Because these traffickers knew they would get away with it, that the news would let the stories die, that the families couldn't afford to fight, that some had no families at all.

And those were just the ones that were reported.

Who knew how many runaways ended up in the grips of traffickers.

Who knew how many women and children were simply never missed?

The numbers, when she made herself think about it, were staggering.

She'd been informed of most of this before, of course. Her aunts—most especially her Aunt Lo who was the badass leader of a paramilitary camp known as Hailstorm who, on occasion, carried out some good, old-fashioned vigilante justice simply because it was the right thing to do—had often tried to start that conversation with her. Discussions full of statistics that had gone in one ear and out the other.

Or so she thought.

Because as she got on the bus and watched her hometown slip away from her, they came rushing back.

An estimated four million people were victims of sex trafficking in the world.

Ninety percent were women and girls.

It was a hundred-and-fifty *billion*-dollar business worldwide.

And it was on the rise.

While prosecutions in all regions—including the US—were on the decline.

Someone was dropping the ball.

And no one was stooping down to pick it up again.

Somehow, while she had been able to feel horror at that fact before yet still move on with her life, now, the knowledge, the firsthand knowledge, was too horrific to avoid. She felt crippled by it. It was all she could think about. All those people stuck in places like she had been stuck in, scared of the things she had been scared of, hoping someone would come to save them. And then no one did.

It was unconscionable.

She couldn't let it stand.

Ferryn might have been young, but she wasn't naive. She knew that a sixteen-year-old girl knew nothing about working on such a huge issue. Even if she did have over a decade of mixed martial arts in her back pocket. She also knew that if she had done what any normal, well-adjusted girl would have done and gone home, that she wouldn't have been able to help, that no one would have let her, that they would coddle her and reminded her she was safe. Even if millions of others weren't.

Eventually, she knew she would have fallen back into herself, would have let the knowledge, let the statistics, the ugly realities of the world once again become background noise.

Which was why she had to go.

She had to.

She had to become someone who could do something about it.

She had to help.

In her mind, she could hear her loved ones trying to remind her that she was just one person, that she could only do so much, that there were experts in the world to help. Or even that, if she wanted to help, she could turn to her Aunt Lo and her team at Hailstorm to help her do something.

From afar.

See, she knew that was the only part they would ever let her have.

A face behind a desk.

Someone chasing down virtual leads.

Again, after some time, it would be enough for her.

Life would come rushing in, stealing her focus, smoothing the edges of her trauma.

She didn't want smooth edges.

She wanted to be sharp enough to cut anyone who got near.

She wanted to rip men like the men who had sneered at her in a basement to shreds. She wanted to bathe in their blood. She wanted to make it so that other girls could go home, could be embraced, could get their edges smoothed, could recover.

She knew that—given enough time, given enough guidance, given enough hard work—she could be the one to make that happen.

And that the only way she could accomplish any of that was to leave.

Leave Navesink Bank.

Her friends.

Her heart-swelling crush.

And her family.

That's not to say it was an easy choice.

What sixteen-year-old girl wants to leave everything good and warm and safe behind to pursue a life of hard and ugly and dangerous?

She cried through several of her bus stops.

She ignored the curious eyes of strangers, the occasional question if she needed help.

She did. Of course she did. But not in the way they were offering.

Something deep inside Ferryn understood that the only way she could truly help herself was to help others who weren't as fortunate as she was, who didn't get away before it was too late.

She didn't *want* to do it.

Yet she *had* to do it.

Given enough time, she hoped to hell she could find a way to explain all of it to her family.

She hated the idea of leaving them behind, of them worrying about her, or them moving on without her.

But she knew it was the only way.

They had all been good teachers to her. Each and every one of her aunts and uncles who had taught her their specific form of martial arts. Krav Maga. Systema. Taekwondo. Street. Sambo. Kendo. LINE. MCMAP.

They hadn't gone light on her.

They had pushed her to her limits. Even over them at times. Just so they knew she could handle herself in a sticky situation.

And it had worked.

But only just barely.

Ferryn knew that she was one extra man or one bad move away from failing, that she didn't have what it would take, that she was still at a disadvantage.

Because while her loved ones would push her, they wouldn't break her.

She needed to be broken.

She needed to know she could live through that, could keep fighting, could become the victor.

It wouldn't be easy.

Or fast.

But she knew that was the plan.

And she even knew where she was going.

See, her Aunt Lo—well, she collected people. People with skills. People who could offer her team something. Hailstorm did a lot of things. A lot of illegal things. And they got paid well for it. But as the years went on, Aunt Lo seemed to take even more pride in finding the damaged people, bringing them in, helping them adjust. She especially did so with many battle-scarred ex-military men and women. The ones who couldn't seem to acclimate to normal life again. The ones who ran away from their families. The ones who could barely function. She found them, brought them in, gave them a safe space. And they, in turn, helped out when they could; they used their special skills.

It was rare that her aunt found someone that she couldn't help.

But there were some.

Men and women like Case File: 34691.

Ones that were so damaged, so fucked up—they were bent in such a way—that they were nearly unrecognizable as humans anymore. The kind of people whom women and children and grown men alike shrank away from on the street, crossed the road to avoid.

They could never be brought in, retrained, reprogrammed.

There was no way to reprogram men like 34691.

Their entire source code was corrupted.

Ferryn remembered hearing her aunt talk to her next-in-command about 34691. About what had happened when the small team she sent out tracked him down, got close to him.

Apparently, what had happened was complete and utter decimation.

As in, they were lucky to leave with their lives.

Their pride? Yeah, that had to stay behind.

Along with a lot of their blood.

And maybe a tooth or two.

This was a team of three large men and a woman.

And they'd all been taken down by this one man.

At one time.

Well, we are going to leave him alone from now on, her Aunt Lo had declared, shaking her head before handing Ferryn the file to go put in the cabinet.

Ferryn, well, she'd always been a bit nosy. She liked to say she was a sponge for any and all information. And that was true to a point. But she was also nosy. You could ask her mother who had learned years before to hide any and all presents in a storage unit two towns over, then had to bury the key for said storage unit because her daughter was too damn nosy for her own good.

So Ferryn had brought the file to the file room, to the file cabinet. Where she had promptly propped it open on an open file drawer and read through it.

34691.

Also known as Holden Ryker. The most badass of names, if you asked her. And she was always a big fan of unique names.

The file itself had little tidbits of information from back in Holden's military days. He hit the service the week of his eighteenth birthday, went in, and seemingly disappeared.

Black Ops was scribbled next to that.

Ferryn was pretty sure at that point that she knew enough about the military to understand some of the very unsavory things that went down in those types of operations. And the kind of people it took to be able to make a living carrying out those orders.

There were various articles pinned in the file, work of the hackers or researchers at Hailstorm, people who had seemed to trace Holden's footsteps all around the globe, pinning certain events on him. Educated guesses, surely, because there was no way one man could do as much damage as the articles suggested.

Of course, she had been very, very naive then.

In those days back before she met him.

She remembered seeing his address as some place in upstate New York, only cataloging that to memory because she thought it was such an odd place for a man like him. Then she had put the file away. And had promptly forgotten all about him.

Until she was on the bus ride away from her old life, heading to a new, uncertain one, knowing she would need a teacher for it.

The best one she could find.

The hardest one she could find.

Then there his file was in her mind, clear as the day at least a year before.

34691.

Holden Ryker.

Suddenly, she was certain there had been no guesswork associated with his file, that every single one of those stories and news articles pinned there were there for a reason, that this man actually was that impressive.

And if he was, well, then he would make a pretty great teacher, wouldn't he?

Adrenaline skittered across each nerve ending when she finally made the trek up the hill in the deepest part of a small forest, sure someone in town had been screwing with her because there seemed to be no actual sign of human life in this area at all.

The rain had soaked through her clothes, making them hang heavy, each step feeling more arduous than it should have. Her newly buzzed head felt a lot colder than she could have anticipated, making her momentarily regret the decision to make her best friend buzz it all off before she headed out of town with only a couple possessions and a few hundred dollars to her name.

She'd all but given up hope, half ready to turn around and start the long trip back home, when she'd seen a puff of smoke about half a mile off in the distance.

Smoke could mean a chimney or a grill.

Oh, God, a grill.

She was so hungry.

And tired.

And in pain.

She just needed to get somewhere, eat, and pass out for ten or twelve hours.

At that point, she didn't even care if it wasn't Holden. Anyone with a spare corner she could sleep in and some old porridge she could eat would do. She wasn't even entirely sure what porridge was, but she was hungry enough to find out firsthand.

"Leave."

The voice was more animal than human, she was sure.

As she started to turn, a part of her was maybe even worried she was so exhausted that she was starting to hallucinate a bit.

But then she found her nerve, turned, and there he was.

34691.

Holden Ryker.

The only picture she'd seen of him—the only one that had been in the file—had been of him in full uniform at eighteen years old. Still a strong-looking guy, but nothing like the man in front of her.

This man was a giant. The kind of big that dwarfed all the men she'd grown up around. And not one of them could be called anything less than huge. But this man was a behemoth. They'd likely used him to model the Hulk after.

He was easily six and a half feet, nearly as wide as he was tall with tree limbs for thighs and linebacker shoulders. His head was shaved. His tanned skin deeply scarred up and down his arms and across the backs of his hands. If she wasn't mistaken, there was a nasty one across the front of his throat. But maybe that was just a trick of the light.

This was a man a full-grown grizzly bear would shy away from. A moose would shy away from. A *Chihuahua* would shy away from. And everyone knew the latter thought they were the most fearsome creatures on the planet Earth.

"H... Hi," she said, choking a bit on her own spit to get the word out as he stood there, towering over her, everything about him seeming just barely able to contain some otherworldly rage.

"You're lost," he declared, cutting off anything she had maybe been about to say. You know, if she could find a way to make her mouth and brain and vocal cords work in unison with those deep eyes of his staring her down much like prey.

"I'm not," she insisted, finding her voice, even if it did sound croaking and awkward even to her own ears.

"You're lost," he insisted once again, voice somehow even gruffer than before, something she wouldn't have thought possible before she heard it.

Holden

Holden, not used to strangers, suspicious of them, fearful *for* them, moved forward, pressing a hand down on the girl's shoulder, turning and pushing her back toward the way she'd come. "That way is the road," he added, brushing past her, mind set on going back to the house, making something to eat, trying to catch some sleep before it got dark again.

"Holden Ryker," the girl's voice rang out, making his feet pause. A deep sigh pushed out of his chest, making his shoulders slump a bit before turning.

"Who is asking?"

"My name is Ferryn."

"Means nothing to me."

"Well, no. But my dad might. Or my aunt."

"Ain't getting any younger here, kid," he growled, finding himself more intrigued than he should have been that this girl didn't cower away from him like most would. Like most did.

She was a *girl*, too. There was no doubt about that. Still had a couple years left before she could even resemble an adult. Tall, skinny, with striking gray eyes and a buzzed head. What girl her age buzzed their head? And sought out men like him?

"My dad is Reign. He is the president of The Henchmen. In Navesink Bank. My aunt is named Lo..." she babbled out the names, but nothing was clicking. "She runs Hailstorm," she added.

Hailstorm.

That did ring a bell.

A paramilitary survivalist sort of organization that was full of men and women much like him, people that had been rehabilitated, people whose skills could be used for hire.

The leader, Lo, had set her sights on him at some point. Judging by her weird fetish for collecting people with skills, he wasn't exactly surprised to find he'd landed on her radar.

He'd quickly put an end to her pestering when her team showed up uninvited one day. He hadn't heard a word from them since.

But he was pretty sure they weren't farming out their dirty work to some slip of a teenage girl.

He could kill her with one blow.

He wouldn't.

Or hoped he wouldn't.

But he could.

Surely, Hailstorm knew that.

Why, then, would she possibly be there?

"And?" he asked, brow arching up.

"And. Ah. Well, I need you."

"For what?"

"So this doesn't happen again," she said, gesturing to her face, drawing his attention to the dark marks he'd missed on his first inspection, her face shaded by the trees.

Then, though, with the sky open above her, there was no mistaking the faded greens and yellows of bruises on her delicate face. His gaze moved downward, looking for any other injuries.

Her wrists were worn raw.

He knew those marks.

Bindings.

Someone had bound her too tight, or she had fought like hell to get out of them. Judging by the stubborn set to her jaw, he figured he would put his money on the latter.

Further down, there looked to be white gauze bandages peeking out of her shoes. Like her feet were wrapped. Wrapped feet meant busted soles. Barefoot running, he figured, not torture like he'd seen, he'd endured, he'd inflicted.

She was the right age for it. Pretty too. Which wasn't necessary. But it jacked the price up.

Judging by the current criminal climate, he figured she'd somehow escaped an abduction or an imprisonment, got herself free from traffickers of some sort.

"Was it bad?" he asked, spit tasting acidic. It was like swallowing back battery acid. It burned all the way down.

He'd lived an ugly fucking life.

He'd seen vile things.

He'd *done* many unforgivable things.

But he'd never put his hands on a woman who didn't want it.

It was one of the few crimes he didn't feel like a hypocrite for condemning with every fiber of his being.

"It wasn't great," she said, rolling her eyes with all the snark of a teenager. "It was, it was a weird situation. Have you heard of V? That was what she went by."

"Trafficker." Back in the day, he recalled. Before she fell off the face of the Earth.

"Yeah, well, apparently, she was my grandma. And she wasn't dead like I thought. She was alive and hidden away.

Until she wasn't anymore. And she took me and threw me in a basement with these other girls."

Her eyes went dark at that.

Bad memories.

He knew those all too well.

Just as quickly as the pain was there, though, it was gone. It was gone and in its place was rage. The kind that boiled your insides, burned holes in your stomach lining.

That was another thing he knew far too well.

It was also much more useful.

"Tough break, kid," he told her because the situation warranted it. He didn't have a lot of sympathy to spare, but he could offer her a small drop of it, he figured. "Go home to your biker daddy and your aunt. You got no business here."

"I need your help."

"I've never been accused of being altruistic, kid."

"I don't need, you know, money or anything."

"What do you think you need then?"

"I need you to train me to be like you."

"You can't," he declared, tone hollow.

"Well, I know I can't be as strong as you. But you can teach me to be as good. Even without your strength, with your training, I could still best most men."

"Your aunt can train you," he insisted.

"My aunt *has* trained me. And her men. And my father's men. And my other aunts. They've all trained me since I was little. And I *barely* held my own. Barely."

"You're out now," he said, shrugging. The chances of escaping traffickers then getting taken again were slim.

"That's not why I need you to train me. I need... I need to be able to hold my own against men like the ones that kept me in a basement."

"Why?"

Ferryn

"Because... because I have a mission," Ferryn insisted, finding the words clumsy on her tongue, silly to her ears. What person spoke like that? Military guys had missions, not girls like her.

"Mission?" Holden repeated, and much to her relief, he didn't seem amused or even dismissive. If anything, she was pretty sure he seemed almost a little... interested. For the first time since she opened her mouth.

"Yeah, a mission. To help girls. Girls who found themselves in basements like me. But couldn't get themselves away. I want to help them. And I want to make the men who did it to them pay."

"Pay," he repeated, seeming to chew on the word, like he found it thick, meaty, something that needed some gnashing before he could choke it down. "With their lives?" he asked.

"Yes," Ferryn agreed, feeling her chin lift a bit, daring him to tell her she couldn't.

"Takes something from you to take a life."

"I've taken a life," she volunteered, meeting his eyes, finding the courage to hold his gaze unflinchingly.

In doing so, she thought he maybe saw something there, something he saw in himself as well, something that started to sway him in her favor.

"You feel bad about it?"

"No."

"See it when you close your eyes?"

"Yeah. But it was the only way. It had to happen. The world is better off this way."

"Why not have your family train you?"

"Because they wouldn't let me do this. And they can't train me hard enough."

"You ran away?"

"Yes."

"So you're serious."

"I am very serious."

"This mission is important?"

"This mission is everything."

Holden sucked his cheek in between his teeth, biting down, trying to find some mental clarity through the pinch of pain.

There was passion in this girl.

Passion was something utterly devoid in his life. It was something meant for other people. He knew better than to desire it for himself.

Yet there was no denying that he was finding himself swayed by hers, intrigued by the possibility of being involved with passion in an indirect kind of way.

He was also all for those who made a life of striking down those who otherwise would get away with their crimes.

He had his doubts that someone like this tiny girl with the determined chin could pull it off.

There was no way to know for sure unless he tried her out.

That came with its own risks, though. Ones he would have to make her aware of.

"I would hurt you. A lot."

"I can take it."

"I'm dangerous," he told her, though he knew that it was much deeper than that.

"So am I."

"I will break you down."

"I will put myself back together."

She knew she had him right then.

The tiniest twitch pulled at the corner of his lips. Not a smile. Surely, he was not a man inclined to smiling. But a hint of amusement. It was the first he'd shown her even the slightest emotion.

So she knew she had him.

For better or worse.

"That all you own?" he asked a few moments later, leading Ferryn through the woods, away from the small main house, something that made her brows knit, but she was too far gone now to go back, to question him.

"Yes. I didn't... I couldn't go home after."

"Won't need much," he told her, shrugging it off.

It was hard to imagine she wouldn't need more than what she was carrying, she a girl who had a bursting closet and a giant book collection. That wasn't even mentioning her makeup and skincare products.

"No one to impress here."

Ferryn figured that was fair enough as a small, well, garage came into view. There wasn't much to mention save for the large metal door and the moss flecked white shake siding.

Holden pushed in front of her, plugging a quick code into the keypad, making the door grumble open, piercingly loud in such a silent space.

"Come on," he demanded, moving inside, leaving her to fall behind.

Where she found, well, a gym.

There was an unyielding cement floor with a nearly paper-thin mat covering part of it, a weight bench, bike, kettlebells, a pull-up bar, leg press, and various punching and speed bags. Everything was familiar, yet she found them oddly intimidating in this space. Maybe because she knew she would have to prove herself, would need to impress him.

"Gym. Self-explanatory. We'll be spending a lot of time here."

His words almost sounded like a threat.

Maybe they were.

"There's a room back here," he told her, leading her through a door toward the back.

It was a small space, all of eight by ten with bare walls and one small, grime-covered window.

"Light," he said, reaching up, pulling a string hanging in the middle of the room, making a bare Edison bulb flash to life, highlighting the dust bunnies along the walls, the webs in the ceiling corners. "Bed," he added, moving forward, grabbing a thin mattress that had been propped against the wall, dropping it down on the floor, kicking up all the dust and dirt in the room. "Can," he went on, waving an arm toward her side, making her gaze shift, finding a toilet and sink combination reminiscent of a prison situated there. "Nothing fancy here, kid. You can't rough it, get lost now."

While a part of her absolutely did cringe at the idea of using her bedroom as a bathroom as well, she understood that luxuries would no longer be a part of the life ahead of her if she continued on this path.

She would have to learn to be okay with a lot of things her pampered former self took for granted.

"Better than digging a hole in the woods," she told him, seeing that little twitch at his lips again. "Shower, though?" she asked.

"Got a tap," he told her, motioning to the toilet/sink combo. "Hose out back. Stream down a ways through the woods. You'll manage."

She would, she vowed to herself.

Because somewhere in the world—many places in the world—there were women living in hellish conditions with no hope of escape, waiting for someone to save them. Given some time, given some experience, she could be that person.

"Yo," Holden growled, shocking her out of her thoughts, turning to find him once again in the doorway as though he was going to leave her. "This door," he said when he got her attention, "this stays locked when you are in here."

"Ah, okay," she said, brows furrowing.

"Not just closed, locked," he went on, pointing to the lock.

"What? Do you have super smart bears in these woods who can plug in door codes and turn door knobs?" she asked, smiling.

"There are worse things in these woods than bears, kid," he said, turning, leaving, slamming the door in his wake.

Even knowing it was coming, she jolted at the slam, feeling something inside do the same thing.

He hadn't outwardly said it, but she knew what he meant. He meant that *he* was the thing in the woods that she should fear.

Her stomach flip-flopped at that realization, wondering in what way he might mean, in what way he could be a danger to her, something she hadn't even started to consider on her way to find him.

She knew he could teach her to defend herself from men.

But what about from him?

Rushing across the room, she turned the lock, then told herself that she would also find something to use to further secure herself. Especially when she was sleeping at night. Because she knew a man as big as Holden could make short work of a simple wooden door.

With nothing else to do, she yanked open the window, then dropped down on the bed, resolving herself to an empty stomach.

It was nothing new.

She'd been starved before.

She had survived.

As soon as she got some time to think, to rest, then she would find a way to get food.

Suddenly, she wished she'd taken her uncles up on offers to learn to fish. Even if she hated the smell and taste of seafood.

She would figure it all out.

That was what she had to do.

Rely on herself.

Become independent.

Make do.

"Grub," Holden's voice grumbled through the door, making her heart shoot up into her throat.

Before she could even draw in a breath to steel herself, she could hear his footsteps clomping away, the grind of the garage door closing once again.

She made her way across the floor, unlocking the door, finding a tray, an actual bright blue school cafeteria plastic tray.

With blessed food piled on it.

A simple white throwaway dish loaded down with grilled chicken, peas, and a plain sweet potato. Not a hint of seasoning. But it might as well have been a decadent gourmet meal.

She tore into it, drinking greedily from the tap with the red plastic cup he'd left with her tray.

She fell asleep some time later, cold, uncertain, sad for the life—and people—she left behind. But also confident in her decision, knowing this was the right path for her, believing she had what it took.

It took only half an hour of training the following day— after getting startled awake by pounding on her door—to genuinely wonder if she had what it was going to take.

She'd sparred countless times in her young life, had fought those her own size as well as men much larger. It was always hard. She often lost. But she had always felt she stood a *chance.*

Holden Ryker gave her no chances.

Heaving, drenched in sweat, every muscle screaming, head pounding from a punch she took to the temple, she couldn't help but wonder if all those people she'd trained with before had truly gone as hard on her as they had claimed. Or, if like a caring parent letting their kid win at checkers, they had simply wanted to encourage her by letting her think she was better than she was.

Distracted by those thoughts, she took another hit to her jaw, flooding her mouth with blood, letting her know that the tooth that had been wiggling from a hit she'd taken in the basement days before was finally knocked loose.

"Are you crying?" he asked, voice frustrated.

"No," she yelled back, though it was clear that she was.

"You wanna quit? You wanna give up on your first fucking day? I thought you cared about all those women."

"I do!" she insisted, raising an arm, swiping the offensive tears off her cheeks, quickly replaced by new ones.

"Right now, somewhere in the world, some woman is being dragged up off the floor, she is being forced down on a bed, she is having her clothes ripped off."

"Shut up," she demanded, feeling her lower lip quiver at the recognition of the truth in his words and also her clear inability to do anything about it.

"Some man is taking off his clothes. And he is getting on the bed."

She learned that first day that she had a trigger. And once even a breeze too strong blew against it, it was engaged.

The rage came from somewhere deep inside, a bottomless well that flooded up through her system, overtaking her entirely, bathing the world in stark contrast, making every sound in the room—the huff of her own breath, the steady cadence of Holden's, the irritating fly buzzing around—louder than they should have been, making her pulse slow, making her instincts kick in.

She still got her ass kicked. Decimated, even. But Holden stopped poking at her, finding himself too busy fighting off her endless advances, leaving him more than a little impressed by the determination he found in this kid with the so easily breakable body but unshakable spirit.

She never cried again.

Not when his fist broke her eye socket.

Not when she'd fallen and busted her ankle.

Not when she got right up off that floor and kept fighting through the pain.

And not when she was utterly alone in her room, nursing her wounds, feeling the girl she used to be slipping away moment by moment, night by night.

The nights were the longest.

The solitude crept in, whispered uncertainties, told her how much easier it would be to go home, forget all this.

There would be no pain.

There would be no uncertainty.

She wouldn't be sweating through the summer and freezing through the winter without heat or air.

She would have body wash and lotion and a warm shower.

Even as she would lie there with those thoughts swirling, even as she listened to Holden tearing through the gym, wrecking it once again, lost in his own memories, lost in his own mind; even when he turned that anger on her door that she had smartly reinforced with three giant planks of removable wood after the first night he almost got in, almost mistook her for some unknown man from his past, almost killed her; even as this new life bent and broke and remolded her both inside and out, she knew she couldn't give up, she knew that all that mattered was the mission, was the difference she could make in the world.

So she stayed.

She stayed.

Until, one day, she didn't.

Three

Vance - Present Day

West was getting his ass handed to him on a group chat with his sisters. It was maybe the highlight of my week—no, month—to see him pacing around the clubhouse, running a hand across through his blond hair, mumbling "Yeah, I know. You're right" over and over, until I was sure the words were burning a hole in his vocal cords.

What can I say, it was a treat to see the club's resident ladies man get taken down a peg by the estrogen-dominant part of his family.

With all but West and Colson—a single father and therefore not one inclined to partying it up—married and the club business relatively stable—as stable as an arms-dealing biker club in a town full of criminal empires could be—I was starved for any kind of entertainment.

"Are you fucking blushing?" I asked, watching as he turned to me, confirming my suspicions but also giving me a look that said if I dared repeat that phrase again—especially in front of our brothers—he would drag me out back and shoot me like a rabid dog.

I was almost desperate enough for some action to take him up on the offer.

Almost.

Let's face it, when it came to a fight, West had a good decade of ass-kicking under his belt while I was busy touring with my band. While there was always the occasional fight when it came to the music scene, I was in no way equipped to take on a furious and embarrassed West.

Sometimes, you had to accept your weaknesses in life.

I'd made my peace with mine.

For the most part.

After all, West had been living a criminal lifestyle, scraping by, scuffling and smacking down, for years while I had been writing songs and playing tiny gigs that slowly but surely led to larger gigs that actually made us more than gas money and pocket change.

I never planned on becoming a biker.

For most of my life, all I could think about was getting out of my oppressively religious household, rebelling, making a name for myself doing what I was passionate about.

Then, well, things changed.

It all started so innocently. Taking my sister and her best friend to a shopping center after they cut school.

Then it all went to hell.

Iggy's best friend was taken.

Imprisoned.

Irreparably changed.

Then she disappeared again.

There had been cracks in me then that afternoon. The literal ones. From trying to fight off the abductors. Those ones healed relatively easily, leaving no lasting marks.

The others, though, I had no idea they were there. At least not after the shock wore off. I thought I had gone back to normal. Or to what had always passed as normal for me.

I couldn't have been more wrong.

It took a while for my foundations to settle.

That was when the cracks started to show.

Little by little over time.

Until they could no longer be denied.

Until everyone else could see them too.

That was where everything changed once again.

And how I ended up at the doors of an outlaw biker club, demanding the president—the father of the girl I had once tried to save from kidnapping human traffickers—to let me prospect, to let me become a brother.

I could never be sure if Reign actually wanted me in his club, or if he was simply letting me in because he felt obligated, because he knew I had once tried to save his little girl.

I would likely never know.

But I was grateful, nonetheless.

The Henchmen MC wasn't exactly where I had planned on landing, but I found security in the clubhouse, in the brotherhood.

Even the pain in the ass West who took it upon himself to be my personal nag, always insisting I was in a dark mood, that I needed to get out more, that the surefire cure for my bad moods was hitting the bar, drinking to near oblivion, finding a hot, willing woman, and taking her to bed.

Sometimes, I placated him. Sometimes, I thought that maybe he had a point, maybe the root of my problem was being on my own too much, getting lost inside my own head too often.

Maybe the cure was time out with friends. Maybe some pretty woman who wanted me was what I needed to replace some of the other thoughts in my head.

Just as often, though, West ended up going home with one or more of the girls while I headed back to the clubhouse to chase a couple ibuprofen with a gallon of water in the hopes that I avoided a hangover.

"So, which of your sisters is now wearing your balls for earrings?" I asked when he threw down his phone on the couch, sitting, cradling his head in his tattooed hands like it was pounding. Hell, it probably was. At the beginning of the conversation, I could hear his sister's raised voices from clear across the room.

All I got from him was a grumbling, pained sound.

In a rare surge of sympathy for the poor bastard, I grabbed a bottle of booze from the back bar, dropping it down on the table in front of him, watching as he grabbed for it greedily, chugging down the contents.

"What are you in the shithouse for?"

"Not coming home for my mom's birthday last week."

"We were doing a drop," I said, brow furrowing. We'd been down in North Carolina for the better part of the week before, dealing with some cheap-ass low-level Irish mob guys who suddenly decided Reign was gouging them on the guns.

"And I sent gifts. And one of those fucking fruit arrangement things. The expensive ones."

"Did you tell her ahead of time that you couldn't make it?"

"Of course I did."

For all of West's faults, he was a good son, a great brother. He had a deep-seated respect for the fairer sex even if he didn't always appear that way from the outside.

"I don't see the problem."

To that, he snorted.

"Man, you know women. They don't want gifts. They want your presence."

Well, that was sage advice if I ever heard it. Even if, in this situation, it was irrational. Work was work sometimes. Everyone had to make a living, even if it meant missing a birthday or holiday here or there.

"I somehow got talked into taking all of them on a long weekend."

"Sounds kinda nice."

"At a meditation retreat."

"Oh, for fuck's sake."

"Yeah," he agreed, tipping the bottle once again.

If there was one place I could not picture West, it was someplace he was supposed to be silent and still.

"Hell, maybe there will be a hot yoga teacher there or something. Imagine the positions you could get her into."

Yep.

There was the West I knew.

"Wanna hit Chaz's tonight? Daddy Reign is away, the kids got to play and all that shit."

He just wanted to be able to bring a couple chicks back to the clubhouse to impress them, and he knew Cash—Reign's brother, the vice president–was left in charge and was a hell of a lot more lenient about that kind of thing.

I'd turned him down a lot lately, finding my mood darker than usual, not able to muster even the smallest bit of interest in going out, and pretending to be into something when all I wanted to do was get back to my room at the clubhouse, play a little guitar.

It had been over a month since I had hit the bar with him. Which I was pretty sure made me a shit friend. Especially since he'd been more tolerant than usual, going off on his own or even hanging back at the club, playing pool with me or initiating a poker game and stealing untold amounts of money from the rest of us.

It was time to get back out there.

Even if I had to try to force the interest at first.

"I think..." I started, hearing the low rumble of a bike coming closer, wondering who was coming back.

Lately, well, the clubhouse had been all but abandoned save for West and me. The other guys dropped in occasionally, but usually not later at night when they had wives or kids to be home with. They left us to do the rounds during the undesirable hours, making sure we kept the clubhouse secure.

It wasn't common for anyone to be heading back to the club after nightfall.

"Uncle Cash checking in on us?" West asked, shrugging.

If anyone were to be heading in, it likely would be Cash. He didn't have any young kids. And his wife was in charge of Hailstorm, which meant she sometimes took off at a moment's notice, leaving him alone and bored.

But from what I understood, Lo didn't do a lot of trips anymore, choosing to stay back, to spend time with Cash, to spend time with her adopted daughter Chris.

Chris who had spent time in a basement, had been horribly abused, who likely would have still been in that basement if not for...

"Something's wrong," West said, already off the couch, making his way toward the door, grabbing a gun out from a drawer under the bar on his way.

He was right.

If it was Cash, he would have been inside the gates and cutting the engine by now.

From the sound of things, whoever was on the bike was stuck at the gates, held up by one of Hailstorm's guards who still stood sentry at the gates for a reason I didn't understand and didn't feel I had the right to question.

If they knew who it was, they would have waved them right through.

"Probably someone who wants to prospect," West concluded as we made our way into the yard, finding someone on a bike in a leather jacket and a helmet, the light on the street casting his face in shadow.

It had been a long while since we got a new member. A part of me was thinking that maybe Reign was having a sort of hiring freeze because in a few short years, his sons, and the sons of the other older OG brothers would be aging up enough to prospect themselves, and he wanted to make sure they would have a place should they want it.

It seemed unlikely there simply weren't any people out there who wanted to join.

We would need to call in Cash after all, neither of us being senior enough to make any kind of decisions on prospects. While Reign generally took into account everyone's thoughts and opinions on things that impacted the whole club, ultimately, we all knew decisions like prospects were made by him, Cash, and our road captain, Wolf.

The engine cut as the rider, clearly frustrated by the obstruction of the guards, climbed off, stomping combat boots on the ground, kicking up dry dirt with the motion.

"What's going on?" West called as we got closer.

"Got someone who says they need to talk to Reign," one of the guards, some young guy I had only seen a handful of times, likely new to Hailstorm, told us.

"Well, they'll have to settle for us," West declared, having a somewhat impressively authoritative voice when he needed to for someone who was usually a lot of light and laughter.

The rider reached upward, unclasping their helmet, pulling it off their head.

Without the shadows cast by the helmet, their face was in perfect view.

A very familiar face.

"Jesus Christ," my voice hissed out of me as my body jolted with awareness, with recognition, with the absolute impossibility of this reality.

"What am I missing?" West asked, and I could feel his gaze on my profile, could hear the understanding that something had just changed, and he was completely unaware.

Because all of this, well, it went down before West was a member of the MC, before West was even in Navesink Bank.

He knew the stories.

But he'd never seen the girl.

No.

Not the girl.

She was most definitely not a *girl* anymore.

She had the same face, sure, the same up-and-down sort of body type. If anything, she was even thinner than she had been when I had last seen her, possessed fewer curves.

The last time I saw her, her shining black hair had been freshly buzzed for the first time. Now, it was cropped short at the sides, but longer on top, an edgy look that somehow fit her very delicate, almost doll-like face, made her gray eyes pop.

The eyes, though, the eyes were so different from the last time I had seen them, from how I thought of them in my memories.

See, when your little sister had a best friend, and you were your little sister's chauffeur, you got to know her friends really fucking well. Whether you wanted to or not.

But she had always been different. Not vapid or catty. She was a reader, a music connoisseur, a bit of a philosopher even at age sixteen.

I didn't mind that she tagged along, that she was always trying to get my attention, always trying to engage me in conversation. Because, quite frankly, the things she had to talk about were usually a lot deeper than the shit my bandmates wanted to talk about. Which usually just had to do with sex positions and which mainstream bands had made it big because they sold out their sound.

She'd always had interesting eyes. Ones that showed everything from excitement to annoyance.

But those eyes, those gray eyes I had been so familiar with all those years ago, yeah, they were completely fucking unreadable.

"Oh, shit. Is this some fucking meet-cute moment?" West asked, voice losing all its authority, going light and fun and sarcastic as was more his nature. "Where is the harp music? Let me guess, she is some big city girl, coming to slum it in our little town to pursue her dreams of making artisanal cupcakes in the shape of sloths. And she just so happens to stop here for directions. And the two of you lock eyes and live happily ever after. Am I right?" he asked, looking between the two of us, both of us seemingly unable to believe what we were seeing when we looked at each other.

"Who are you, beautiful?" he asked, and there was still a smile in his voice.

"Ferryn." The name rushed out of my lips, as airless and unsure as I was feeling at that very moment, the entire world seemingly thrown off its axis, knocking everything sideways.

In what world was Ferryn here, now?

How the hell was I the one to first see her?

Why was she back after all this time?

When her parents were out of town?

"Whoa, fuck. Hold up. *Ferryn*. As in *the* Ferryn? Little runaway Ferryn?"

To that, those lifeless eyes of hers shifted from my face, letting me snap out of the stupor I had been stuck in—time and life and my damn heartbeat standing still.

"And who the hell are you?" she asked.

Again, I knew that voice.

But it lacked something.

It seemed colder.

It shivered over my skin.

It left goosebumps in its wake.

"West," he supplied, seemingly unaffected by her tone, by her dead eyes. But, then again, he hadn't known her when her voice was honey sweet, when her eyes danced and smiled. "I was starting to think you were just a girl from a story. Just a tale the old guys told."

"Well, *that* girl is just a story now," Ferryn supplied, making West's brow quirk up.

"Yeah, I think I am getting that, pretty lady," West agreed.

Ferryn was someone discussed often. They'd share old anecdotes, tales of her escapades, always followed by a collective solemnness from all those who had known her, those who had missed her, those who felt acutely the hole her absence had left behind.

In those stories, Ferryn was often painted as a little girl by her aunts. One who was loud and opinionated and who did shit like put dinosaur heads on her Barbie dolls and bossed all the boys around like her little minions.

From her uncles, the men I now called brothers, they often talked of her as a rebellious teen, someone who could kick a little ass, who could win every debate, who once kicked a guy in the nuts because he cat-called one of the other club's daughters when she was all of twelve years old.

Ferryn was always a larger than life personality, someone full of life, someone who always had something to say, some story to tell, someone both fiercely independent, yet incredibly loyal, someone badass, but also sweet and soft.

There was no sweet or soft in the woman standing before us.

This woman was not full of life.

If anything, she almost vibed of death.

If that made any sense at all.

"Hey, man, didn't you know her?" West asked, breaking the crushing silence.

"Back in the day, yeah, you could say I knew her," I agreed, watching as her gaze slid back over toward me.

"Yeah, yeah, it's coming back. You tried to save her, didn't you? Got your face all busted in doing it."

"Yeah, that's the way it went," I agreed, looking for something in Ferryn's face. Some emotion. Hell, even just a little acknowledgement would be enough.

"That was the last time you saw her, right?"

No.

No, that was not the last time I saw her.

The last time I saw her was several days after she had been taken. I had been on my way to pick up my sister from our parents' house, knowing she had been as big a wreck as I had been about Ferryn's abduction, about her unknown whereabouts. And then I saw my sister walking out of the house with someone that, with their shaved head, I momentarily mistook for a boy.

I remembered even feeling a swelling of pride. Because our parents were strict fucking nut jobs, having lived it wild and free—maybe even a little *too* wild and free, hence naming their children Vance and Iggy—for a long time before becoming born again and shunning everything they had once loved and prided themselves on. And Iggy had found herself wholly inept at proper rebellion, no matter the very clear path I had blazed for her to walk in. I figured she had maybe gotten the balls to have a boy over the house.

But then I got a closer look.

It wasn't a boy at all.

It was Ferryn with a shaved head and bruised face and odd eyes.

Before I could even understand what was happening, she was stalking over toward me with the determination I had once seen in her gait when she was cutting across a park to confront a group of kids picking on a small girl with glasses.

Then she had grabbed me.

And kissed me.

There were several reasons Ferryn was off-limits.

Like her scary-ass father.

Like being the best friend to my little sister.

But the biggest one, of course, was the fact that Ferryn was underage when I knew her.

So, despite the clear crush she had held for me for a long time, and despite how interesting I had always found her, there had never been anything anyone—least of all her intimidating as fuck father and all his friends—could misconstrue as inappropriate between the two of us.

Hell, I barely looked at the girl. Even when we were having long-ass conversations in my car after I drove her home from hanging out at my parents' house or back from one of my shows where she had always been our biggest fan right there in the front, singing her heart out.

So, because of that—because there had just been some kind of block in my mind about her—nothing had fucking shocked me more than the zing that went through my body at the contact of her lips on mine.

I would have stopped it, of course.

I *would* have.

But then it was over.

And she was gone.

And no one, fucking no one, ever saw her again.

I had gone right on to tell Reign about seeing Ferryn, made Iggy tell him everything she knew about where she was going, what was going on in her head, but I had never told anyone the part about the kiss.

I valued my life at least a little bit.

Even if I hadn't initiated it, had been too shocked to even respond to it, I knew that was what it would cost me if anyone found out.

That was the last time I saw Ferryn.

Seconds before she ran away from her life.

Not to be seen again.

For nearly nine fucking years.

Yet here she was.

Alive.

Seemingly... well enough.

At West's words, as though she could hear the memories racing through my mind, I swear something sparked in her eyes then. Something familiar.

A challenge.

Like she was daring me to tell West when was the last time I saw her.

Like she was daring me not to.

I decided to avoid both options.

"Ferryn, where the fuck have you been?"

"That's a long story," she told me, putting her helmet on the seat of her bike. "What are you doing here? With a cut on?" she asked, eyes going to my chest.

"That's a long story too," I told her.

"I have a feeling there are going to be a lot of long stories in store for me," she said, and it was impossible to tell if she was dreading or excited about that prospect.

"So, I am just going to cut through all this fun cryptic shit," West interjected. "And ask what you're doing back here all a sudden and unannounced."

To that, her chest rose as she sucked in a deep breath.

Looking for courage, maybe?

Though there didn't seem to be a bit of this new woman standing before us that could possibly be uncertain or insecure.

"It was time to come home."

And just like that, after almost nine years, Ferryn was home.

Four

I don't know what I had been expecting heading home.

Honestly, I wasn't sure I even really let myself mull it over too much. I knew that doing so would make it impossible to drive into Navesink Bank after all these years.

Once I bested Holden, the decision was simply made. I didn't sit around, wondering what it might feel like to go back to the place that raised me, the people that raised me.

I wasn't sure I was prepared to feel much of anything at all.

There had been a drought in the softer, mushy sort of emotions for years for me. My life was too hard, too dark, to allow such weaknesses in.

So when I turned my bike to head down the main street, I had been woefully unprepared for the unexpected surge of nostalgia.

Maybe a part of me had expected so much to change. After all, so much about *me* had changed. And towns, well, they were a fluid thing, always growing, always evolving. Stores went in and out, faces changed, buildings were torn down and rebuilt.

It should have been different.

But it was almost a time capsule to my youth.

There were the same places.

She's Bean Around, the coffee shop where my friends and I had spent so much of our time. The Garage, a local, well, converted garage that served as a venue for all the local bands to practice and perform on weekends. There was the floral shop, the convenience store, the fancy lingerie store that my Aunt Elsie took me to when I turned fifteen to get me some cute sets my father would have had a conniption over if he knew I owned.

Then, of course, there was my destination.

The clubhouse.

The place I had spent a huge chunk of my childhood. Hanging out with my father and uncles and my aunts and the women who I knew would eventually become aunts.

There had been cookouts and birthday parties and Christmas extravaganzas.

I'd snuck my first taste of alcohol inside those walls with my best friend Iggy. I'd broken my first bone jumping off an old car my uncle Repo kept in the back in an attempt to prove I was the ballsiest of the group. I'd spent time in the glass room on the roof used for guard duty just to watch the stars and talk with Iggy about how cool it would be if I married her brother, and we could become sisters for real.

So much of my formative years was behind the gates, inside the walls. So much of who I was was created there.

Was.

Who I *was*.

I was not the same girl that had last seen the Henchmen MC compound.

My stomach, usually so steely, flip-flopped as I pulled my bike up to the gates, finding the Hailstorm guards situated there like they always were.

They were a familiar sight with unfamiliar faces.

Which meant that they had no idea who I was.

How humbling it was to finally come back home after so long and not be recognized in a place that had been like a home away from home for me.

Then just as I was trying to explain who I was there to see, why they should get out of my way, there were two new men there.

Both were tall, fit, wearing cuts. Only one was familiar.

A ghost from my past.

The boy I had once fantasized about marrying.

At the club.

Wearing a cut.

One of my father's men.

It so far from made sense that I was having trouble actually stringing my thoughts together in a way that could suss out what, exactly, was going on.

"So, where's my dad?" I asked into the awkward silence, my people skills definitely lacking thanks to no one but Holden to talk to. And, well, let's face it, Holden was not exactly an expert conversationalist. "What?" I asked when West shifted his feet, when Vance's arm rose, his hand rubbed across the back of his neck.

I knew that motion.

He did it when he needed to tell you something he knew you didn't want to hear.

At least some things still made sense to me.

"You've always had pretty shit timing, Ferryn," he told me, and memories suddenly flooded back. Missing school buses. Getting there ten minutes late for the movie. Mixing up dates.

"Why? What's wrong?" I asked, feeling my stomach pitch at the idea that one of them was in the hospital or something.

"Nothing, breathe," Vance demanded, voice soothing, like I was some prickly stray he was worried of frightening.

And, well, it wasn't an altogether ridiculous thing to think, was it?

Except that little, very fucking little, actually frightened me anymore.

"Where are they?" I demanded, voice sharp even to my own ears.

"On a cruise," Vance told me, face apologetic.

A cruise.

If there was one place on this entire planet I couldn't picture my father, it was on a cruise.

Then again, he was hopelessly in love with my mother. If she wanted to go on a cruise, he would take her. He might do it whilst brooding and openly mocking various cheesy elements of such a vacation, but he would go. He would do whatever it took to make her happy.

"Their anniversary was last week," he added.

I wanted to snap that I didn't need to be reminded when my own parents' anniversary was, but, well, I guess I did. While birthdays were still deeply burned in my brain, the other dates started to slip away without a calendar to remind me.

"Where did they go?" I heard myself ask, heart sinking a bit.

"To the Caribbean. Left from Florida two days ago. It's a seven-day cruise."

And there would be next to no way for them to get back earlier.

Which meant if the word spread, they would be trapped on a boat for five more days, anxious to get home, ruining their much-deserved vacation.

"No one can tell them," I blurted out, hearing the urgency in my tone, knowing it was a weakness, but unable to bring myself to care, to rein it in.

"Beautiful, your parents have been waiting for your ass for years. They'd want to know the minute you came back," West reasoned.

"This is not your call," I reminded him, pinning him with a glare, finding myself a little annoyed when he didn't immediately look chastened.

"Pretty sure it is more my call than yours, pretty biker princess," West went on.

The thing was, he wasn't exactly wrong.

I had grown up in the club.

I knew how it went.

Brotherhood over everything.

Sure, those rules kinda bent a teensy bit when the men married and had kids because you would be a shit husband or father if you chose your friends over your blood, but almost as a rule for all the younger bloods, the single guys, they took that rule very seriously.

Clearly, West felt the same way.

A part of me respected that, was happy that my father still had such loyal men.

The other part of me, though, bristled. Because I knew if this was one of the men I had grown up around, they would have considered my side of things before simply shooting me down.

"Alright," Vance cut in when my mouth opened to snap at West. "Let's just think about this for a minute, alright?" he suggested, looking at West. "You know Reign can handle having to wait," he added. "But think of Summer," he said.

"That's a fair point," West agreed. "But... what? We tell Cash and everyone else, and he comes home to find out all of us have been keeping this from him for a week? You want to deal with the backlash of that?"

"That's fair," Vance agreed.

My father was never quick to anger, to overreaction. He had been in charge of an outlaw biker gang for a long, long time, dealing with all the wars, all the external and internal conflicts, he had learned to let a lot of things roll off his back.

That said, maybe I as only having a hard time picturing him making Vance and West's lives a living hell for keeping a secret because he had always been careful about not showing me those darker sides of his personality, his life.

It was something that almost seemed funny to me now, knowing that his dark and ugly looked light and fluffy compared to mine.

"Maybe it would be better to tell no one," I suggested, feeling a sort of balloon deflate inside me.

Even if I hadn't known what I was going to be expecting, I guess I at least anticipated a reunion of some sort. With my parents, my brothers, my aunts and uncles.

It was childish to crave it.

I hadn't even been aware it was there.

But there it was.

"Yeah? And do what about them?" West asked, jerking his chin toward the Hailstorm guards.

Biting into my lower lip, an old tell that had been long-buried, and I was sure dead, I reached for my phone.

"I can handle that," I assured them, not a drop of doubt in my voice because I had none.

In a place where I felt wholly off my footing, I did know that I could handle the guards, keep them quiet.

And, for once, I wouldn't even need to use my fists to do so.

"Where will you go?" Vance asked as my fingers moved across the keypad of my phone.

"I'll find a place," I assured them. "I'm not a little kid anymore. I can make my own way."

"I wasn't questioning that, Ferryn," Vance assured me. "I just want to make sure you aren't running off again."

"I'm not."

"We're just supposed to take you at your word?" West asked.

"What other choice do you have? Tying me up and tossing me in the basement? I'd like to see you try."

"Alright. That's enough of that," Vance cut in, a sigh in his voice. "How about you crash at my old place? It's there. Empty. I'm here all the time. It's not much. Got it back when I was done with the band but before I started here. I kept it just in case your father realized I had no place in the club and kicked me out."

To that, I snorted. "No one gets kicked out of a club, Vance. They get taken out of one."

"Never heard you talk about your father like that."

"I've learned a lot of harsh realities over the years. Even about my own family. Where's this place you have?"

"I will bring you."

"I can bring myself."

To that, he let out his breath, deflating his strong chest. "How about you humor me, Ferryn?" he suggested. "You can follow me on your bike."

That was fair.

I was being argumentative for no real reason.

"I'll be damned," West said, making us both turn, finding the Hailstorm guards both lifting their phones, listening to the voice on the other end, looking back at me, nodding, then hanging up.

In my hand, my phone buzzed.

I got the confirmation I needed.

My secret was mine until my parents got back.

"Alright. Let's go," I declared, tucking my phone, putting my helmet back on.

Without anything else, I turned over the bike, pulled out on the main street, waiting for Vance to do the same.

A week.

That was it.

I just had to lay low for a week.

I'd been laying low for almost nine years.

A week was nothing.

Yet it somehow felt like a lifetime.

So close to everything I had left behind, but still so far.

Vance pulled out ahead of me, and I couldn't help but wonder how the hell he had found himself on a motorcycle, in a club, running guns for my father.

Last I had seen him, he and his band had been paying their dues. They weren't big time. They weren't even hinting at big time. But they had a large local following. They were making plans to start doing some touring. They would have made something of themselves if they kept on the same path. There had been nothing to suggest they wouldn't. No internal battling. No one letting their ego get the better of them.

How did he go from promising rockstar to an outlaw biker?

Those thoughts were pushed away as Vance turned off the main drag, leading me down toward, well, the bad area of town.

Growing up, my father had always made it clear that none of us were ever to go near Third Street territory.

A local and unpredictable street gang known for constant changeover in leadership, roughing up the girls they pimped, and selling whatever drugs they could get their hands on—my father always had worries about them one day rising up, getting a leader who would set their sights higher than the drug and pimp game, who would try to find a way to take over the much more profitable gun-running. I guess he figured one good way for them to so would be to take my brothers or me, use us as pawns to get what they wanted.

We were banned from the area.

Of course, that meant very little to me. I was always looking for ways to bend or break rules. But after a trip of two, finding nothing but sadness, and people desperately trying to scrape by, well, I saw no reason to keep bending that particular rule.

If Vance had needed to rent a place in Third Street territory, well, the transition between being a band member and a biker had to have been a rough one.

We drove toward the very end of the road where there was a sad little house that looked as though a slight breeze might blow it down. In the backyard was a line of what looked to be shoebox apartments, all connected and sharing a slab porch.

"I know it isn't much," he admitted when we both cut our engines, our bikes parked in front of the last one on the right, a light on inside like he had decided that a lamp on a timer would fool anyone into thinking someone was actually living there. Why he bothered, I wasn't sure. What could he have possibly stored there that he needed to protect from intruders?

"I've stayed in worse," I admitted. Because it was true. And because, apparently, some small, deeply buried part of me still wanted to be on his good side.

Those first crushes, they never fully die, do they?

"Maybe you can tell me about it sometime," he offered, but kept moving, not letting it get awkward, reaching into his wallet to find a key.

"How long were you crashing here?" I asked as he shouldered the stuck door.

"Four, five months. Something like that. It wasn't as bad as it looks, really. I was used to sleeping in the back of a van a lot of the time. With five other guys. At least here I got some solitude. Alright, here we go. Welcome," he said, moving inside, leaving me to fall behind.

I had maybe been too generous in calling it a shoebox. It looked just about big enough to house a family of squirrels.

Predominantly one room with a closet of a space to the back that I figured to be the bathroom, there was a pretty badly worn brown material couch that, judging by the blanket draping it and the pillows butted against the arm, also served as the bed.

Would it be lumpy and uncomfortable? Yes. But also likely more cozy than my old mattress on the floor.

Behind the couch was what must have been considered the kitchen which consisted of a mini-fridge, a sink, and a microwave.

That was just as well.

I didn't have many cooking skills to speak of either.

Once upon a time, I had been a pretty decent Christmas cookie baker.

In another time, another life.

I hadn't even seen a chocolate chip in the better part of a decade.

The heat seemed to come from a small space heater tucked a few feet away from the couch. There was no AC. Not that those things mattered. I had gotten on well enough without them for many years.

"Everything is empty," he told me, waving a hand toward the cupboard and the fridge. "Except there is likely a bottle of whiskey in the freezer. I will grab you some stuff."

"I can—"

"No," he cut me off, shaking his head. "If we are going to pull this off, you have to lay low here. There's not much in the way of entertainment. Got my old record player and some records I left here that I had repeats of. I can maybe grab you some books. You still into the true crime and history shit?"

Was I?

I hadn't had access to books in years.

But I still remembered, of course, all the endless hours I had once spent with my nose buried inside them, escaping from the real world when it was not exciting enough.

Now, though, the real world was plenty exciting. Maybe it would be nice to escape to something calmer.

"Not true crime or thrillers," I decided. "Anything but that."

"Anything but that," he repeated, mulling over the words, looking for the meaning behind them. "Got it. What about food? You still all about the coffee and crunchy cheese puffs and half-sour pickles?"

More memories, ones that had been so buried under flavorless chicken, sweet potatoes, and the rotation of green beans, peas, broccoli, and asparagus.

I'd had coffee.

Plain black coffee.

The kind that could damn near put hair on your chest.

Everything else, though—just part of my past. Cheese, sugar, most carbs. I hadn't touched them in years. Holden was in charge of obtaining and cooking food. I was simply grateful to eat after a hard day of training. I stopped dreaming of junk food years ago.

"Yes," I told him without hesitation. "And Devil Dogs."

"Devil Dogs," he repeated, lips curving up slightly.

That wasn't one of my public junk food binges. Devil Dogs were my secret binge food. The thing I feasted on in private after a bad day.

Doing poorly on a test.

Getting that look of disappointment from my mother.

Having a silly fight with Iggy.

Watching Vance hit on another girl in front of me while it was painfully clear I was mad for him.

I would stop at the convenience store, grab a box, hide it in my backpack, lock myself in my room, and plow through the entire thing.

I shouldn't have needed the comfort.

I hadn't needed anything even resembling comfort items in so long that I was sure I was above such things.

Even when I had seen and done the most horrifying things a person could imagine.

I managed.

Without a soft blanket.

Without music.

Without books.

Without fucking Devil Dogs.

But all it took to bring back old habits was simply stepping foot in my hometown?

What would happen after a couple hours, a couple days?

Would it make me soft all over again?

No.

No, of course not.

I couldn't let it.

"Alright, well, I can manage all that. What about clothes? Doesn't look like you brought much in that bag on your bike."

I hadn't.

Because I didn't own much.

Three days worth of clothes. A notebook I'd taken from the workout room because Holden wasn't using it, a place I used to write once every year. On my birthday. Why, I wasn't sure. To remember? For my family to have should I die, to know why I ran, what I ran to do, all the things I had been through?

I don't know.

But I did it.

And I kept it with me most of the time.

Otherwise, well, I didn't have much to my name.

A little cash.

Some sharp objects.

A big old bottle of ibuprofen.

A little wooden bear statue Holden had carved for me one day. After that night.

The night the lock on the door failed.

The night he came barreling into my room with his demons racing through his veins.

I'd taken a blow to the head before managing to scramble out through my window, falling down wrong, twisting my ankle, but having to run on it regardless because he was coming. I still to this day wasn't sure how I got away from him in the woods he knew so well but I was just starting to learn, but by some miracle I had, hauling myself high up into a tree, lying flat and still against the trunk, just waiting for day to come.

When I had finally hobbled back to my makeshift home, I'd found my breakfast there waiting for me along with the wooden bear on the tray.

Holden wasn't good at words.

But sometimes his gestures spoke volumes.

He was sorry.

He, in his own way, valued me, didn't want me to leave, wanted me to know it wasn't him that had broken into my room, that it was a part of him that existed in dark moments.

And, well, I had started to understand.

I kept the bear.

I treasured the bear.

But I made sure I secured that goddamn door.

"I can get by with what I have."

"I think we can do better than just getting you by, Ace," he said, the word seeming to shock us both the moment it was out of his lips. It had slipped out naturally, out of habit, old and familiar.

He'd always referred to Iggy's friends by nicknames he associated with us. Sometimes, when he was being a condescending ass, he'd call us kids. Or he'd call us punks. Or nerds.

But me?

Me, he liked to call Ace.

I was Ace.

In my silly, girlish mind, I was *his* Ace.

My heart always fluttered when I heard it.

There was no flutter now.

I didn't flutter anymore.

But there was a jolt, something electric. Something stronger than a flutter.

Maybe the old me letting me know for the first time that she was still around, buried deep, but not as dead as I thought she was.

"Since you are as skinny as ever, I think I can figure out your size."

"Here, let me give you some cash."

"Fuck off with that," he scoffed, rolling his eyes.

He'd always paid when we were kids. Even though I knew he wasn't rolling in it. I always thought it was rather gentlemanly of him. One of the many traits I had admired.

But that was then.

This was now.

Things had changed.

Maybe he hadn't.

But I had.

"I insist."

"You can insist all you want. You're not paying for shit."

"Vance..."

"I'm afraid it's not up for debate."

"Everything is up for debate."

"Yeah? How are you going to convince me to let you pay, huh?" he asked, lazy smile tipping up. Familiar. Charming as it always had been.

All words seemed to fail me in an instant.

"That's what I thought," he agreed, making his way to the door. "Give me a few hours. And lock the door."

I felt my lips curving up a bit at that. At the idea that any monster that showed up at my door could be anywhere near as vicious as I was. Even in this neighborhood.

"Will do," I agreed to appease him.

"Hey, Ace?" he called, standing in the open doorway, eyes a little lost, a little far away.

"Yeah?"

"It's good to have you home."

With that, he was gone, the rumbling of his bike speaking of his departure.

I poked around, making sure I wasn't sharing the space with any four-or more- legged friends before making my way back out to my bike, and finding I wasn't alone.

"Think if he's looking to screw you, he'd at least spring for that sleep and fuck off the highway. Thirty bucks a night and it has better amenities than this shithole."

"Maybe I like it rough and dirty," I declared, rummaging into my bag to pull out my double-bladed hunting karambit, letting it catch the light.

"Well, then you fit right in here, don't you?" he asked, flicking open a lighter, holding it up to the cigarette between his lips.

This was a man you thought about when someone said a man looked like bad news.

Tall, fit, scruffy, wearing scuffed up boots and sporting a scar straight down his left cheekbone.

"I was born and raised in this town. With that accent, though, you weren't."

I knew a twang when I heard one. Even if it had gotten roughed up a little by spending some time on the upper east coast.

"Louisiana, darlin', since you want to know so bad."

"What the hell are you doing all the way up here?"

"Looking for some trouble."

"Then you're probably going to find it. You my neighbor?" I asked, jerking my head to the shack directly connected to Vance's.

"For now, yeah. Finch," he offered, though wisely didn't extend his hand, didn't come close. Men tended not to do stupid shit like that when you were holding a weapon sharp enough to sever a limb without much effort. "You got a name?"

"Not that you need to know."

Another of those devilish smirks.

"Fair enough. Well, you can rest easy tonight knowing you got a real devil one room away."

"Finch, I have a real devil living right in my skin. But it's nice to know the neighbors."

With that, I shut myself inside, realizing that in the course of an hour, I had spoken more words than I had likely spoken over the past month. Six months.

My throat actually felt scratchy.

Closing myself behind the door, locking it to humor Vance, I dropped down on the couch, head spinning.

Things had been so simple for so long.

Train, eat, sleep, research.

When I had trained and researched enough, I followed through on the mission.

That was it.

That was all I had to think about, all I had to digest on a daily basis.

I overestimated my ability to handle my reintroduction into polite society. I was pretty sure I had been as impolite as possible.

I was trying not to be too hard on myself. I hadn't needed things like pleasantries in ages. In fact, the harsher I was, the better it worked out for me.

It was something I needed to work on, clearly. And it seemed like I had about five days to do it. Before my parents got home. Before everyone would know I was back. Before everyone would want to talk to me.

I couldn't be snapping at them all the time.

They didn't deserve that.

I wasn't the Ferryn they knew and loved anymore. But maybe I could play her. For a while. Maybe I could give them what they needed. Then get back to my mission.

I owed them that.

The face of the girl they had raised.

My father, well, I was pretty sure he could handle this new me, could understand what life could do to a person.

But my mother? My mother may have suffered more than I ever realized when I was growing up, but she had stayed sweet, generous, loving through it all. She had a strength I clearly had not inherited.

She wouldn't get it.

She would try to.

She would love me regardless.

But there would be a part of her aching for her little girl.

I had to give her that. For all I had put her through over the years.

I wasn't sure how I would manage it, but I had a feeling a good start was with coffee with cream and sugar, and pickles, and crunchy cheese puffs, and Devil Dogs.

And maybe being less of a dick to Vance.

Really, he'd been nothing but good to me.

Then.

And now.

Kicking out of my boots, I climbed off the couch, moving over toward the record player sitting on a TV dinner stand in the corner, a moving box full of old records below it.

Music had once been a huge part of my life. I'd sat endlessly listening to everything I could get my hands on, widely discussing the merits and pitfalls of each genre, whether bands deserved the recognition they'd gotten or not.

I hadn't heard music in almost a decade. Sure, there had been caught snippets from passing cars, but mostly pop crap, mostly soulless words sang over electronic instruments.

I hadn't heard real music in so long.

Holden liked—no, needed—silence.

And I simply never sought it out.

Maybe a part of me was worried it was something too deeply steeped in who I had been, that clinging to it would make it impossible to change the way I knew I would need to.

My hands flipped through old, familiar favorites, making me wonder if they were favorites because Vance and I had the same taste or because I modeled my taste after his. It wasn't so far-fetched an idea. Young girls bent themselves into the shapes men most desired of them all the time. Sometimes so much so that they no longer recognized themselves anymore.

I liked to believe I was too headstrong for that, but now with everything being a time-soaked memory, I couldn't be certain.

Somehow, though, I was very, very certain about what I wanted to listen to when my hands found a record I had never seen before.

One belonging to Vance's band.

Turning it over, the date was the year I ran away. But none of the tracks had names of the songs I knew they had been working on.

Curious, eager, I slipped it out of its sleeve, putting it in the player, dropping the needle.

I think I ran through the whole album twice before I finally heard a bike rumbling down the road, snapping me out of the album that was really just seemingly one long story.

My story.

It was *my* story.

It started with a track called *Young Girl* all about the younger version of me being infatuated with an older guy who knew she was too young. It was a sweet, slow song, almost a ballad. Or as close to a ballad as a rock band could get.

From there, though, the story took a darker turn. Much like mine had.

Taken was about a man standing by helplessly watching a woman be taken to an unknown fate.

Don't Cry was another sad song of helplessness, a woman who saw no way out of a bad situation.

The next track was about the bad guys, about their predatory ways.

Closer to the end, there was a blood-soaked, brutal story about a woman fighting her way to freedom.

It concluded with a song called *Runaway* , this time in the perspective of all the people she left behind. Lines about her mother crying, about her father worrying, about her friends picking up a phone to call her only to remember they can't. Which had to have been a nod to Iggy. Then, finally, the man she left behind, lips still tingling from a stolen kiss goodbye.

If I were being critical, I would say it romanticized an ugly reality.

But I wasn't being critical.

In fact, all I could feel was awe.

Vance had always been a good songwriter. The only lyricist of the group, he always explored interesting topics, always had a way of weaving words together that was both blunt and beautiful at the same time.

But this?

This was something else entirely.

Maybe because this stemmed from an actual experience, something he had clearly felt deeply.

For a few hours, I actually felt myself transported back, felt the darkness, the loneliness, the helplessness.

It had been so long since I felt such things. I had been consumed by the rage for so long that it was almost hard to remember that the rage had stemmed from the even more uncomfortable feelings Vance portrayed in his lyrics.

More pieces of me I had lost along the way.

As though the record wanted to keep our time together a little secret, the music cut just as Vance's engine did as well.

Shutting off the player, I moved back over toward the couch, trying to wipe any lingering emotions off my face, out of my eyes, knowing that he had once been able to read me so well.

"Don't ask how I managed to get all this back on my bike," he declared after somehow managing to unlock the door with his arms and hands loaded down with bags.

Bags fell to the floor and I felt my hope drop a bit too. Though I should have anticipated it. There was no way for him to get me a coffee from She's Bean Around on his bike.

A slow smirk pulled at his lips as he stooped, rooting around in a brown paper bag. "Worried I didn't get you your coffee?" he asked, producing a deep purple stainless steel reusable travel mug. "I had to get inventive on the bike. This said leakproof. I decided to gamble with it. Seemed to work." I nearly lunged at him, hands cradling the cup for a long moment before pushing the button to open the mouth. "Drip with vanilla almond milk, caramel syrup, and two sugars," he recited.

"You remembered." Hell, I barely remembered. I had just been excited about the idea of cream and sugar.

"So did Jazzy. She was like 'You know what's weird? That's the same drink the missing girl used to order years back.' Even she remembers you."

"Iggy and I practically lived there for a year. Oh, my God," I moaned as I took my first sip. Yes, moaned.

Judging by the awkward cough Vance let out, it sounded as sexual to him as it did to me. "Good as you remember?" he asked, a slow smirk pulling at those lips I had spent endless hours fantasizing of kissing.

"Better," I corrected.

"It's the little things you miss," he told me, seemingly from knowledge. Like maybe he had left Navesink Bank for a while as well. Long enough to miss the little things about it.

There was so much I didn't know.

And what was maybe even more surprising, things I wanted to know.

Where had he been?

Why had he written an album about my life?

Why did he become a Henchmen?

Burning questions all, but I somehow felt I had no right asking, demanding anything from these people that I had left behind.

"I think I did pretty well," he added, stooping to retrieve a few of the bags that belonged to the local grocery store. "I got the shit on your list, but grabbed a few extra things. You can't exist on Devil Dogs and cheese puffs. This fridge doesn't hold much, but I got some stuff to throw in the cabinet. And I can always pick up anything else you want. Or bring by some takeout."

Takeout.

God.

I had nearly forgotten about takeout.

Chinese.

Pizza.

Fried stuff.

Oh, fuck yes, fried stuff.

"I can..."

"No," he cut me off. "You can't," he added.

It had been a long, long time since someone told me I couldn't do something.

Maybe Holden had done it in the early years to piss me off, to try to get me to fight harder, but after a while, we had become almost equals in life. We trained together. We ran together. Sometimes we hit the town together. But we lived wholly independent lives outside of that. Really, even after almost nine years, I had no idea what the hell he did all day in his house.

Suddenly, I felt like I should have maybe tried a little to know him better, to connect with him more.

Everything between us had always been about the mission. About molding me to be able to do it on my own.

We didn't sit and have long conversations about our paths or our hopes and dreams for the future.

It never even occurred to me to try before.

Just like it had never occurred to him to tell me I could—or could not—do something.

Inwardly, I bristled, feeling a telltale tingling on my nerve endings. The start of anger, before it went deep, infected everything inside me.

"I'm not sixteen anymore, Vance. You can't tell me what to do."

"Ferryn, I don't think you ever let me tell you what to do," he told me, shaking his head. "And I'm not trying to tell you what to do now. I'm trying to remind you that you need to be here in this shithole for a few days. If someone drove down the street and saw you picking up food somewhere, it would be all over this town in ten minutes flat, and you know that. There is no anonymity here."

"That's true," I agreed, feeling the anger fizzle out as suddenly as it had started.

"I know it has never been in your nature, but you're just going to have to let me take care of you for a bit."

Take care of me.

Once upon a time, those words would have given me shivers, would have made my heart full to bursting.

Now, though, there was mostly a void where that heart used to be. But, much to my surprise, I did feel a bit of a warmth spread across my entire upper chest, a flush that was both comforting and alarming at the same time.

My tongue felt fat and clumsy in my mouth as my lips formed around words. "I, ah, I guess that will work. I could probably order in, too. The delivery kids have to have changed by now—What?" I asked when his smile spread a bit as he moved across the room to stoop to retrieve the other bags, making me suddenly realize that I probably should have been helping out.

"Kids. Last time you were here, those kids were all older than you. I remember you saying you wanted to get a job delivering for the pizza place but your dad said absolutely not."

"He said 'absolutely-fucking-not,'" I clarified, smirking at the memory.

"You were so hot about that."

"It was sexist of him to say that I couldn't be a delivery person."

"Maybe."

"Definitely. I bet Fallon and Finn were allowed to do deliveries. Such a double standard."

"Sometimes those double standards exist to protect you, not to take away your freedoms. What?" he asked, making me realize I was small-eyeing him pretty hard.

"Nothing. You just never used to be that backward."

"Backward," he scoffed, shaking his head, deliberately turning away, moving so he could have his back to me as he shuffled through the bags.

"Yes, backward. Weren't you the guy who once told Iggy that she better not save herself for marriage? Weren't you the guy who told us both that we would learn a lot more about the world by being exposed to it than we would reading about it?"

"Yeah, babe, but that was before the world threw you into a basement then ripped you away from everyone who cared about you, okay? Shit changes."

"I don't see why my shit would change your shit."

"You're fucking kidding me, right?" he snapped. Snapped. Vance, the Vance I had always known, was someone incredibly slow to anger. He was always the sort to let things roll off his back, to shrug it all away. And the girl I had been—so easily riled, so reactive to everything—had always appreciated his inner calm, his easy self-assurance.

There was no mistaking, though, that Vance was most definitely the riled one right in that moment. His blue eyes blazed. His jaw tightened so hard that a muscle ticked there, something I found almost alarmingly fascinating.

"I'm not kidding you," I told him, arching a brow just because I wanted him to keep going, I wanted to get a rise out of him, I wanted to see more of his rage. I didn't stop to wonder why it was so important to me that he even had any. Had I maybe considered it in the moment, I likely would have concluded that a small part of the girl I used to be was thinking that if he had a little of his own rage, he might be able to accept mine.

"You fucking *left*, Ferryn. We worried ourselves fucking sick about you for days after you were taken. And the minute we know you are safe again, you tear out of town and we never see you again. We are going to skip right over the bit about how selfish that shit was because I'm sure one of your aunts or uncles will unleash into you about that since your parents will be too relieved to do it themselves. Putting that aside, your shit, whatever that shit was, it affected every fucking person you left behind. Just because you needed to start a new life didn't mean you got erased from all of ours. We couldn't just move on like there wasn't something always missing. Your shit was our shit too. Thought in about nine years, you would have grown up enough to see that."

The anger this time rose up out of embarrassment, out of shame, out of the bone-deep recognition of the truth in his words.

Yes, my mission mattered.

Yes, I was making a difference in the world.

Yes, my life was mine to do whatever I wanted with.

And, yes, it was okay to be selfish sometimes.

But that didn't mean I hadn't been rash and maybe even cruel with my decisions, with the way I cut everyone out.

I wrote my mom.

Every week.

I didn't miss a letter. Not even when I was trapped in a hospital bed recovering from surgery.

I tried to convince myself that was enough.

Even if a part of me knew better.

"I don't know who the hell you think you're talking to like that," I started, feeling my lips quivering in an old—and up until right that moment, seemingly overcome—reaction to strong emotions. "I understand I have things to explain and apologies to make. To my family. To people who love me. I get that. But you don't get to act all holier than fucking thou with me. I mean who the hell were you? The big brother to my friend? I didn't mean anything to you. If you took my shit on, that was a *choice*. You can't blame me because you wanted to be a martyr in a situation that had nothing to do with you."

"Nothing to do with me," he repeated, voice chillingly cold. An actual shiver moved up my spine. "You know what, fuck this," he said, tossing down the bag he had been rifling through, long legs making short progress from where he had been standing to the door. "Believe whatever the fuck you want, Ferryn. You always have. Guess some shit never changes."

The door slammed hard enough to shake the panes of glass in the windows, a sound that made me jerk a bit, not because I was even prone to startling, but because violence was not something I could have ever anticipated coming from Vance.

Apparently, I didn't know him as well as I always thought.

Or maybe he had changed.

It wouldn't be too surprising.

I sure as hell changed too.

Sitting there in utter silence, I could feel something foreign. A burning at the backs of my eyes. A hint of something impossible.

Tears.

Blinking hard, I fought them away, standing up, making my way to the bags he had abandoned, needing something to do to distract myself.

There was a loud banging on the wall to my side before a newly familiar voice carried through the apparently very thin insulation.

"That was a great prelude to an upcoming hatefuck if I ever heard one," Finch called to me, making a snort burst out of me as my hand moved upward, running my fingers through my newly longish hair on top.

"Mind your business, Finch," I called back, but couldn't even muster a little firmness to back the demand.

Not more than five seconds later, the door to Vance's apartment was opening, Finch taking up the whole doorway, leaning against the jamb, smoking, a beer in his hand.

"But your business sounds a lot more interesting, sweets."

"There's nothing sweet about me."

"All that sour, gorgeous, there is always sweet underneath it."

"Oh, a chainsmoker and troublemaker and philosopher to boot," I mumbled, folding the yoga pants Vance had picked up in simple neutrals—gray, black, deep brown, green—into a pile on top of the tees and tanks he had picked up as well.

"So, you've been gone a while, huh?" he asked, taking a long swig of his beer, still not moving from his position on the doorjamb. Intrusive, but with boundaries. I found I didn't hate the combination. And it was maybe nice to talk to someone who didn't used to know me, who didn't have all these expectations of how I was supposed to behave.

It didn't seem to matter how old you were, when you went home, you were an unsure teenager once again, apparently.

"You could say that," I agreed. Time was subjective. It had gone by in a blink for me. For those I left behind, maybe not so much.

"Homecomings can be rough."

"You have no fucking idea," I promised him. This was just the very tip of the iceberg for me. Vance was right, one or two or a half a dozen of my family members were going to ream me out. And I would have no real defense against it. But that was a problem for another day.

"Shit will shake out. It usually does."

"That is very naive coming from someone with a prison tat on his hand," I told him, rolling my eyes. I'd missed it before outside, the light casting everything but his face in shadow. But there was no mistaking the cobweb covering the whole top of his hand, a sign of doing a long stretch. And with the shitty, inconsistent lines, it had to have been done with a pen and lighter. Maybe that was how he knew a thing or two about homecomings.

"Yeah, maybe," he agreed. "So, you been gone for a while, what have you been up to?"

Five

- Journal Entry - 18th Birthday -

I caught Holden staring at me.

It was something he had done a lot the first year. Not in a creepy, predatory way. But in a way like he couldn't figure me out. Like I was a clock that refused to tick like he wanted. Like it bothered him.

After a while, though, we seemed to sort of come to an understanding about each other. He was there watching me evolve from the hurt, unsure girl who had shown up at his door.

He stopped looking at me like I didn't tick right.

So it was weird to catch him staring at me with that intensity again.

"What?" I asked, brow furrowing.

"Fresh as fallen fucking snow."

Now, this was a man prone to not saying much. But when he did speak, he usually spoke plainly and bluntly. He was not a flowery person. But those were oddly flowery words.

"What? Like I'm pale?" I asked, scrunching up my nose.

"Like you're a virgin, kid."

I was officially not a kid anymore. As of four a.m., I was—in the eyes of the law—a full-fledged adult. But I knew that compared to him, I was a kid. And he would likely always see me that way.

There was no denying the fact that those words directed right at me—along with the truth behind them—made a flush move across my chest, up my throat, over my cheeks.

Clearly, we'd never discussed sex.

He'd been a grown man and I a child, after all.

It was all kinds of inappropriate. It was the kind of gross stuff we were both in agreement was wrong with the world.

A part of me was more than a little worried that he was saying it now because I was legal, because he had those sorts of feelings about me. And, well, Holden had sort of become a stand-in uncle-figure for me, reminding me a lot of the uncles I had left behind, finding a sort of comfort in that type of relationship.

I never had anything even remotely resembling feelings for him.

The idea of him having them for me made my stomach churn.

"For fuck's sake," he growled, slamming a hand down on the table, making our bottles of water teeter and topple. "Don't look at me like that. I didn't mean it like that."

"How did you mean it then?" I demanded, crossing my arms over my nothing-there chest, feeling my pride sting just the tiniest bit. No, I didn't want him to be attracted to me, but he'd made it sound like such a thing was absolutely revolting. I'd worked hard to shake off any need for external validation, but I was pretty sure it was encoded into our DNA not to want to be thought of as disgusting.

"I mean it as... have you really given this shit thought?"

"What shit? The mission shit?" I asked, still feeling a little jolt in my stomach when I cursed, only ever having done so with friends in the past, never around my elders.

"Yeah."

"That's *all* I have been thinking about for two years. You know that. I wouldn't still be here if I wasn't."

"Clearly, you haven't given it as much thought as I have."

"How do you figure?"

"I walk in there one day, try to make some waves, save some girls, take out some shitheads. I get outnumbered. I get my ass kicked. That's what happens to me. You ever really stop to think how what might happen to me and what might happen to you are very different fucking things?"

The stomach dropping to my feet sensation was proof in and of itself that, no, I had not given that particular thing enough—or any—thought.

Why, I wasn't sure.

It should have been something at the forefront of my mind.

Human traffickers and the men who paid to use the women being trafficked were rapists. They raped. That was what they did. That was what they were capable of.

And if they got the better of me, that would be my fate too.

Of course it would.

A swirling sick feeling moved up my belly and throat, bile catching at the back of my tongue before I forced myself to swallow it back down, refusing to get sick.

I had to be harder than that.

I read a book once about a female field agent doing covert ops who used to always wear a pearl necklace. Except one pearl wasn't a pearl at all but a fatal dose of poison should she bite into the hardened shell it was safely encased in.

The book had claimed she had the precaution in case of capture, in case she was worried she might spill state secrets.

Suddenly, I knew better.

She wore it because she understood the kind of torture that could be inflicted on her was very different than the types typically inflicted upon men who were captured.

Rape was a weapon used against women in so many different ways.

It was one that could be used against me.

Sure, that was why I had to train harder, be better, but that didn't guarantee anything. Something could always go wrong.

Short of wearing a chastity belt, there seemed to be no way of ensuring it would never happen.

A bit uncomfortably, I cleared my throat, willing my voice to come out stronger than it felt as it built inside me. "What does... why does my virginity have anything to do with it?"

"Christ," he growled, raking a hand down his face. "Didn't you have some sex education or some shit back home?"

My mother had called in two ladies from our town—Fiona who owned a local phone sex operating business, and Autumn who owned the local adult toy store—and let the experts and some of my aunts give me all the details. I knew more about sex than I *cared* to know at thirteen. But no one could say I wasn't well informed. My mom had been sure that knowledge about sex was power, it enabled me to make smart decisions about it, instead of jumping into it too young because of pure curiosity.

If a fact existed about sex, I knew it.

They'd even given me a little gift bag of toys so I could learn to pleasure myself so I didn't think guys were the only ones who could do it.

It was all a bit over the top and incredibly embarrassing at the time. But good. I ended up giving Iggy the talk because her parents refused to have any kind of frank and honest conversations about sex with her, believing it was still reasonable to expect everyone to wait until marriage.

"Yes, I had sex talks. I am fully aware of all the mechanics. And everything else," I admitted, chin lifting a little, daring him to question me.

"Then you know what a first time is often like."

That was the one place where my aunts all had differing experiences. Some had excruciating pain, others just a little discomfort, some no pain at all. But the general consensus was it wasn't super pleasant the first time or two.

"Yes," I agreed.

"Look. Just fucking look," he said, turning back to me, planting his giant fists on the table across from me, completely drawing me, pinning me with his dark eyes. "Your first time should be given, not taken. Okay? That is all I am going to say about it.I am going to be there for your first mission. I am going to make sure shit doesn't happen to you. No matter the cost. But when you are on your own, kid..." he trailed off, shrugging his shoulders, making his way to the door. "Just something to think about," he added. "Be ready at dusk," he finished, moving outside, door grumbling closed as he hit the button.

He was right.

It was something I needed to think about.

But not right then.

Right then, I needed to focus.

Because it was my eighteenth birthday.

And Holden's way to celebrate was to take me on our first mission.

I had a little hand in the researching. He'd brought a laptop into the garage one day, firing it up, opening up a dark web browser, and showing me how to find the scumbags.

And find them, I did.

So, so, so many scumbags.

My head hurt just thinking about it. About all the women and kids who were out there suffering. About the fact that no matter how hard I worked, I couldn't save them all.

I could, though, save some.

So Holden and I chose an operation as our target.

We spent weeks researching the players, finding locations.

And then we trained harder as we waited for me to be officially of age.

So that if I landed in a hospital, no one could call my parents. Or even if I got caught and locked up.

It was time.

Tonight was the night.

We were going in.

I had taken a life.

One life.

My grandmother's.

With a gun.

Holden wouldn't even let me hold one of his guns. He told me that since we wouldn't be able to use them on missions, there was no reason for me to 'play around with' them.

We trained with sharp and blunt instruments.

And he constantly drilled it into my head that taking a life with a bullet was a detached kill. And that taking a life with a blade was close and intimate. It would be different. I would be different.

Not having any experience, I couldn't contradict him. So I steeled myself. I reminded myself all the evil things they had did, how they had shown the women they captured no mercy. And that they deserved none from me.

I would be changed maybe.

But I had already changed so much.

The idea of more didn't scare me like it once might have.

If anything, I was ready to make the full transition.

From trainee to master.

Maybe normal people would think it was a fucked up thing to want to be a master in. But I wanted to be a master.

At taking lives.

At sending them back to hell where they belonged.

I ate plain toast to keep my stomach settled.

I took another makeshift bath.

I re-buzzed my head.

I put on a tank top then a long-sleeved tee, the jeans Holden had picked up for me in the men's department so they fit just the right kind of saggy.

The plan was to appear like a dude.

And to get in the doors with Holden doing the same.

And then taking over.

I shrugged on a leather jacket, checking out my reflection in the window, both relieved and a little bothered by the fact that I could pass for a guy. A pretty guy, but a guy nonetheless.

Hearing Holden's door close, I took a deep breath, moving out into the gym, waiting for him to open the door.

"What's this?" I asked when he handed me something wrapped in a brown bag from the supermarket.

"Birthday present, I guess you can call it," he said, shrugging it off. "Careful, it's sharp," he added when I eagerly went to reach inside.

It was.

Sharp.

So fucking sharp.

And beautiful in a lethal sort of way.

A double-bladed hunting karambit.

It had a slightly curved wooden handle in the center for your hand and then two fierce curved blades- one that went across the fronts of your knuckles, the other that curved around the back of your hand.

Making you deadly in both directions.

"Wow."

"Just a glide across the skin will cause major damage."

With that and nothing else, we climbed in his truck.

In utter, almost unbearable silence, we drove four hours to our destination, an old warehouse from some bygone era when it had helped employ local townspeople.

Lots of windows.

Lots of exits.

Lots of ways for things to go sideways really quickly.

We'd trained for this, I reminded myself.

I could do it.

I *had* to do it.

I didn't get much time to let my fears get to me. Because as soon as Holden cut the engine, he was climbing out and making his way down the street we had parked on for protection, making his way toward our destination.

"Women are in there getting raped as we speak," he mumbled to me as we got close, as I felt my body tensing, my stomach plummeting.

He knew I needed to hear it.

He knew how the mere mention of that reality made my vision go red with rage.

It burned through my system savagely, singeing everything in its wake.

We each made our way to the door, giving the code we'd agreed to online at separate times, looking like we didn't know each other.

And just like that, we were led inside.

"You can each pick a girl and then we will talk money. More for certain things, you know."

Oh, I knew.

More for virgins.

More for 'spirited' girls who would put up a fight.

More for younger.

More for tag-teaming.

More for certain kinks.

More to rough them up.

My fire didn't need more kindling.

But every slimy word out of his mouth made me burn hotter.

Until I simply got engulfed when he opened a door showing us a row of unclothed women. Some drugged. Some lost in their own minds. A few openly crying.

And that was it.

Any worries I had about my ability to get the job done disappeared as I reached into my pocket, slid my hand around my new double blade, pivoted, and swung my arm out.

He didn't even have time to gasp before the knife dug in, casting arterial spray across my chest and the side of Holden's shoulder.

Holden didn't move to act at first, to go back outside to handle the other men we'd crossed paths with.

He shushed the women with a finger to his lips.

They had no reason to trust us, but they seemed to understand without us saying anything that we were there to save them, to get them free.

The sound of the body slamming to the ground, breathless, dead, was what triggered others to rush inside.

There was no thinking, just action, just pure instinct that Holden had drilled into me for the past two years.

Four men were on the ground in the single room in the span of a few short moments. Three dead, one gasping for a few final breaths.

"Are there more?" Holden spoke, not the least winded while I gasped for some air. Not as badly as I once would have, but enough to annoy me, make me vow to take up some more cardio.

"One," the tallest and oldest of the women declared, desperately trying to cover her nude body. There was nothing in the room, no modesty I could give them. There would be time to comfort them later, though. We needed to finish the job we came to do.

"You lead," Holden demanded, jerking his chin toward the door. "You all stay here until we say it is safe," he added to the women, getting a firm nod from the tall woman.

Holden pulled the door closed behind us, shockingly loud in the quiet space.

There was a TV on somewhere further down the hall.

I followed it to find a cracked door and a man sitting on a chair, a woman on her knees before him.

Bile rose up as I took a steadying breath, willing my footsteps to be silent as I moved forward, thankful for the loud cheering of the football game, allowing me to move directly behind the chair.

The movement caught the girl's attention, making her stop the act she was being forced to perform, eyes bulging, gasp sucking inward.

Her surprise worked in my favor.

The man turned to try to look.

The tension made the blade slide into his neck like butter.

"It's okay," I murmured to the girl as she scrambled backward across the dirty floor, hands grabbing for her own throat, worried I would turn my blade on her. "It's alright. We were only here for the men. We are going to get you girls home," I added, watching as the words landed, as they sank in.

I could tell the moment they did because her entire body started quaking, a hysterical hitch catching in her throat.

"Got some shirts," Holden mumbled, digging through a backpack near the door.

"Here, put this on," I told her, holding out a tee that would at least offer a small bit of modesty.

While she shrugged into the tee, my gaze went to the man, his brilliant blood covering his neck and chest.

I wasn't sure where the urge came from, but my gloved finger moved out, sinking into the plasma, then moving toward the wall.

F was X.

It was a sort of vanity to want to mark your job like that. And I knew it was always smarter to stay as anonymous as possible. But I couldn't seem to help myself.

"We got to go before more clients show up," Holden reminded me as we led the girl back to the other room where we handed out shirts and blankets.

"Take this phone," he said, speaking to the tall woman once more, now much more comfortable wearing an old white tee that barely skimmed the tops of her thighs. "Call the police after ten minutes, okay? Can you give us ten minutes?"

"We need to get away," I added, willing her to understand how important this is. "So we can keep taking out monsters like these."

"Ten minutes," she agreed while one of the other girls lowered to the floor, cradling her knees to her chest, rocking as she sobbed.

I wanted to believe they all had loved ones at home, people who could help them recover, love them through their path to healing.

I knew it was naive.

I knew that some of them would likely be on their own, would have to fight their demons alone.

But anything, I was sure, absolutely anything was better than being stuck here until they were no longer useful.

"Let's go," Holden demanded.

When we hit the front door, we took off at a dead run.

Holden was stronger, but I was leaner, able to keep up as we made our way back to the car.

I grabbed the black bag he'd placed under the wiper blade, slipping our gloves into it, my jacket, my outer shirt.

Holden had the foresight to wear black, hiding the bloodstains he sported.

My heart was in my throat the entire ride back to his place, sure we were going to be found out, positive cops would pull up behind us, lights and sirens spelling out our doom.

It was almost hard to accept that we'd gotten away with it when we finally pulled up to the garage.

"I have to clean the clothes. Detail the car. You get some rest," he told me, dismissing me. "Hey, kid," he called when I was about to slam the door.

"Yeah?" I asked, feeling a little buzzy, a little foreign in my own skin.

"You did good. You got what it takes," he added. "Get some sleep."

With that, he pulled away, door slamming on its own as he went.

It took a long time for the shock to slip away, for my mind to seem to be able to grasp what had happened on a rational level.

I couldn't bring myself to move inside, feeling a layer of filth coating me from head to toe.

I took myself to the hose, finding the bar of soap I hid in a plastic container beside it, stripping out of my clothes, and scrubbing every single inch of me.

Two times.

Three.

Ten.

Fifteen.

I lost count.

But I knew I had to stop when my skin felt raw and sensitive.

I walked like that, stark freaking naked, back to the garage, going inside, locking myself into my room, and lying alone on my floor mattress, still feeling the grime all over me.

It was many hours later that I realized it would never go away.

It was a part of me now.

I would have to learn to get used to it.

And that was how I spent my eighteenth birthday.

Six

Vance - Present Day

She was different.

Maybe I should have expected that.

I mean, of course she was different.

She'd been gone for almost nine years.

I guess, to an extent, she had been preserved in my mind as the sixteen-year-old who was never short on topic for conversations, never shy with her strong opinions. Confident. Interesting. Deep.

She still seemed confident and deep.

But she didn't speak much.

She just sat there with those deep eyes that I used to read so easily. There were still sparks there at times, but for the most part, they were blank, seeing but showing nothing.

And while, years before, she had been passionate and even a bit heated, she hadn't been angry.

Angry was very much something she appeared to be now, though. And quick to it.

I'd never been one for anger either.

There was no denying that I'd snapped at her, though. Not that she maybe didn't have it coming. But it was still unlike me.

I'd made good points.

But maybe it wasn't my place to make them.

Maybe she was right and I had no reason to be so resentful about her attitude.

I had no idea what she had been through.

I think that was why I had written so much about it. I think I had been trying to understand what she'd been through, what could have prompted her to not only flee, but to stay away for so long.

I guess I never did come to any conclusions.

And any theories I had at one point flew out the window because, clearly, everything she had been through had been much, much worse than I had imagined if they had changed her so entirely.

"The fuck put you in such a shit mood?" West asked, making me realize I'd been slamming around the kitchen making something to eat. "Did you and Daddy Reign's girl have a nice reunion?" he pressed.

"Let's hope that a couple days in my old place gives her time to remember who she is."

"People change, man," West said, shrugging. "I imagine girls who spend time starving in basements then run away to do fuck-knows what tend to change more than usual."

"Maybe," I agreed.

"Gotta wonder why you are so bent about it."

"No, actually, you don't need to wonder about that."

"Still," he said, sighing, barely holding back a grin, "I find myself wondering."

"Well, don't."

"It seems it is not in my control."

"Try harder," I grumbled, pretending to ignore the shit-eating grin on his face.

If there was one thing West liked, it was when he got a rise out of someone. He chose opposite sides in an argument just to fuck with you even if he personally agreed with your stance. He pulled pranks on the girls. He taunted the shit out of the guys when they got lovesick over some chick they were getting serious with.

I had made the mistake of letting him know that Ferryn could be used to get a rise out of me. I was in for a lot of shit when no one else was around.

He'd keep the secret.

Until Reign got back.

Then, well, who the fuck knew what he was capable of saying or implying.

Not that there was anything to imply, of course.

There wasn't—and had never been—anything between Ferryn and me. We'd been sort of friends. As much as a nineteen-year-old guy can be friends with his little sister's sixteen-year-old friend.

That was it.

Sure, I mean, yeah, she had wanted it to be more. I wasn't stupid or blind and she had never been all that subtle.

I liked her mind.

And, well, that was all I could like.

That was all you could like when someone was too young for you. And it was sick to even harbor thoughts like 'in two years she will be eighteen.'

My mind didn't go there.

But there is no way to tell that should she and Iggy have stayed friends, and she therefore continued to be a part of my circle, that once she turned eighteen, something might not have progressed.

It's impossible to say.

I had been a different person then as well. A little too full of myself. A little careless with hearts. I hadn't been a relationship sort of guy. I liked fun and casual, and I hung around girls who liked fun and casual.

So who knows. Maybe she'd have turned eighteen, decided she didn't have any interest in just being one in the line of other girls, and found some other more serious guy to shine all her attention on.

But a part of me still believed that had she stayed, had my life continued on the same path it was on back then, we might have started something up at some point.

We just always clicked. We liked the same things. We always enjoyed each other's company. And Iggy had always made it clear she would love it if she could have Ferryn as an actual sister one day.

But even though there was no history in more than a platonic sense, she was absolutely a trigger for me now, something West could use to torment me endlessly with.

"Inquiring minds have to know," West said, and I didn't trust the smirk on his lips. "Did you diddle the president's daughter?"

I'd never had a short fuse.

Or so I thought.

This night was teaching me some things about myself that I maybe never wanted to know.

Like how easily I could snap.

Because one second, he was across the room from me.

The next, I had him pinned to the wall by his throat.

"Watch it," my voice hissed out of me.

A reaction was slow to cross West's face. For someone who often did flit around his emotions quickly, it was strange to see the brow arch ever-so-slowly.

"We're friends, brothers, and I thought this went without saying," he started, choosing his words carefully, something vaguely threatening in his tone, showing me a side of him that I didn't often get to see, "but you don't want to fuck with me, man. You throw hands at me again, and this is going to get ugly fast."

I didn't doubt him.

West was let into the club for legitimate reasons. Reign didn't owe him a marker like he did with me. West didn't have an *in* like Colson did since Virgin shacked up with Freddie.

He was patched in because he had things to offer.

And, from what I heard, those things included violence.

"Fuck," I hissed, remembering myself, releasing his neck. "Shit, West. I don't know what the fuck is wrong with me," I admitted, raking a hand through my hair. Every ounce of me felt off-kilter. My mind was racing from one thing to another so fast it was giving me mental whiplash.

"Really?" he asked, cracking his neck. "Because I've seen these signs a few too many times."

"What signs?"

"Oh, the pacing, the crazy eyes, the fits of violence. Always have one thing in common. A woman."

"She's been missing for almost nine years, West. Shit is different."

"Shit might be different, but some other shit seems like it is starting to make sense."

"What are you talking about?"

"Your moody ass," he told me, smiling as he snatched a bottle off the back bar. "I never made the connection. But then I saw that girl out there. It's all falling into place."

"I don't know what you're talking about."

"Always noticed you eyeing these chicks. Short black haired chicks. But you never approached them. Just looked at 'em all longingly. Last I saw a picture of Ferryn, she had long-ass hair. It never clicked. She shaved her head. And so you've been looking for her in every bar and club and every town we've done a drop in. Eight and a half years, you've been haunted by this chick. Or the memory of her. And now she shows up unexpected and she's nothing like the girl you knew and were pining for."

"I wasn't pining for her. It was never like that for us. She was my little sister's best friend. That's it. We got along. But it was platonic."

"Platonic because she was jailbait maybe."

"Don't," I snapped. "I don't like what you're implying."

"Just thinking out loud," he said, shrugging, tipping back a bottle. "But I am going to throw this out here because it is something you might need to keep in mind for the next week."

"What?" I asked, feeling like I didn't want to know.

"No matter how fucking tempting it might be, you don't touch the president's daughter."

With that, he moved out of the common space, going down the hall where the rooms were situated, leaving me alone with my own swirling thoughts.

I didn't need the warning, of course.

I had no plans on touching Ferryn.

Unless it was to grab her and shake some fucking sense back into her, that is.

Too amped up to rest, I told West I would take the night shift, deciding that if I was going to be pacing, pacing the grounds doing rounds was at least a useful.

By the time the sun came up and Cash's bike was rumbling up the road, I was near dead on my feet.

Thankful for the break, and happy I would be able to sleep instead of lie to his face about his niece, I headed to bed, not waking up until late in the afternoon.

Groggy and disoriented, it took a long time for everything to click together in my head.

Ferryn.

My old apartment.

Her not being able to leave.

Skinnier than ever, the food I had brought her was probably more than enough to sustain her, but that didn't mean she should be forced to exist off of chips and junk food cakes and peanut butter.

I took a shower, gave Cash an excuse about having to meet Iggy for lunch, then picked us up some food and coffee—investing in a couple more of those steel containers—then making my way back toward my old place, wondering what she might have done to pass the time, to keep herself occupied. The lack of entertainment had never bothered me much. I had always been playing music, writing music, listening to music. I didn't need a TV.

Had she plowed through the books I had gotten her? Back when she was younger, she was never without a book in her purse, in her backpack. She would constantly ask if I could drop her and Iggs at the library to hang out, or if I could drive her past it so she could return books or pick up something she'd been on the waiting list for. I'd heard her say she went through one on a school day and two on each day there was no school. She'd been an insatiable reader.

Unfortunately, it was slim pickings at the box store. The majority of the books were paperbacks that seemed like thrillers or crime fiction. I ended up having to get her a couple that looked like historicals, a biography of a 1920s socialite, and a couple ones with couples embracing on the cover. Thankfully, so late at night, the only lane open was self-checkout, so I didn't have to get eyes from the cashier over the smut.

It was proving hard to picture Ferryn picking up and reading them. I guess because it was proving hard to think of her as a full-grown woman with her own sexual history.

The recognition of that made my stomach drop a bit, something I chose to blame on a bump on the road I was speeding a bit down.

"Might not be up yet," a voice called out toward me, masculine, with a hint of a southern twang, making my head move to find him leaning against his front door, smoking lazily.

Last time I had been to my place, the guy who had been living there was all of eighty with a wet cough and rheumy eyes.

Who this new guy was was anyone's guess, but I had a feeling he wasn't hanging out in Navesink Bank for the proximity to the beaches. He looked like he was here for trouble.

"Excuse me?"

"Your girl. We were up late drinking. Drank me under the fucking table," he added. "Got a tolerance I've never seen. But you would already know that, wouldn't you?"

There was an odd inflection in his tone, like he was suspicious of something. What, I wasn't sure. Since there was no way he knew who Ferryn was or that she had once been missing.

"Yeah, she's always been able to hold her own." In more ways than one. "Who are you?"

"Finch," he supplied inclining his head.

"Right, well, Finch, I would appreciate you staying the fuck away from my girl."

"Don't worry, man. I'm no threat to you. Like my girls a little meatier. And with duller claws."

"Duller claws? In this town?" I asked, lips curving up. "Good luck with that."

With that, feeling a little bit better that Ferryn was not Finch's type—even if I knew it was none of my business who was or was not interested in her, that it wasn't my job to protect her, that I had no reason to feel possessive over her—I made my way into the apartment just as Ferryn was walking out of the bathroom.

In nothing but a pair of the polka dot red panties I'd bought her and a white ribbed tank that left very little to the imagination.

Her somewhat corded arm was twisted up, rubbing at her wet hair with a towel.

"Do you know the hot water is out?" she asked, not sounding entirely bothered by the fact. As though a cold shower didn't bother her in the least. When I previously heard Iggy tell me that when she slept over at Ferryn's house, she would take such long—and hot—showers that her little brothers would bitch that there was no warm water left.

Again, I couldn't help but wonder what kind of life she had been living since she'd left? Fleabag accommodations where she got used to a lack of basic human necessities?

Just the idea of that made my stomach twist, not liking that image, not wanting to picture her living such a fate.

"I would call the owner, but it is probably easier just to fix it myself."

"You know how to fix things?"

"You don't need to sound so shocked," I told her, lips curving up, finding all the anger from the night before dissipated. She seemed to feel the same, taking the offered coffee with a simple *Thanks* before walking over to the brown bag of breakfast sandwiches and hash browns on the counter. Without even a thought to putting pants on.

I couldn't decide if I found it charming or incredibly distracting. Or, well, both. I'd never known Ferryn to be shy, but there was something in the way she moved around without a single care in the world about the bottoms of her rounded ass cheeks hanging out of her panties that was very indifferent. As though she either didn't consider the fact that it was sexy, or that she was so confident in her sexuality that it was simply a part of her, something she felt no need to feel odd about. Even in front of someone who was all but a stranger to her the past several years.

"I had to go through the prospecting period, remember? Turns out, none of the older guys want to spend their time hammering on pipes or cleaning out drains anymore. They left that up to West and me. I learned quick."

"Are these cinnamon rolls?" she asked, her eyes going wide when I nodded, like she'd been in some parallel dimension for eight and a half years where they didn't have such things at pretty much every fast food or coffee shop in the country.

"Don't worry. I didn't want any," I told her as she plowed through two and reached for a third.

"I wasn't worried," she told me over a full mouth, making my smile stretch wide.

I'd been too distracted by the strangely ravenous way she was devouring her food to notice much else until she took a break from shoving food into her mouth to reach for her coffee once again.

Then, well, then I noticed something.

Her arm.

Sure, she had strong arms. She always did. Muscled, but long and lean. But that wasn't what caught my attention.

Oh, no.

It was the puckered scar right near her left shoulder, still pink, but not new.

I knew that scar.

A couple of the guys in the club had that scar.

An old bullet wound.

"The fuck is this?" I heard myself demand, reaching out instinctively, moving to grab her upper arm to get a better look.

It was the wrong move.

One second, I was standing there with her arm in my hand.

The next, my arm was arched up between my shoulder blades, my head was slamming into the counter, and some curved fucking knife thing was pressing into my throat.

"Jesus Christ, Ferryn, what the fuck?" I asked, too stunned to think better of speaking, making the knife slice into my skin slightly. Superficial, but stinging.

"Fuck," she hissed, releasing me all at once, scuttling backward so fast that by the time I turned, she was by the couch.

My hand reached up, sliding over the wet on my neck, glancing at the blood before looking up at her.

"Don't grab me," she warned. But there wasn't anger there like you'd expect after such an aggressive display.

No.

There was a haunted sound to her voice, something that made a shiver course over my skin.

My hands moved out instinctively, palms facing her. "My bad, Ace. I was just surprised. I didn't mean to grab you like that."

She nodded a bit tightly at that, moving back to the table, tucking the curved blade under the book where it must have been in the first place.

"When the fuck did you get shot?"

"Um... four, no, five years ago," she told me, tone conversational, indifferent, as she picked up a sleeve of hash brown circles, popping a few into her mouth, slowing down a little.

Five years ago.

She'd gotten shot when she was something like twenty years old?

How? Why? By whom?

I wanted to know, but I somehow understood that if I asked, things would hit the fan again.

We seemed to be getting on alright. I wanted to keep the peace as long as possible. If I wasn't careful, I might scare her off before her family even got to see her. And then, well, then I would be in some deep shit.

"You got more of them?"

"More of what?"

"Scars. And not from falling out of trees or some shit like that."

"Yeah, I have more of them."

Again, no inflection.

Like it was no big deal.

"Ace, about last ni..."

"No," she cut me off, shaking her head.

"No?" I repeated, finally reaching for my breakfast sandwich as well.

"I think we can both chalk that up to being off last night," she explained.

"I think we both made some valid points," I added, not willing to say that I was wrong because I knew I wasn't.

To that, I got a shrug as she finally put her food down, focusing on her coffee.

"Is Iggy still in Navesink Bank?" she asked, not making eye contact.

"She... yeah. Yeah, she's still here."

"Is she mad at me?" she asked, and it was the first time I heard a hint of vulnerability in her.

"I think mad is the wrong word. I think Iggs was worried and maybe as time went on, a little resentful. She loves you though, Ace. You know she wants to see you."

"I don't want to screw with her life."

"You won't."

"You don't know that."

"Yes, I do. I know her. And I know what you two had together. Yeah, it's been a while. And you two have grown. You will need to get re-acquainted. But I know you two will fall back into it."

"I wish I..." she started, trailing off when her phone dinged on the couch.

Considering the fact that she cut herself off from everyone for her old life, it shocked me when she shot across the room, reaching a bit frantically for her cell. I couldn't help but wonder who was in her life now to make her jump-to so quickly.

Her finger scrolled for a couple seconds before she was dropping the phone, grabbing for a pair of pants, pulling them on, then grabbing for her jacket.

"What are you doing?" I asked, fearful I already knew the answer.

"I have to go."

"No."

"Vance, I'm going," she said, giving me eye-contact for a long moment before slamming her feet into her boots.

"You just fucking got back and you are going to leave without seeing anyone?"

"I'm coming back."

"When?"

"I don't know. A day. Two days tops."

"Ferryn..."

"I'm coming back," she insisted, voice harder as she moved toward me.

I didn't want to know why she was taking her knife. I had a feeling I wouldn't like the answer if I asked.

"Wait," I demanded when she went to rush past me, reaching out to grab her arm before thinking better of it and holding my hand up. "Let me give you my number," I told her, watching as her brows furrowed as though the words didn't make sense. "Text me when you're on your way back," I added.

"Oh. Ah. Okay," she said, pulling out her phone, jabbing the numbers in. "I have to go," she added when she was done, making her way to the door.

"Ace."

"Yeah?"

"I don't know what you're up to, but be careful."

"No promises," she told me with a solemn shrug.

With that and nothing more, she was gone, the door slamming behind her.

I couldn't focus the rest of the day.

Figuring that Cash and some of the other guys would call me if they needed me, I spent my time working on the apartment. Getting the hot water going took longer than I anticipated. In checking to see if it was working, I noticed the tub needed re-grouting. And the whole place in general was in desperate need of a scrubbing.

Living on the road being a musician had been a filth-filled adventure. Prospecting The Henchmen had left me in charge of all the dirty work. It was something that made me not only aware of filth when I came across it, but much more likely to grab a vacuum or mop and handle it than I once had been.

By the time the sun had gone down, the apartment was immaculate, and I was kicking myself for giving her *my* number when I should have gotten hers instead. At least that would have left me with a little bit of control over the situation. Or a way to ensure I could get in touch with her to make sure she was on her way back.

"Should I ask what—or who—you were doing all day?" West asked when I walked back into the clubhouse.

"I was fixing a hot water heater," I told him, rolling my eyes. And, oddly, choosing not to tell him about Ferryn skipping town once again. Considering he was my only confidant in this situation, you'd think I would want to keep him up to date on everything, offload some of the stress onto his shoulders. "Do you know a guy named Finch?" I added, trying to remember if I had heard anything about him before.

"Finch? First or last?"

"Didn't say. Just introduced himself as Finch. Southern accent. Tennessee, maybe?" I guessed. Having done a fair amount of touring, I had gotten pretty good at telling accents apart.

"Not ringing a bell. Why?"

"He's my new neighbor at the apartment. Just don't peg him as someone in Navesink Bank for no reason. Was wondering if he had ever popped by trying to prospect or something."

"Not that I've heard. But we're not the only game in town."

Well, that was for damn sure.

Bikers, and loansharks, and the mob, oh my! really should have been the town slogan. And that didn't even mention the PIs, the fixers, the gangs, or the for-hire enforcer types. If he was looking for a job, he would likely find it.

"Do you think he's going to be a problem for us?"

"I don't think so. But it is something to maybe put on Cash's radar if you see him before I do. Have Lo check him out just to see what he might be up to. Everything's been relatively quiet around here for a while. It would be nice to know if there were about to be waves in the water."

"Are you asking because you genuinely want to check him out, or because your girl is moon-eyeing him?"

"She's not my girl. And I don't think Ferryn is capable of anything even resembling moon-eyeing anyone."

At least, not anymore.

There had been moon-eyes once upon a time.

Watching me from the passenger side of my car.

Watching me from the front row when I was on stage.

Watching me as I climbed out of my parents' pool.

Watching me as she made me listen to her new favorite songs.

She'd once been the queen of moon-eyes.

Now, though, now I wasn't sure there was enough of that girl left in her to allow that kind of open vulnerability, that rare honesty of emotion.

"Dunno. Thought I maybe saw a flash when she realized who you were. Old crushes and all that cheesy shit. Where you going?" he asked when I went to go down the hall to my room. "Gonna write some more music about her? Because two albums weren't enough!" he added just as I got to my door.

No one brought up the albums.

I honestly wasn't even sure anyone had thought to look it all up.

There hadn't been a vetting process before letting me into the club, so all my secrets were mine to keep. Not that the albums were a secret at all. They'd done well, actually. They put the band on the map.

They'd also been my undoing.

But that was a story for some other time.

Or never.

Never worked for me just as well.

I preferred my life in two parts.

During the band.

And after the band.

It made everything easier to deal with. Made lost dreams less of a jagged pill to swallow. Made this new life an easier transition without everyone knowing and bringing up all that old shit.

As I walked into my room, though, I felt an old, yet familiar, itching in my fingers. Not just to play. I played music all the time. But never my own. Always someone else's thoughts and ideas and feelings. I stopped writing my own music ages ago. But right then, my fingers were itching to get on my guitar, to grab a notebook and start writing things down.

I was choosing not to think too hard on why, for the first time in many, many years, words and music were finally coming back to me.

Because I was pretty sure I would find the common denominator if I did the math.

And that the answer was one that would complicate the fuck out of everything.

Seven

Ferryn - Present Day

I didn't intend to leave.

I mean, at least not so soon after getting back to Navesink Bank, not before I at least made contact with my parents and siblings.

The nature of my job was that when you got the call, you had to pounce.

Lifelong criminals get to be lifelong criminals because they are good at what they do. Because they are smart.

Stupid criminals end up behind bars or in shallow graves.

So if you were a smart criminal, you knew that keeping the same home base for any length of time was a surefire way to have shit trace back to you. What does your fellow neighborhood criminal do to prevent getting traced? They moved. They moved frequently.

If your plan was to try to get to one of these types of criminals, you had to be flexible with your time. You had to pounce when you finally got a pin in them. Because, chances were, if you missed the opportunity, you would never be able to find them again.

I had to go.

It was that simple.

This was an operation I had on my radar for over a year, had been turning over every rock to try to find their slimy asses. With no luck. Not even a trail of breadcrumbs.

And, well, when this mission was all that your life was based around, you didn't just shrug it off and keep on sitting in some old apartment trying not to overthink the way your girlhood crush still managed to get a rise out of you when no one else was capable of such a feat.

You had to go.

You had to do what you do.

In my case, that meant I had to drive across two states, throw on a baggy shirt, slap a hat on my head, and once again impersonate some guy looking for a 'good time.'

I couldn't even think that phrase without grimacing. I wasn't sure how it wasn't a dead giveaway that I wasn't an actual, real client when they opened the doors to me.

But, well, scumbags tended to think all other men are scumbags, didn't they? That because they had sick, sadistic fantasies, that all men were like them.

I couldn't even be too mad about it because it worked in my favor.

I took a deep breath as I walked down the wood-paneled walls, breathing in smoke and pot and cheap beer, things so familiar that I barely registered them anymore.

It was a slow night.

I liked slow nights.

Especially now.

Especially because I was completely on my own.

It wasn't unheard of. Holden knew this was my path in life. And I understood that it wasn't his. We still did big jobs together when we came across them, but most of the smaller ones were just me on my own.

I simply had to hope that the nights I got there were slow. Because no matter how good I got, no matter how sharp a weapon I had made myself become, there were some odds that were not only not in your favor, but impossible to accomplish.

I'd been outnumbered a few times.

I'd been outnumbered in a nearly fatal way twice.

Once, I only lived because I'd been saved.

And the second time because I had needed to do the unthinkable.

I jumped ship.

Literally threw myself out a second-story window and ran like fucking hell because I knew what would happen to me if I got caught.

I'd called the police anonymously.

Those women *did* get saved.

But the men had cleared out.

I'd never gotten a trace on them again.

Even just thinking of that night put a sour taste in my mouth.

I'd always been competitive. I always liked winning. I wasn't the best loser. These were traits I always allowed in myself because I thought they served me. Now more so than ever.

I wasn't entirely sure I would ever rest easy until I finally tracked down those bastards and put them down like the animals they are.

"You lucked out, buddy. We just got a new boat in this weekend."

As a whole, you found American women being trafficked on American soil. It was too hard to get girls in from other countries, unlike other parts of the world where women and girls were just driven over country borders in the backs of trucks like chattel.

But there was a subset of American men who had a fetish for young, petite, quiet, doll-like Asian women. Massage parlors were still very much a thing in modern culture, stocked with women dragged from their home continent, or swept up when their work visas expired and they had nowhere to turn to.

Tonight, I was Austen who had a thing for Asian women.

Austen also liked groups of girls.

Austen was all-too-happy to pay for them.

Which was why the night was slow. Because I was a big spender who was going to occupy a lot of the girls' time.

I hadn't come across a set-up like this one in a while. A place where girls were being held and you could rape them on premises. It had been a lot of catching guys trying to ship out American girls for the past year or two. I had spent a lot of time in coastal towns just waiting. You never had to wait too long.

This, though, this was a case I had been tracking for a while. Just because the guys who ran it were so ballsy. It was a hard as fuck time to get anyone without papers into the country. The fact that these guys were doing it said they were really friggen smart. Or they had important people in their pockets.

It would surprise exactly no one to know some of the worst criminals are those we, the public, have given power to. Because power makes people ugly. And it makes them think they can get away with anything they want to because they so often do.

It was easy, after all, for men in power to say they were hitting another country for political reasons when, in fact, they were going to places to indulge in their sick need to force themselves on women and girls.

Men like that, well, they tended to help make it easier for other men to traffick women.

So it was hard to get women on our soil from other places to exploit, but it wasn't exactly impossible.

These assholes were proof of that.

The guy who led me down the hall was tall and lean, Chinese in heritage, but American-raised judging by his accent.

"And they're not drugged," he added, carefree about the implications of his words, the hell these women had likely already been through in such a short period of time. "I know you said you like them more... reactive."

I had told them that I liked a fight.

Because they loved hearing that.

Because they were the fucking scum of the Earth walking around in the flesh of men.

"Perfect," I agreed, using as few words as possible. Despite trying for years, Holden informed me that even my man-voice sounded too soft to be believable. So I used as few words as possible. Just to get me in the door. Just to get me into the space.

Each step was a cannonshot in my head, each sleazy comment from the trafficker making my rage bubble up to a rolling boil.

By the time the key was in the lock, my hand was around the handle on my blade. A sizzle accompanied the touch every single time. Like the wood and metal and I were connected, like we recognized the rightness when we were in contact.

It was over in the span of one breath.

Before the door could push open, making an audience of the women, increasing the chances of screams that would make this harder than it needed to be, I closed the distance between us, grabbing his hair, and yanking back and to the side, elongating his neck, exposing the weak spot, then slicing hard and deep and ruthless, catching the body so it didn't crash to the ground.

I re-closed the door, knowing the only people to be found inside were the girls I was supposedly coming here to brutalize, then slowly made my way through the rest of the space.

Two guards.

One client.

Clients don't get any mercy either, Holden had told me in those early days when I was still working out the fine print of the mission. *If it weren't for them, there would be no trafficking because there would be no demand for it.*

Your old ideas of morality had to go out the window when you were going to make a life out of taking lives.

Yes, these men likely had lives and wives and children and grandchildren.

But that didn't make them any less guilty.

It didn't make them deserving of mercy.

I had precious little mercy to offer anyway after all these years, seeing the things I had seen, barely able to keep food down at times because I knew the terrible shit that was going on and knowing I couldn't stop it all.

I tucked away the blade, bringing the one girl who had been with a 'client' back to the room where my group of girls were situated, putting them together, standing there feeling lost.

It was harder with girls and women from other countries, ones who didn't speak the language, who didn't know where to go or how to get help even if they did get free.

With nothing else to do, I plugged what I had to say into a translation app, hoping it would get the basics across to them.

You're free.

You need to run.

Go to the police or Chinese Consulate in New York.

In the end, as it always seemed to go, many women froze up or broke down, but one always managed to keep herself together, take control, try to organize everyone else.

I gave them the phone.

I gave them numbers and addresses.

I made sure that once they were dressed, I walked them to a safe space where they wouldn't be found by any other traffickers in the organization.

And then I jumped back on my bike.

Normally, I would get a room after a job. Clean up. Get rid of any evidence that wouldn't come clean enough. Watch the local news to make sure my description wasn't too accurate if they got one at all.

But I couldn't seem to make myself wait.

I didn't want to stay another night in another cheap hotel.

I wanted to go back home.

And since my family was not currently there, the only real conclusion one could come to about that desire was that I wanted to see Vance again.

I didn't know what that meant on a technical level, how a shrink would sort that out. Was it just because he was a familiar face? Was it because he was the connection I currently had to my family? Was it because there was still some long-buried feelings attached to him? More than friendly feelings? I had no idea.

The latter seemed the most unlikely, though.

I didn't have feelings for men.

My brain wasn't wired like that. Not anymore. I think my brain stopped being wired like that after that first trip out on my eighteenth birthday, when I had been forced to face the reality that had sent me on this path in the first place.

I knew as I sat in that dingy room of mine that Holden was right. That if I continued on this path, the likelihood of having a man use his power against me got higher.

That very weekend, I walked into a local bar/restaurant place, went up to the first halfway decent looking man I could find, and lost my virginity in the backseat of his car.

Romantic or pleasant, it was not.

But there had been a sense of power in it.

A choice was made.

It was followed through.

I owned that part of me.

No one could take it.

Sex had become a catharsis for me. Maybe someone with a degree would argue that it became about power to me. That it was just another sort of weapon I yielded. That I removed any possibility of a man having power over me by controlling the sexual narrative completely.

It was only ever about an itch being scratched, about needs being met.

The second they were, I was dressed and out the door.

I didn't want connections. I wasn't even entirely sure I was capable of them. I barely got to know names; I damn sure had no interest in learning what your favorite color was, what songs set your soul on fire, what books made an impact in your formative years.

I guess the difference here and now was that I already knew the answers to those questions.

Vance loved hunter green.

His favorite songs list was a hundred titles long.

He loved all things E.E. Cummings and Charles Bukowski and the poetry books of Jim Morrison.

I knew that his most embarrassing moment was his first performance when his mind went blank and he forgot the music he had written.

I knew the thought of any kind of meat coming from a can made him look green in the face.

There was no way to feign disconnect when the connection had always been there.

So many things I thought long-buried clawed their way back to the surface. Long conversations we had. The fact that I had once made suggestions to a song he'd written, and he'd implemented the changes. The way his body looked when he'd gotten out of the pool. The lazy, sexy smile he'd beamed in all women's direction. Except for me. And how I so dearly hoped that once I was old enough, I would be the recipient of one as well.

I'd been sappy and girlish, sitting there picturing him making a move, realizing I was the one girl he wanted to get serious about, getting engaged, getting married.

I had spent untold hours both with him and fantasizing about him.

And while I had buried that under the years of hard work and self-denial and devotion to my cause, it was still there, still a part of me.

Being around him, it was making me feel things, things I didn't know I could feel anymore. The scary thing was that this was just the beginning.

If Vance could bring this old stuff up, what about Iggy and my parents and my siblings and my aunts and uncles and my cousins?

I had grossly underestimated how big a deal this would be, how much of an impact it could have. Which would therefore alter everything. Meaning my plans for the future.

As I turned my bike back down the road that would lead me to my temporary home, I promised myself to keep the visit as short as possible, to minimize the potential for too many changes, for too much emotion.

I could visit, make some amends, then head out with the promise of stopping by for big events.

I could handle that.

A night or two here or there.

Then get back out again before I started feeling too much, before it broke down the shields I had built up.

Because I needed them.

If I didn't have them, everything would fall apart.

I would fall apart.

And then I wouldn't have what it took to do my job anymore. No one would be there to save those women and girls and the occasional boys. They would be stuck in hell with no hope of getting away. More and more traffickers would pop up because they had nothing to be afraid of.

Now... now they knew my name.

They knew my signature in their comrade's blood on the walls.

They knew I was looking for them, coming for them.

Every shithead should have someone on this Earth that they were afraid of, someone who kept them awake at night, someone who made them look over their shoulder when they were walking alone.

That was who I was.

That was what I did.

I didn't get to just give that up. It was too important.

Important things required sacrifices. Those sacrifices were mine.

It had been wrong, I was coming to see, to force my family to sacrifice so much as well. Especially because my job had a high rate of a short lifespan. They would never recover if I got killed on a job before they got a chance to spend time with me again. So, I would give them time. Just enough. Enough to make their lives feel like something wasn't missing anymore. But not so much that it softened me too much, it made my shields start to disintegrate.

"I've got some bleach if you are out," Finch's voice called, once again smoking out front his apartment.

I wore black.

The blood that was on me wasn't visible. I wouldn't have gotten back across two states if I was covered in red on a bike, plain for all to see.

I figured it said a lot about Finch that he knew when no one else had looked at me twice. Maybe he smelled it. I swear I could smell blood from twenty yards after all of these years getting so acquainted with it.

"Good to know," I agreed, not wanting to say too much, always aware of the possibility of being found out by the wrong kind of person.

"Supposed to pour tonight," he added, looking casually up at the sky, though it was clear his words had more meaning than they did at surface level. "If someone just happened to, you know, accidentally spill some soap on their vehicle, it would be cleaned like magic."

That wasn't exactly a bad idea since I wasn't supposed to hit the car wash and even standing out in the open hosing down the bike might be a bad idea in a town where dozens of people knew who I was and would report back if they happened to see me.

"You're just a fountain of weird information, aren't you?" I shot back, giving away nothing, still having no idea who this Finch guy was.

"That I am, babe, that I am," he agreed, and I got this gut drop sensation that made my step falter, having the absurd thought that maybe he knew who I was. When my gaze slipped over, though, he was back inside his apartment, his cigarette smoke dancing up through the air.

There would be time to research Finch later. Right now, I had to clean up.

Without a washer in his unit, I filled up the tub, washing, rinsing, rewashing, rinsing, over and over until the stains were gone, until I felt satisfied that every crevice on all the clothes was thoroughly washed, then wringing and hanging them to dry as I got in the shower.

I wouldn't lie, it was refreshing when, after a job, I could actually take a hot shower to scrub off the blood. It definitely beat out the cold, makeshift hose showers of my past.

No matter how hot the water got—and Vance had fixed the heater enough to make the water almost skin-blisteringly hot—there was no getting it off.

The grime.

That coating I had been wearing around on my skin for years. The filth that covered me, that sometimes I swore sank down into my skin, became a part of my soul.

I never felt clean even after scrubbing my skin raw.

I figured it was a small price to pay—never feeling wholly comfortable in my skin, carrying around these blood-soaked hands, not being able to sleep soundly—to be able to make a difference in the world.

I slipped on fresh clothes, ate a couple Devil Dogs, went ahead and poured some soap on my bike like Finch had suggested, but only after having heard him leave for the night.

Then, tired down to my bones, I dropped down on the couch.

I wasn't sure if it was the thunderclaps or the nightmares that finally woke me up. All I knew was I woke up with a fist lodged in my throat, with my heart hammering in my chest, with a cold sweat covering my skin.

I'd tossed and turned for hours, catching snippets of sleep here and there, not nearly enough to take the ache out of my muscles, the heaviness off my eyelids.

On a sigh, I unfolded my body, climbing off the couch, moving out toward the door, opening it up.

I had always liked the rain.

Reading Weather, my Aunt Reese, the local librarian, would say.

Maybe that was part of it. It was an excuse to curl up in pajamas and ignore the world.

At least, that was part of it back then.

Now, though, I liked it because it matched my mood. Especially after a job. Especially after slathering on another layer of filth.

Taking a deep breath, I stepped out into the downpour, sliding down onto the cement slab that acted as a shared porch for all of us, though no one bothered to put out cute rocking chairs or planters filled with happy flowers. This was not the kind of place you lived in because you wanted to, that you wanted to spruce up. It was a stepping stone to someplace else, somewhere that you would put effort into.

All there was, instead, were old cigarettes or cigar stubs or even half-disintegrated joints from the unit to the other side of Finch.

I appreciated the honesty of this shithole of an apartment building.

Almost as much as I appreciated the fact that when they looked out the window to see me sitting there in the rain, they said nothing, did nothing, minded their own damn business.

My eyes drifted closed, my head leaning against a half-crumbling railing, feeling the water soak through my clothes, wash over my skin.

I wondered if I sat in a storm for long enough if it could take a layer or two of the slime away.

I figured it was worth a try.

"Ace, what the fuck are you doing?" Vance's voice asked, shocking me out of my half-consciousness, making a surge of adrenaline course through my system.

I blinked up at him, a towering shadow with glistening hair. "Enjoying the rain," I heard myself mumble.

"People enjoy the rain from the window, not sitting out in it. It's fucking freezing," he added, suddenly making me aware of the chill moving through me. "Come on," he said, going to reach for me before remembering himself, offering me his hand instead. "You're going to get fucking sick," he added.

"You can't get sick from the cold," I told him, my old know-it-all self rearing her giant head.

"No, but it can lower your immune system so that the next time you are exposed to a bug, you can't fight it off as well," he shot back. "This girl I used to know told me that," he added, eyes twinkling a little.

God, that was a good twinkle too.

Something a part of me responded to, making my hand raise, settle into his, letting him pull me back to my feet, lead me inside.

"Here," he said, finding a pile of clothes, handing them off to me. "Go get dressed. I'll order some food. Something hot to warm you up."

I realized as I made my way to the bathroom that he hadn't been pissed. That I hadn't texted. That I didn't tell him I was on my way back.

Truly, I meant to. I was so unaccustomed to answering to anyone that it had completely slipped my mind in my race to get back, to get clean.

"I know better than to ask where you went," he said when I walked back into the room. "But how about I ask if you're alright."

I felt my lips curve up a bit at that, not sure the last time someone asked how I was.

Holden cared. In his way, he cared. But he wasn't a touchy-feely "is everything alright" sort of guy. He wanted to know if you had any gaping holes anywhere that needed to be stitched up, and that was about it.

I guess how could he ask me if I was okay—mentally, emotionally—when he was clearly anything but?

"I don't really know how to answer that," I admitted. Because, physically, I was just fine. A little banged up. I had a bruise the size of a foot on my side. But it was just a nagging sort of ache if I moved the wrong way. Emotionally, mentally, well, I wasn't even sure. Could anyone who took lives for a living ever be truly alright? No matter how noble the cause.

Surprisingly, Vance nodded his head at that, accepting it as an answer. I was pretty sure most of the people in my life would have pried, would have demanded more of an explanation.

"Are you going to be running off again like that anytime soon?"

"I don't have any plans to." I always had feelers out, was always looking for the next big bad, the rising star in the trafficking world, and a couple of elusive cases that had been nagging at me for years. But I had no current leads, no one on the horizon that I knew about.

If the emails came in, if the information was there, then, yeah, I would need to go. But I figured I had a few weeks before that happened.

"I guess I will have to learn to live with that uncertainty," he said, shaking his head.

"Unpredictability keeps you on your feet. What kind of pizza did you get?"

"Quarter plain, quarter pepperoni, quarter mushrooms and onions, and a quarter veg."

My old favorite order. I had needed to beg the pizza place to make it every single time because it wasn't something that they offered. You got toppings on the whole thing or half and that was it.

"Why didn't I hear any pleading?" I asked, brows lowering.

"Perks of being a member of an outlaw biker gang. People just do shit when you ask them to."

Apparently, being the offspring of an outlaw biker president didn't afford me the same courtesy.

"Bastards."

"They are throwing in a liter of soda too," he added, rocking back on his heels, pleased with himself.

"I haven't had pizza in years," I admitted, not knowing why I wanted to do so. If I just didn't want the silence to grow awkward, or if I genuinely wanted to give him little parts of myself.

"I noticed you look a little thinner than usual," he agreed. "On a strict diet?"

"You could say that. I wasn't cooking my meals. Everything was very basic, very healthy, and very plain. I hadn't had cheese in like... eighteen months until I got back here."

"I have to ask because it is going to make me sick not knowing... were you being held by someone?"

"What? No. Of course not. Would a captor let me write letters?"

"True. Your mom was always so excited when they came in. She would bring them to the clubhouse to let your aunts and uncles read."

"Oh, God. There was never anything interesting in them. Definitely not enough to spread around."

"They were all she had. All they all had. They pored over them when they showed up." He paused at that, and I had a feeling he was trying to let that sink in, like he figured I needed time to process things. Which I did. "Can I ask you one more thing?"

"Well, you're buying me dinner. I think that means I owe you small talk."

"I want to say that you don't owe me anything, but if social obligation gets some information out of you, I'm not above utilizing it."

"Very pragmatic," I agreed.

"Why the flowers?"

"The flowers?" I repeated, lost.

"On the letters. There were always flowers drawn in the margins. Roses. Daffodils. Lilacs. Daisies." The favorite flowers of my aunts. I honestly didn't even remember doing that. "It just always seemed odd to me. You never liked flowers. It made you sad when they died."

It did.

He remembered so much about me. Some things I even forgot about myself.

"I wish I could give you some meaning. I guess they were just... things that reminded me of my aunts. I really wasn't conscious of doing it." I must have doodled them after I finished writing the letters, while my mind was still in places other than the present situation. Then when I snapped out of it, I'd thrown it in an envelope after without glancing over it again.

I never wanted to stay in that Navesink Bank headspace for too long. I knew it would be too hard to leave it behind if I did.

"Are you excited to see your parents?" he asked, following me as I dropped down on the couch.

"I think the predominant feeling is worry."

"Worry," he repeated, brows knitting. "You're worried to see your parents? Why?"

I couldn't seem to make eye-contact, pretending instead that inspecting my ripped cuticles required my utmost attention.

"I'm not who I was, Vance. You see that. I know they're going to see that."

"It doesn't matter who you are. You're still their daughter."

"You don't understand," I objected, shaking my head.

"Then help me understand."

I wanted to.

God, I wanted to share it.

Which was all the more reason I couldn't. The desire to talk about it, to spill all the pain and heartbreak and fear and sacrifice over the past several years was just more proof that being here, that being around these people who had known me so well, was going to make it impossible to keep myself as detached as I would need to continue to do my job.

"I can't talk about it. Not really. But... it's just. There's not as much to love now."

"Ace, there is plenty of you to love."

There was no stopping the scoff that escaped me. "How would you know?"

"Maybe you've changed. Maybe there is some coldness and some guards, honey, but you're still you. You still have the same likes and dislikes. You're still sharp. I get that you've changed. But we've all changed. That's what time does. You might find some things different about your parents and aunts and uncles. And you damn sure will find things different with your siblings. Your life didn't stop when you went away. And none of our lives stopped either. Everyone is going to have to get reacquainted."

"Why did you quit the band?" I blurted out.

"What?" he asked, jolting back at the change of topic.

"You said I would need to get reacquainted with everyone. That we've all changed. You're here. You've changed. So why did you quit the band?"

This time, it was his turn for his gaze to slip from mine, staring forward toward the front window, the blinds much cleaner than they had been when I had left, leaving me to wonder if he had somehow also inherited his mother's and Iggy's habit of cleaning when they were stressed or restless.

"I didn't quit. I was forced out."

"Forced out," I scoffed. "You were the only one with any talent in that band. You *created* that band. How could they force you out?"

"Pretty easily, it turns out," he admitted, shaking his head.

"Tell me," I demanded, knowing I had no right to ask when I wasn't willing to give him anything, but finding I needed to know, I had to know what he'd been going through over all these years.

"I saw you had picked up our *Waiting* album," he started, looking at me, almost daring me to deny I had done so.

"You told my story."

"I tried," he admitted, nodding. "I think it was cathartic, a way to help me sort through the situation. I didn't really mean for it all to become an album. But the guys came across it all one day. They loved it. We decided to go ahead and make the album. We expected much of the same thing we'd always had in the past. Sell a couple CDs to the local fans, get a few further away gigs to try to expand a little. But it blew up. We literally couldn't keep stocked. We had lines at our shows. And then there was a record producer and a contract and some serious shit. I think we were all too stunned to do anything but sign the papers and agree to everything."

"Understandable. That must have been very exciting."

"You'd think," he agreed, nodding.

"That was your dream. How were you not excited?" All I ever remembered him talking about was making a name for himself, following the greats, making music, playing shows, going on wild adventures. Once someone was offering him all of that, he should have been over the moon.

"I was in a weird place. In my own head a lot. It was kind of dark days back then. I just... went with the flow. It sort of happened around me instead of to me. If that makes sense."

"It does."

"So we just kept touring and all that. Did some bigger shows. Signed some fucking autographs," he added, shaking his head like he still couldn't believe it. I could, though. I always could.

"Then what happened?"

"Then we cut our second album. Even then, I was getting a lot of push back, a lot of shit for the songs I was writing. They were too 'whiny' or 'longing' or shit like that. But it had worked for the first album, so they just let it ride for that one. But when it was time to start brainstorming again, they all cornered me and told me if I write any more of 'that shit' that I was out."

"Your bandmates were always kind of assholes," I told him. I'd kept my mouth shut about it back in the day because I knew they were important to him. And every girl knew that if you wanted to eventually start a relationship with a guy, it was important that his friends like you and that you at least pretended to like them.

"In retrospect, yeah, they were. At the time, they were my friends. I gave a shit about their opinions. And I wasn't feeling too sure of myself to begin with. So I agreed. And then I couldn't write a single fucking thing. I was dried up. Had nothing left to offer."

"You had a lot to offer," I objected. He had dozens of notebooks full of rough drafts of lyrics. More than he would need for a lifetime of record making.

"It wouldn't come to me, though. And you kind of need the music to come to you. It's hard to force it. And if you force it, it's crap anyway. I started getting threats from our manager, the record label saying shit about me neglecting the contract. Eventually, I guess they found a big enough of a loophole to push me out but keep the name, keep the rights. And I was out."

"Those fucking bastards," I growled, angry for him.

"I get it to an extent. This was their dream too. I was fucking with it. I was the only thing fucking with it."

"Yeah, but without you, they never would have had that dream."

"They managed well enough without me."

"They're still making music?"

"Have you been living in a hole for eight years, Ace?"

"In a way," I told him. "I haven't been in touch with anything popular culture," I added, not wanting him to think I'd literally been in a cave or something.

"They are still hitting the tops of the charts," he told me. "The guys are millionaires. Drive around in a half a million-dollar tour bus."

"Who replaced you? Who is writing the music?"

"Two different guys last I checked replaced me. And the music is picked from whoever is a big name in the lyricist game at any given time."

"Soulless crap."

"Pretty much."

"It's all about fucking and fighting and doing drugs."

Vance and I had talked about music a lot when we were younger. About the validity of rock-and-roll culture. The songs about fucking and fighting and drugs. But only when it was a reflection of the struggles of the members of the band. If everyone in the band was in a monogamous relationship and sober, they had no business faking it for sales.

And, well, I knew the drum player had been with his middle school sweetheart for ages. And the singer was straight edge.

And, well, we'd always one-hundred-percent agreed that when it came to rock, you had to write your own music to be legit.

"How did you handle the fallout?"

"You're looking at it," he told me, waving a hand around. "I packed up my shit, headed back home. Used what I had to rent this place as I tried to figure out what to do."

"Did you try to form a new band?"

"No."

"Why not?"

"I had no music left in me. Not any unique music, anyway. I still played. I still play. But other people's music."

"But... you could have joined a band that already had a lyricist."

"I think it was all or nothing for me, Ace. Without the words and music in me, there was no dream."

"I'm sorry," I told him, voice with more emotion than I had heard there in ages.

I'd never had a dream like his. Unless, of course, you counted the dream I cradled to my chest of being *with* him, sharing his dream and life with him.

But I hadn't grown up with a surety about what I should do with my life. I didn't have a secret talent or a bone-deep passion. I'd been one of the few people I'd known, actually, who didn't have a plan for their future.

I hadn't been concerned. With my large extended family—many of whom had their own side gigs—I figured that I would always end up somewhere.

I couldn't imagine what it had been like to possess the kind of passion that he had for music only to one day lose it all. It must have been devastating. It must have left him feeling like his world had collapsed around him.

"What did you end up doing?"

"I bounced around a few jobs. Nothing worked out."

"How did you end up with a Henchmen cut on your back?" I asked. The question had been niggling at me since I first saw him in the front yard of the clubhouse.

"I just couldn't find a place. Years ago, your father told me if I ever needed anything, to come to him. I needed a new focus in life. He gave it to me."

"That's quite a shift, though. A musician to an outlaw biker?"

His lips curved up at that. "I think you are one step in the wrong neighborhood in this town away from being some sort of criminal. Plus, because of you and Iggs, I was even more exposed to that kind of lifestyle. It was more normalized in a way, I guess."

"Did you like it? Or was it just a compromise?"

"I didn't expect to like it at first. It just seemed like a sure path, a way out of this shit apartment, some way to belong again. But it didn't take long to start to really like it, to think it was a good decision. The brotherhood is nice. The family of it all—with the brothers as well as the wives and kids —was something I no longer knew. I mean, I've always had Iggs. But that shit, well, it hit the fan with my family and Iggs and therefore me. I haven't spoken to our parents since."

My stomach plummeted at his words. At the idea of my best friend in the whole world being without me when the seemingly inevitable blowup happened with her family.

Iggy had always been a good child. She rebelled in small ways usually thanks to my or Vance's nudging, but she bent to her parent's ridiculously strict rules with little or no protest in the vast majority of the cases. I always thought that she would one day hit her wall, would have enough, would give them a lifetime worth of her pain and anger and resentment.

I always wanted to be there for that.

"Hey," Vance said, voice soft, hand reaching out, closing around my knee, giving it a reassuring squeeze. "It's okay. She's okay. I don't... I want her to be able to tell you her own story. It's not my place. But she's good now. I think we both knew it was going to happen eventually."

"I should have been there for her."

"You know what, Ace, fuck shoulds. I think you are only going to make yourself miserable with them if you let them in. And what good will that do?"

"I don't really see a way around them," I admitted, curling up, pulling my knees to my chest, a makeshift shield against all the feelings suddenly swirling around me.

"Ace, it's going to be alright," he told me, voice sweet.

His hand moved out, snagging my chin between strong yet gentle fingers, carefully tipping my head up, making my gaze find his.

One beat.

Two.

Three.

I'd swear the world could stop right then and I wouldn't have even noticed.

And, what's more, I wasn't sure he would have either.

"Christ, were you always this bea—"

The knock at the door might as well have been cannon fire the way it sent us shooting apart.

I didn't know about Vance, but my heart flew into overdrive.

"P-pizza," Vance declared, clearing his voice as he folded up, moved away from the couch and toward the door.

As I watched his back, there was only one thought in my head.

A desperate, needy sound.

Always what?

Had I always been so... what?

It had been so long since someone mattered, since someone's thoughts and feelings about me mattered.

There was no denying, though, that while conversation curved toward lighter topics as we devoured the pizza, that it mattered.

He mattered.

And I wasn't entirely sure he ever *stopped* mattering.

Maybe I had simply forced it down, pretended to ignore it.

Suddenly, all those nights alone in my bed, emotionally dead seemed a lot less triumphant and a whole lot sadder.

Eight

- Journal Entry - 20th Birthday -

Maybe I could blame a night without sleep the night before the job.

There was no accounting for them. No matter how much I tried to analyze it, it made no sense why some nights I slept like a baby while others my mind flashed through a catalog of memories. Mostly ones I didn't want to relive. The ones soaked in blood and screaming, full of abused women.

The night before the job I was finally supposed to do on my own, I couldn't sleep.

Maybe that had been a factor.

Especially because it was the first time in a long time that the bloody shit was somehow cut with other images. Ones from my past. Ones of my family, my friends, and Vance.

You want to really fuck up your psyche, have images of a man choking on his own blood followed by kissing the guy of your dreams followed by a head bashed in with a ten-pound hammer.

There was no sleeping when you had maybe started to get a little turned on by the kissing memory then immediately made queasy by the memory of looking down and finding brain matter on the top of your shoe.

In retrospect, I should have put the mission off one more day. The intel I'd gotten had suggested it was a relatively new location, so they were likely to be there a while still. I had the time to wait until I had gotten a decent night of rest.

I was headstrong, though, sure of myself, hungry to prove I could do it on my own, that the past four years of training were more than enough.

I didn't want to wait.

Impatience was one of my flaws.

So I shook off the tired with a large black coffee, had a small meal, then hit the road.

The Alpha brothers had been a name in the trafficking world for years, had managed to stay just below the radar, never getting caught because they never stuck around for very long. Their greatest asset was the fact that the younger brother, Patrick, was a ridiculously good looking guy. Mix that with a little charm, and that made him the guy who could lure countless unhappy runaways and foster kids into his car, could earn their trust. Then drug them and send them off to be trafficked overseas.

The older brother, Thomas, was the mastermind of it all, the muscle, the shot caller.

Both of them took advantage of the women they were to traffick. Sometimes at the same time. That disgusting little tidbit was information I had gotten from a girl who had managed to jump off the ship she was bound to be transported in, swim to shore, and scream for help, creating a big enough scene that the brothers had simply taken off without her, knowing that trying to retrieve her would only end them both up for a decent stint in prison.

She claimed the only ones who got away without being raped by one or both of the brothers were the ones they determined to be virgins, knowing they could get a much higher price for them if they served them up intact.

I was itching to finally get to take them down.

I was sure it would be one of the easier gigs.

It was only ever the two brothers and this one hired hand.

Three guys wasn't too big of a deal.

Oh, how very, very cocky I had been when I got ready for the day, when I took off, when I walked up to the door of a small three-bedroom that, from the record I found online, was in the middle of a foreclosure and supposedly abandoned. From those records, I also knew there was an unfinished basements.

Traffickers liked basements for obvious reasons. One way in and out. Really fucking thick walls to keep sounds from being overheard by neighbors.

This place didn't have neighbors, though. On a deep cul-de-sac, the closest house was half a mile down, and from the looks of it as I passed—crumbling front steps, holes in the roof, and shutters hanging on for dear life—abandoned.

See, I got in the door.

In the past, getting in the door was all that I had needed.

It was a pattern that had given me a false sense of security. Like nothing could go wrong during the introduction process.

I miscalculated.

Got sloppy.

Missed the way his eyes had roamed over me.

I'd noticed him glancing at me, of course, but had written it off as a typical man-inspecting-man look. Not a predatory look. Not a look that found hints of breasts, a subtle flare of hips, a certain softness of ass, the thickness of thigh.

Men who made money off of women's bodies became a sick sort of expert on appraising them.

In the past, Holden's presence had secured me my place in the door, had validated my claim. Or maybe they were simply too busy eyeing his herculean size to pay me much mind.

The door was closed behind me.

I was led through the abandoned living room, dining room, and into the kitchen. A formica nightmare straight out of the seventies with hideous dark wood cabinets and holes where all the appliances were supposed to be, the only redeeming quality I found was an ornate scalloped wooden detail around the window over the sink.

"Right through here, Frank," he said. And I missed the sneer. I missed it. But when I replayed it in my head later, I wasn't sure how it hadn't sounded like a blaring siren in my ears.

He moved in behind my left shoulder, reaching in front of me to open a door.

Which should have been another warning sign.

No one had a bedroom off of the kitchen.

What was often off the kitchen, though, was a basement.

This was something I figured out when the door swung open.

Just slightly too late.

Because hands planted at my hips.

And I was flying forward down steep wooden stairs.

I felt the impact.

And the crack.

A rib.

I'd bruised and busted a rib or three in my time, but this one felt different. The pain was sharper. It was hard to think beyond.

But I had to think beyond it.

I had to get up. I had to scramble back up those stairs.

Behind me, I could hear the shrieks and whimpers of women, lost somewhere in the dark and cold.

Before me, though, I still saw an open door.

And I knew.

Oh, I knew that if that door closed, I would be in for some deep shit.

I ignored the deep pain.

I ignored the heavy feeling in my chest.

I got on all fours, forced my body to straighten, charged forward, ramming my body weight in the lower body of Patrick, knocking him backward, seeing his back crack against the counter as my hand sought and found my karambit, charging forward on pure instinct.

I was vaguely aware of clamoring behind me. Bare feet on wooden stairs. A slapping noise everyone would recognize.

But I was too distracted by the whirring of my heartbeat and the tightness in my chest and the curses being hurled at me to dig too far into it.

Patrick's body slumped.

I'd missed the artery, but he was losing fast, he wasn't going to make it without intervention.

One down.

Two to go.

The guard barreled in from the back door, sweaty, eyes wild as he caught sight of the girls running off.

I could worry about them later.

If they were runaways or foster kids, they were probably pretty street smart. They would get safe, get help.

I had to finish this.

The guard was smaller, but wider than Patrick, all shoulders and thighs, barreling toward me, hand reaching behind him.

He was a better fighter than his boss, more street, more natural.

He was taking every bit of my focus.

And when I saw Thomas charging into the room, I had a feeling I was officially in over my head, that there was no way I could fight them both off. Not with my chest feeling so tight. Not with the screaming in my rib.

Apparently, though, I wasn't the only woman in the room bent on vengeance.

I thought they all had fled, but one had stuck behind. Maybe to try to help me. Maybe too in shock to think of running.

I didn't know.

What I did know was she was present enough and angry enough and smart enough to reach the only weapon lying in plain sight in the room.

See, I had seen a lot of shit by this time. I had doled out so much violence. I had been witness to pure evil.

As such, I wasn't really sure what I thought of a higher power anymore. I wasn't sure I could believe in something that allowed so much wickedness, so much cruelty, to flourish in the world.

But right then, in that moment, I saw it.

God was the righting of wrongs by any means necessary.

God was vengeance.

God was a woman with a butcher's knife.

I saw the blade sink into Thomas's back just as my karambit flew from my grasp, dragging my attention back to the fight at hand.

My other blade was in my boot.

But something inside me told me there was no way I could bend down with the screaming in my chest.

My arm flew out instead, a scissor to the throat, cutting off his air much like my own felt restricted.

Catching him momentarily distracted, my arm grabbed his neck, slamming it down onto the corner of the counter, the whack loud even to my ears.

It might have been enough.

But I didn't take chances.

Especially not if it might be my last job. I was starting to feel a little lightheaded from the lack of oxygen.

I wasn't feeling great about my chances.

If I had to go I was taking all of them with me.

Jerking his head back, I whacked him against the counter.

Two. Three. Four more times.

I was too winded to keep going.

And the entire front of his skull was bashed in.

It was done.

"Hey," I called, voice coming out a lot weaker than I intended, even more evidence that I didn't likely have a lot of time left. "Hey, he's dead," I called again to the woman in the black tee with her tumbling red hair, her arms covered in red too. Blood. A lot of fucking blood.

Thomas's body was spread over a half-wall that led into the dining space, his entire front carved open, the flesh there resembling mincemeat.

"You need to go," I added, finally dragging her attention over to me, seeming to process everything at once. "Listen to me," I added, knowing I didn't have long to tell it all to her. "You need to get that shirt off. You need to clean that blood off. If you're going to the police. You need to get that evidence off of you."

"He... he *hurt* me," she cried, waving her hand with the knife toward Thomas's body.

"I know. I know he did. And you had every right to do that. But our judicial system hasn't been great about this kind of thing. Victims who kill their captors end up in jail. You don't deserve that. Take the money out of his wallet. Get a hotel room. Take a shower, get all the blood off. Dry your hair. Then walk to the police like the rest of the girls likely are, okay? Then tell them your story. But leave out this part. This part was me. Tell them that."

"But you don't deserve to be behind bars either."

"I don't think I have long," I told her, desperately trying to suck in the right amount of air. Failing miserably. "It's okay. Don't worry about me. Wipe off that knife then hand it to me. Then find a shirt, and help put that one on me."

Thankfully, she didn't fight. Her survival instinct was as strong as mine had needed to be for a long time.

She ran off, finding a shirt, pulling off the blood-stained one, swiping off the blood from her neck and arms and legs with it, then coming over to help me put it on since I was barely able to raise my arm on my own anymore.

"I need your pants," she mumbled, pulling me out of my lightheaded stupor.

"What?"

"Your pants. I need your pants. I can't go to a hotel without pants."

That was true.

So she took my pants.

And my boots.

She gave me one long last look. "Thank you," she told me, then tore out of the house.

Alone, I lowered myself down to the floor, finding a small bit of relief in laying flat even as I felt blood moving up my throat, making me turn my head to the side to cough it up.

This was how I was going to die.

Of all the ways, it could have been worse.

It could have been more drawn out.

It could have been something as sad as a car wreck or terminal disease.

At least I was going to go out in a blaze of glory.

At least I took these bastards with me.

It wasn't a terrible death.

I found a small bit of comfort in that as the blood kept coming, as my chest got tighter, as my eyes started to close.

I found an image behind them in those last moments of consciousness.

Piercing eyes.

Cocky smile.

Calloused fingers.

A raspy, sexy voice.

Vance.

Consciousness came to me slowly, a place I had to claw myself to from somewhere deep, somewhere floating and cool and numb.

I'd never done drugs, but I was pretty sure I knew high when I felt it.

I was really, really high.

I tried lifting my head from the pillow, finding it lolling to the side instead.

My eyes stayed stubbornly closed through all of this, a strange weight holding them closed.

Sound came first.

The quiet chattering of the television. The footsteps from the other side of a closed door. The beep of a monitor.

A monitor.

Holden had a decent amount of medical supplies. Stitching kits, prescription drugs, casting material, braces, even a defibrillator.

But he didn't have monitors.

If there were monitors, I was in a hospital.

That thought seemed to be enough to push the drug stupor away, allowing me to surface, jerking awake, relieved beyond belief to find my wrists weren't attached to the rails of the bed with handcuffs.

The cops hadn't gotten me.

But if it wasn't the cops, who was it then?

"Thank fuck you got friends with deep pockets," Holden's voice called to me, deep and familiar and more soothing than I could have anticipated. "Because you got no idea how fucking expensive your surgery was."

"Surgery," I repeated, blinking my eyes open, finding him sitting there at my bedside. Things were hazy, but starting to clear.

The mission.
The house.
The missed signs.
The fall.
The fight.
The girl.
The surety of my death.

"I punctured a lung," I guessed, thinking of the tight chest, the screaming pain, the blood.

"You never do shit by half. Small puncture could just mean a re-inflated lung. Just a tube. Not a huge deal. But you did a good job. Nice big fucking hole that meant they had to open you up to repair the damage. Recovery is going to suck."

"Am I in a real hospital?"

"As opposed to an imaginary one?"

"I know there are doctors that can be bought. Facilities that can be used." For the right price.

"Don't have connections like that."

Glancing around the room, I made sure we were alone. "What about the blood?"

"Couldn't save your modesty kid. Had to get you clean. Then get you here. Was it just Thomas?" he asked, voice rough, closest to emotional I had ever heard.

"No. I got them all."

"Not what I meant, kid. You know what I mean."

"I don't," I countered, shaking my head a little, finding my vision a bit swimmy with too much motion.

"Your pants," he growled, unable to even look at me.
My pants.
The girl had my pants.
But Holden, Holden had found me without them. And thought the worst.

"No," I objected, voice forceful. "No. I mean it could have happened. I missed so many signs. But no. I gave my pants to one of the girls. I thought... I thought I was done. I told her to take my clothes, give me hers. It would all fall on me."

"Thank fuck," he grumbled, shaking his head.

"How did you know?"

"Didn't," he said, shaking his head.

"You just didn't trust that I was ready." I couldn't help it, my temper flared a bit at that.

"You weren't," he agreed, shrugging. "I followed just in case. When you didn't come out after the girls ran off, I came in. Found you on the floor half naked and coughing up blood."

"What about the evidence?"

"I work fast," he said, shrugging. "Took that shirt off of you, mopped up most of your blood with it. Put you in something fresh. Wiped you down with paper towels and fucking Windex in the car on the way to the hospital. Said saw you getting mugged. Scared the guys off. Grabbed you. Brought you in. You had no documents on you, of course. They took pity on me and let me visit with you. They're going to kick me out eventually though."

"What am I supposed to do from here?" I asked, suddenly afraid to be alone, something I hadn't experienced in ages.

"You go with the cover story. You have all the documents." The fake documents. Everything from driver's license to social security number. I had an identity to fall back on for situations such as this. "You're gonna be here for five to seven days. I can visit during the right hours. Make sure you're keeping it all straight. From there, you get discharged, take your shit, and meet me out front. You're going to be down for two months. Then we can start training again."

Somehow, that was reassuring. That things hadn't changed. That this didn't take away Holden's faith in me.

In the end, he'd been right.

I stayed there six days.

I went home on my twentieth birthday.

I celebrated by sprawling out on my mattress, staring at the ceiling, trying to remember that all of this was worth it

That it wasn't about me.

That my life wasn't about me.
That my pain didn't matter.
That my fear didn't either.
Because those girls out there were in pain and scared.
My life was about them.
I knew that.
I believed in that.
But I just really, really wanted a fucking ice cream cake.

Nine

Ferryn - Present Day

I couldn't breathe.

It was laughable, really.

I'd been in the most dangerous situations anyone could imagine. I had legitimately faced death time and time and time again.

And I had done that with a sense of calm coursing through me.

But the thought of walking into the compound to see my parents was making it feel like someone had a hand around my throat.

"Hey, Ace," Vance called, voice sounding far away even though he was just a foot or so away from me. "Hey," he tried again, hand reaching out, tipping my chin up, a move that sent a little shiver through my insides.

I remembered once seeing him do that to a girl at a show. And then went ahead and spent eighteen months fantasizing about him maybe doing it to me someday.

Now he had done it twice.

And it was proving just as effective as I imagined it would be.

We'd found a relative truce over the remaining few days.

He showed up in the late mornings. He brought various foods. We talked. Mostly about the club, about Navesink Bank, about the new club members and their women, about all the dramas I had missed. It was all enough to fill up a dozen books, I swear.

But there was a sort of comfort in the chaos. My childhood had been full of it. My mom shaking us awake in the middle of the night, telling us to grab our favorite toys—or as we got older, electronics and books—then shuffling us into Dad's bullet-resistant SUV, and driving us up to Hailstorm.

As kids, we thought it was some sort of planned adventure

Oh, how naive we had been.

As we got older, though, we knew what was really going on. There was some kind of drama in Navesink Bank. And as a precautionary measure, the women and kids were shipped off to the safest spot in the area.

Eventually, I started to be able to piece together the drama, figure out the new bad guys in town, what they wanted, how my family or their connections dealt with it.

It had been a while since I learned about it. And it felt good to be in the know again. Even if it was so after the fact.

Vance carefully side-stepped information about my parents or siblings, wanting me to hear all that from them, and I gave as little as possible about my past.

Though I had maybe told him one or two small things.

Like I'd told him I had punctured a lung once. But I hadn't given the details of how.

I'd told him that I had made a sort-of friend along the way. But didn't give names.

The fewer people who knew about what I was up to in my private time, the better.

I knew that.

But, somehow, there was no denying that it felt incredibly *wrong* not to tell him.

I wondered if I would feel the same with my family.

Or if there was simply something special here. Something leftover from how things had been in the past, full of possibilities we'd never had a chance to explore.

"I can't breathe," I admitted.

It was amazing how much emotional turmoil could have the exact same sensation of a collapsed freaking lung.

My chest was tight, my head fuzzy.

"They love you. And they have been waiting for this day for almost nine years."

"That's not a lot of pressure or anything," I grumbled, turning away, pacing the kitchen.

"No pressure."

"Easy for you to say. They aren't going to be disappointed in how *you* turned out," I reminded him as I placed my hands on the counter, head ducking down.

A snort sounded from behind me. Close. Very close. So close that I could feel the air on the back of my neck.

"You forget who my parents are? How disappointed they are in me?" he asked, and I could feel his body behind me.

"We're both just a couple of fuck-ups, aren't we?" I asked, turning, feeling my shoulder brush his arm.

"Guess you can say that," he agreed, arms moving forward, grabbing the counter on either side of my body, trapping me. Making that breathing thing I had been struggling with a moment ago a complete and utter impossibility.

In the past, attraction had always been centrally located in one region of my anatomy. It was a tingle and an ache.

It never went beyond that.

I didn't get breathless. My nerves didn't jumble. I damn sure never got butterflies.

Yet there I was, heart pounding, belly fluttering, chest tight, shivers coursing over my skin.

Just because of proximity.

His brilliant gaze held mine.

And all ideas of this being a big mistake, my possible undoing, disappeared.

My arms rose, a hand going behind his neck, pulling down, the other resting on his cheek, then sealing my lips over his.

There was a short moment of stunned non-reaction before his lips came alive under mine, before his arms curled around my lower back, crushing, pulling me off my feet as his lips got harder, hungrier, stripping away any ideas of not going down this route with him.

And, what's more, stripping away the shields I had worked so damn hard to build, to keep in front of me.

And what's most—I didn't even care. I welcomed the decimation.

Because that wreckage allowed warmth to flood my system, something starting at the base of my spine and spreading outward until it overtook me completely, until it chased away all the cold, until I was sure I would never be able to exist without it again.

Vance's hands slid down, sinking into my ass, yanking me up and off my feet, dropping me down on the counter. Then he was moving between my welcoming legs, everything in me honed in on his closeness, the need emanating from him as strongly as it was assaulting my system.

My legs angled up, slid over the sides of his hips, curled around his lower back, pulling him closer, eliminating any space between us, making his hardness press up against my need, something that made a shiver course through my body, making my hips do a shimmy, creating the friction I was dying for.

Vance's hands went to either side of my face, keeping me captive.

The very idea, just a few days before, would have sent panic coursing through me, would have made me fight to get away, to take back control.

In the moment, though, I wanted to be guided, I wanted him to own my body and soul. I wanted fulfillment to a wish I made something like twelve years before.

To touch him.

To be touched *by* him.

It was everything I had imagined.

More.

Better.

Maybe made especially so by the distance, by the changes life had thrown our way.

His body curved over mine, arching me back, letting me angle my hips just right to grind against his cock, to feel the pressure build, an acute, nearly painful sensation that promised completion like I had maybe never known before.

His hips shifted, pressed, pushed against me. More pressure. More need.

One arm released me, sliding down my side, teasing over the side of my breast, the slope of my waist, the subtle flare of my hip, down the side of my thigh, then around the knee, curving inward. Moving up.

Up.

My lips broke from his as his fingers pressed in at the juncture of my thigh, a surprised whimper escaping me, making his gaze find mine, eyes heavy-lidded, hungry.

The sexiest thing I had ever seen.

His hand shifted, his thumb finding the right spot, pressing.

"Vance..." My voice sounded airy, choked even to my own ears, making his breath sigh out of him.

His thumb went to do another swipe as my fingers clawed at his upper arms.

Then, ringing.

"Ignore it," he demanded when my body started to tense. As if to punctuate his point, his finger did another press as the ringing stopped. But just as I began to get back into it, it started up again. "Fuck," he growled, wrenching away from me, stalking over toward the living room to snatch his phone off the couch. "What?" It was a vicious, angry growl, something that managed to send another shock of desire through me as I tried desperately to bring some control back into my body, some focus back to my mind. Vance's gaze found mine, regret plain in his eyes. A sigh. His hand raking across the back of his neck. "Shit. Yeah. Okay. On our way."

Just like that, it was all over.

We had to go.

My Uncle Cash and Aunt Lo were picking my parents up at the airport. They said they would text my brothers when they were close. From there, West would let us know so we could get there first while he distracted my brothers.

We would wait out back until things calmed a little then we would go in.

Nerves twisted in my belly, snaked around my chest and throat.

"Everything is going to be fine," Vance told me as he shrugged his cut back on. "The sooner we get there, though, the better."

"Right," I agreed, hopping off the counter, looking down at myself.

I hadn't considered things like outfits and my overall appearance in a long time. Everything had sort of come down to utility, what was easiest to fight and train in. It didn't matter what I looked like. In fact, the less approachable I looked, the better.

This was the first time I could remember fretting about my slim wardrobe choices in ages.

I had on a simple pair of bluejeans and a white tee. I had my combat boots and my leather jacket. But that was it. Nothing soft. Nothing warm. No jewelry or makeup to speak of.

I would be a far cry from the daughter they remembered, the one who spent hours in front of the mirror, who had enough clothing to clothe an entire village somewhere.

"Ace," Vance called, making me shake the thoughts away. Even an unkempt daughter was better than no daughter at all, I imagined.

"Yeah?" I asked, shrugging into my leather jacket, taking a steadying breath.

"We got some shit to talk about now too," he told me, gaze full of meaning.

We'd finally crossed that line.

And I didn't think either of us wanted to go back.

Which, well, was problematic, wasn't it?

In more ways than one.

If we kept it up, he was right, there would need to be some talking.

But I had to take one uncomfortable interaction at a time.

"Let's get going," I said, brushing past him, moving outside, not bothering to wait for him to follow. I knew he would. We'd planned this in painstaking detail. The guards at the gate had even been told ahead that we were coming, to let us in.

There was a sense of urgency in me as we hid out behind the building, as I heard the SUV pull into the yard, the doors opening and closing, the sounds of my family reuniting in the clubhouse. I wasn't sure if that urgency stemmed from how much I really did want to see them, or the bone-deep need to get the initial interaction over with—or both—. But there was no denying it was coursing through my system as we finally heard things calm down, as West loudly declared it was nice to have everyone back—a not-so-subtle cue for us to finally make our move.

Vance went first, as we decided, moving in, saying hi, holding the door open.

And then it was my turn.

My heart skipped into overdrive as I forced my feet forward, as I moved into the doorway, then back into the clubhouse.

My mother saw me first.

She'd been giving Vance one of her warm, familiar smiles. Then saw a figure move in beside him.

The smile stayed there for a second as she searched my features, as she made them make sense.

And then the smile fell entirely, her whole face becoming a mask of shock."Ferryn?" the sound shrieked out of her. And she was running even before it was finished coming out of her lips.

Just before we collided, I saw the face of my father, my brothers, my Uncle Cash, my Aunt Lo.

But then my mother's arms were around me, and mine instinctively went around her.

And she was all there was for a long moment. My mother and her familiar scent, the warmth of her embrace, her hot tears soaking through my tee.

A moment later, my father's arms were around the both of us, strong and reassuring as I always remembered them, holding his family back together again.

My brothers, understandably, were standoffish.

It was a different relationship, a different bond. And I had left them during the—arguably—most important years for siblings, the years that made or broke the deep friendship that was possible to be found there.

My gaze lifted, finding them watching the scene.

I didn't know what to expect. They'd still been gawky, awkward things when I had left, all arms and legs and pimply faces, still too young to take on any hints of manhood.

But now, well, they were both men, weren't they? Tall and wide as our father, judging by the way their bodies looked under their shirts, they'd been hitting the gym, they'd been working on themselves.

Fallon was the spitting image of Dad. The same sharp angles, the same sort of cocky, almost indifferent glare. The kind that said he had seen it all.

Seen it all.

God, what had he seen?

What stories did he have to tell that I wasn't a part of? More than he could ever tell me himself, surely.

Finn, though, was more a mix of Mom and Dad. His face shape was more our mom's but with a stronger jaw, with a broader forehead. He was a little thinner than Fallon, a little less bulky in the muscle.

Both of them seemed almost wary of me.

Wary.

"Baby, we're so happy you're home," my mother cried into my neck, squeezing me tighter.

"I'm sorry it took so long," I whispered back, feeling a sting at the backs of my eyes, closing them tight to fend off the tears.

I wasn't sure how long we stood there like that, just embracing, just listening to my mother say over and over how much she missed me, how happy she was, how much she loved me.

"I love you too," I assured her, feeling like the absolute scum of the earth while I did so, not nearly worthy enough of the love she had for me.

With that, they pulled away, my mother swatting at her cheeks, my father throwing an arm around her, leaning over to kiss her forehead.

My uncle was the next to hug me, squeezing me so tight I could barely breathe before releasing me.

He'd changed his hair.

I remembered thinking before I was taken that I needed to find a way to tell him he was getting a little old for his haircut. I wondered who finally got the guts to inform him. He'd grown the shaved side out, having a head full of long hair instead, hair he had pulled back at the moment.

"You look good, kid," he told me, eyes a little glassy.

My Aunt Lo was next, moving toward me with purpose. I prepared myself for another rib-crushing hug.

I really should have known better.

She didn't hug me.

She slapped me across the face.

The sting was immediate. But more than the physical pain, the emotional pain was like a stabbing inside.

Outside of training, no one had ever laid a hand on me. They didn't believe in it. So the fact that my aunt got angry enough to slap me, well, that said a lot, didn't it?

"That was for staying away," she told me, giving me a firm nod.

"I deserved it," I agreed.

"Good. We agree. Now, this is for coming home," she said, giving me that hug I had been expecting.

When she stepped away, it was Fallon who spoke next. "So, you're back," he said, voice hollow, a little cold.

"I'm back."

"And when are you leaving again?" he asked.

Sharp. He was sharp. I should have expected that. He was our father's son. He was who was likely going to take over the MC one day.

"You can't leave," our mother insisted, her voice sounding choked.

A sound that made me shoot daggers at my brother.

"It's a valid question," he insisted, crossing his arms. A muscle was ticking in his jaw. So much like our father.

"For another time," I shot back, daring him to push it, to make a scene right here in front of our parents.

"Yeah, man," Finn agreed, shouldering our brother. "Relax. The Prodigal Daughter returned. We should get a cake or some shit."

Some shit.

Some weird, big sister urge inside me wanted me to tell him not to curse. At least not in front of our parents. I was instantly transported back to my teens, always trying to big sister them, to assist in making them tolerable human beings.

But, I needed to remind myself, that wasn't my place anymore.

They didn't need help raising.

They were grown fucking men now.

They could curse in front of our parents if they wanted to.

"You celebrate," Fallon suggested, making his way toward the door. "I'm going for a ride."

"Thanks for the room," Finn told me, coming in for a quick man-hug. "Fallon used to slay dragons in his sleep. It was fucking obnoxious."

"When did you get back?" my dad demanded, the first words he'd said directly to me.

"Five days ago," I admitted, watching his brow arch up as his gaze moved over toward West.

"Don't look at me, Daddy Reign. Vance was the mastermind here."

"Gee, thanks, asshole," Vance shot back, shaking his head.

"We didn't want to ruin your vacation," I cut in. "If they told you, you would have spent the rest of the time wanting to get home instead of making memories. It was just a couple days.

"That was very considerate," my mother told us, giving me a watery smile.

My father, though, still sent a stern look in West and Vance's directions. There would be a talk later, I was sure. But I think my father was going to go light on them given the circumstances.

"Where have you been staying?" my mom asked. "Since you came back," she clarified, like a parts of her knew it was too soon to start talking about where I had been, what I had been up to.

Thankfully, the night went much the same. We discussed the things Vance had already filled me in on, but I acted as though the information was completely new.

We ordered Chinese and Finn went out to get coffee.

Eventually, West brought out the alcohol.

"Do you want something, honey?" my mother asked, words a little awkward. "That still feels so weird," she added, grimacing. "Offering your adult children alcohol. I don't know if I will ever get used to it."

I didn't drink much.

Once in a blue moon, I would hit a bar, throw a few back when my mind was a too-ugly place. Despite things going well, I honestly did feel like I needed the edge taken off. Because there was no telling when things might get rough, might get awkward for me.

"Whiskey," I told West who was fetching drinks. "Straight," I added.

"Well, you are your father's daughter," my mom declared, wrinkling her nose.

"She still likes her coffee full of sweet crap," Vance supplied. "She's got a lot of you in her too," he added, giving her a warm smile.

I wondered a bit then if Vance had started to see my mother as a sort of foster mother to him. He'd been motherless for a long time from the sound of things. And their relationship had never been close in the first place.

I could see it so easily.

My mom was the ultimate mom. Sweet, loving, generous almost to a fault. She was the kind of mom who baked you cookies for no reason, who took you out of school early to take you to get ice cream because she thought you needed a mental health day. She let you bend rules. She let you become your own person without judgement. She was quick to hug and offer an ear or shoulder.

I could totally see why Vance might be so drawn to her, wanted to make her feel better when she maybe worried her daughter didn't have a lot of her qualities in her.

"I forgot how much I like sugary crap," I added.

"You *are* thin," she responded, eyes going worried.

"Don't worry. I've been eating. It has just been healthy stuff."

"I've been stuffing her full of fat and MSG for you, Summer," he told her, gaining a warm smile from her.

"Thank you for looking out for her for us. It must have been so depressing to finally come home and not have a welcoming committee."

"I, ah, no. It wasn't depressing. I was surprised is all. You guys never take a vacation."

"Were you surprised to see Vance?" she asked as Dad called Vance away.

"Well, ah, yeah. I had no idea he patched in. He, you know, he never showed interest in that before."

"We were surprised too, I think. His band had been doing so well. Then he was just out of it. When Daddy came home to tell me he asked to prospect, I was shocked."

"He seems to have settled in well."

"He has. I think he really needed the family dynamic here. Were you happy to see him here?" she asked, leaning in closer, voice dropping lower.

"Ma..." I said, shaking my head, feeling my neck get warm, an old familiar feeling when she said something I felt was inappropriate for her to say. Which was just about anything she said when I was a teenager.

"I know it has been a long time. And maybe you have a man. Or a woman..." she added at the last second, shrugging.

"No. No man."

"He still looks at you like you hung the moon."

"Still?" I asked, brow furrowing.

"He always did. Even though he barely ever looked at you. When he did, it was clear how much he cared about you. And, well, you didn't exactly hide how you felt about him."

"I made a fool of myself, huh?"

"You know... I think it is really admirable to be so open about your feelings. It says something about you to be able to do that. I always thought it was really lovely how unwavering you were with him. Even though you knew nothing could happen. Even when other guys paid you attention. It was only ever Vance for you. Have you two been... reconnecting?"

My inner teen couldn't help but utter a typical *Ew, gross mom*.

And I felt my lips twitch at that.

Warm and familiar.

"We were trying to lay low so no one saw me before you guys, so he was kind of taking care of me."

My heart squeezed at that.

At the truth of it.

At how it was the culmination of my girlhood dreams coming true.

"He's a good man, baby."

"I see that," I agreed, nodding.

"I hate the cliche of the meddling mother, but if you still find yourself interested, I think he would be a great partner."

"Plus, could you imagine your father's head exploding when he realized his girl was dating one of his men?" Aunt Lo asked, smiling wickedly.

Aunt Lo could always be counted on to enjoy all parts of a new romance. Including the drama.

She'd been the one to start slipping me romance novels as a teen. Which had only managed to further encourage my hopeless romantic dreams of a happily ever after with my girlhood crush.

"I think we are getting a little carried away with ourselves," I said. Even though *carried away* was exactly what I wanted to get with Vance. I tried to convince myself that it was just an itch that needed to be scratched, that I was simply holding onto a need from years ago that needed fulfilling.

"Carried away sounds fun," Aunt Lo said, giving me a knowing smile before moving off.

"Ferryn?" my mom called, voice hesitant, making me turn back to find her watching me with worried, uncertain eyes.

"Yeah?" I asked.

"Can I ask something of you?" she asked.

In that moment, I was sure I would promise her anything to get that look off her face.

"Sure."

"Don't do that to us again."

"Mom..."

"I get that you are an adult now. I get that you built a life. I get that you have other obligations now. But don't do that to us again. Take off for years with no way for us to contact you. Without dropping in to let us see you."

I didn't want to make promises. I didn't want to say that I could always be here. Because my life, the nature of my work, offered no guarantees.

"As much as I can control it, Mom, I will try to be around more."

"One day, and I am not asking right now, but one day, I would like to know what that means," she told me, giving me a one-armed hug. "Where are you going to stay tonight?"

I knew what she was really asking.

Do you want to come home with us?

And, quite honestly, I wasn't sure I was ready for that.

"I was thinking maybe we could all camp out here. Like old times," I added. "That way, when word gets out to everyone else, we will already be here when they want to stop by."

"That's a great idea. Maybe we can arrange a big breakfast. See if I can get some of the girls together to help me make a big spread once they hear."

"That sounds amazing."

It did, too.

Some of my favorite memories as a girl were of hanging around while my mom and aunts—the ones who liked cooking—hung out in the kitchen, chopping, mixing stirring. They were always very open and blunt when cooking, sharing really silly or embarrassing or sexy stories.

I would always flit back and forth between the kitchen and wherever the men were congregated, usually cursing, watching the game, playing pool, being ultra manly. I always loved the contrast.

The idea that I could get to be a part of that all over again made that warm feeling move through my chest again.

"Have you picked up any cooking skills over the years?" she asked, knowing it had never been my strong suit.

"Not a one," I admitted, giving her a smile that she so readily returned. "But I am good with a knife. I can chop things for you guys."

She skimmed right over the meaning behind my knife skills with a wobbly smile. "That would be great, honey. Anything special you want?"

"Are you going to make West go and get it?"

"It never ceases to be fun to boss the younger guys around," she admitted with a conspiratory grin.

"In that case, what is the most obscure, really hard to find ingredient we can sent him on a hunt to find?"

"Oh, that's my girl," she said, eyes warm as we tried to come up with a plan.

"You're evil," Vance declared, dropping down on the couch beside me after my parents had gone off to bed. Only after my coaxing because they both looked dead on their feet from travel and the excitement of the day.

"Oh, come on, I have heard a lot of stories now about how much of a pain in the ass West can be. Someone has to give it back to him."

"Organic Seedless Strawberry Pop-tarts. They almost sound real."

"Which is exactly the point," I agreed.

"And three-percent whipped cream."

"That should have him hitting all the grocery stores in the area until he finally tries to Google it."

"He's going to get you back for it."

"I'm counting on it," I agreed.

"You know, from the sound of things, it kind of seems like you might be staying for a while."

"I have a lot of catching up to do still."

"I'm happy to hear that, Ace. I think all of you have a lot of recovering to do. Fallon..."

"Yeah," I agreed, nodding. He'd never come back. And when Mom had texted him about brunch the next morning, he had said '*Not a fucking chance in hell*'. That was going to be a long, hard road to travel up.

"He's just a royal pain in the ass in general," Vance told me, shrugging. "Hungry to prove himself but has no opportunity to do it. Makes him a moody bastard a good chunk of the time."

"Well, at least I know it's not just me."

"Are you excited about the breakfast? Or nervous?"

"Both, I guess. Not as nervous as I was today. But I think a couple of my uncles are going to have a lot to say. And maybe some of my aunts too."

"And you have to hear them out."

"Exactly," I agreed, nodding.

"Sounds like you need to get some sleep."

"I guess," I agreed. Even if sleep was the last thing on my mind with him so close by.

"Finn changed the sheets out before he headed out. You're all set."

Finn didn't technically have a room. Only patched members had rooms. But with so few of them needing to stay at the clubhouse much anymore, the guys who used to crash there cleared out their stuff which let Finn claim a room right beside our parents. Fallon, a stickler for rules and clear stick-in-the-mud, refused to claim a room until it was in an official capacity.

I think he was secretly hoping Dad would step down. Which would allow him to move into that role. Traditionally, in this club at least, presidents didn't step down. They lost their place because of death only. But our father had always been a little looser with the rules, so it wasn't entirely outside the realm of possibilities that he just might give his place away.

I had to wonder, though, if he truly thought Fallon was mature enough to take his place. It wasn't my business. It wasn't my place. But I couldn't help thinking about it at least.

"Alright," Vance said a moment later, stopping outside Finn's door. "I know you know your way around here probably better than I do, but if you need anything, I'm right there," he said, pointing a few doors down, the second to last one in the hall in the opposite direction of my parents.

"Vance," I called at his retreating back.

"Yeah, Ace?"

"Thank you," I told him, voice a little thick, the events of the day clearly catching up to me quickly.

"Anytime, Ace. Anything," he added, turning and walking back to his room.

Those words were the ones rolling around in my head as I lay on the bed in the very bare room, staring up at the ceiling, hearing the distant sounds of a TV droning on. Likely in my parents' room. My mom tended to fall asleep with it on. And Dad thought she slept better with some background noise, so he left it on when he conked out too.

Other than that, though, the place was quiet.

Or so I thought.

Until there was a brief pause in the TV sound and I heard it.

Music.

The slow, soothing thrumming of a guitar.

I didn't think it through.

I simply followed the urge.

Out of my bed, across the floor, out into the hall, down to his door.

My hand rose, rapping my knuckles gently against his door.

"Yeah?" he called, music still playing.

"Pushing open the door, I stepped in, closing it silently behind me, leaning back against it.

"I can't sleep. I heard you playing," I added. "Can I listen for a while?"

To that, he gave me a lazy smile, nodding his head toward the empty foot of his bed.

I didn't need any more encouragement. I stretched out at the end, my legs cocked to the side to make room for his feet, staring up at the ceiling, just listening.

I couldn't count how many times I'd sat listening to him playing. Sometimes his favorites. Sometimes mine. Other times music he was working on, starting and stopping over and over, jotting down notes, trying to get it right.

There were no words to this unfamiliar song, but Vance hummed along occasionally, a sound that shivered through my insides, turned them warm and gooey.

"Ferryn," he called some time later. Maybe it was only minutes, maybe hours.

"Yeah?" I asked, hearing a certain dreaminess in my voice, feeling it in my eyes as my head shifted on the mattress to look over at him.

"You're fucking killing me," he declared, voice barely more than a whisper.

"Hm?" I asked, confused.

His gaze slid from my face, moving over my chest, covered by the very thin material of my gray tank top, then over my thighs, perfectly bare.

I had long ago stopped thinking of things like proper sleep attire, generally choosing to sleep in the least amount of clothing possible for comfort reasons.

There had never been any reason not to, any eyes looking at me.

Vance's eyes were definitely looking at me. Reminding me that we had unfinished business.

Swallowing hard, I met his gaze once again. "Do you want me to go put more clothes on?" I asked, challenging him to say yes when we both knew neither of us wanted that.

"No," he admitted, voice rough as his hand moved his guitar, gliding it down onto the floor beside the bed.

I rolled over, moving onto all fours, gaze holding his as I crawled up the mattress, arms and legs on either side of his body, until I settled on his lap, slowly raising my arms above my head.

In my girlish fantasies, he'd always been the ones making moves, always the one initiating kissing, touching, undressing.

But there was something about the way his eyes burned as I made moves that lit me up in a way I never could have anticipated before.

His body folded upward, chest nearly brushing mine, hands snagging the hem of my shirt, slowly sliding it upward, knuckles grazing my ribs, the sides of my breasts, the undersides of my arms.

My shirt slid off my wrists, was tossed carelessly to the side.

Vance held my gaze for a long moment before lowering back down, happy to let me take the lead.

My hands moved down, grabbing his, sliding them up my sides, settling them over my breasts, the calloused tips of his fingers sliding over my sensitive skin, settling them on fire even as goosebumps covered my skin.

"Ace," he called, voice rough.

"Yeah?"

"I fucking missed you," he told me.

I couldn't have prepared myself for the impact of those words, touching down deep in places I didn't even know existed any longer. But they did. And he had managed to find them, fill them, make me realize how empty they had been for so, so freaking long.

"I missed you too," I admitted, moving down over him, sealing my lips to his.

There didn't need to be any more talking.

His lips were passive under mine for a long moment before his control finally seemed to snap, making him lift, roll over, roll me under his weight, press me deep into the mattress as his lips burned into mine, demanded more from me, refusing to settle for anything but all I could give.

And give I did.

Happily.

Wholly.

My legs wrapped around his lower back, holding him to me as my hips shamelessly ground upward into him while my hands tugged at his shirt, yanking it up, waiting for his lips to break from mine to allow me to remove it, watching as he pressed backward between my legs to remove his arms, tossing it to the side to mingle with my tank on the floor.

His hands glided down my calves, uncrossing my ankles from his lower back, pressing my feet down on the mattress at either side of his body, fingers sliding up the tops of my thighs, air hissing out of him when my breath caught, his fingers curling into the material of my panties at my hips, pulling.

My hips lifted up, allowing him to slide them down, pressing my knees into my chest to slide them off my ankles, leaving me perfectly bare before him.

Vance took a breath so deep it expanded his whole chest before folding downward, pressing his lips into my throat, tongue moving outward to glide down, running along my neck, clavicle, down over the hardened bud of my nipple, making my back arch up off the bed almost painfully before his lips sealed, sucked, made everything go white.

This.

This was something entirely new to me.

I knew sex.

I'd experienced pleasure.

But it was almost painfully clear that this, this was what I had been missing since the beginning.

Intimacy.

Connection.

The intoxicating combination of physical pleasure and emotional affection.

My body was buzzing with it.

My soul felt lifted with it.

Soon, though, all those flowery thoughts flew from my head as Vance's head shifted, lips blazing a path down the center of my belly. Lower.

An almost pained gasp escaped me as his lips sealed over my clit, sending shocks of pleasure through my system, nearly pushing me over the edge right then and there.

My hand slapped down on the back of his neck, holding him to me. As if he had any intentions of moving away.

He didn't.

His tongue moved over me with single-minded purpose, driving me quickly up to the edge, throwing me recklessly over, leaving me gasping through the orgasm, too breathless even to call out his name as the waves crashed savagely through me.

His body moved over mine, his lips claiming mine once again, pressing harder, deeper, bruising in.

My hands clawed down his back, yanking mindlessly at his pants, too lost in the need to have more, to have him, to feel him inside me that I couldn't seem to remember that the button and zip needed to be undone.

Vance, luckily, managed to remember himself, pushing up enough to undo them with one hand. Mine took over from there, yanking his pants and boxer briefs down over his hips, ass, down his thighs.

There was a short shuffle for protection before his body pressed into mine fully again, his cock dangerously close to where I needed him most.

"Now," I heard myself beg, hands sinking into his ass, trying to shift him, trying to put an end to the clawing need building inside me.

"Baby," he called. "Babe... Ferryn," he tried finally, managing to break through the growing desperation. "Ace, look at me," he demanded softly, refusing to budge until I forced my desire-heavy eyes open, finding his gaze on me. "There you are," he said, lips curving up ever so slightly as his hips shifted, as his cock pushed, then pressed inside on one slow, deep thrust.

I nearly shattered right then and there.

As a rule, I was not an eye contact person during sex. It was too close, too personal.

But I wanted nothing but close and personal with Vance.

My eyes stayed on his while he moved inside me.

Another first.

Slow.

Sweet.

Almost—dare I even think it—loving.

"Shh, babe, shh," he demanded as my whimpers turned to moans, as my moans became pleas. "Shh," he tried again as my orgasm started to crest. His hand pressed down over my mouth just in time, muffling out my cries as he pressed deep, as he came with me.

Bodies spent, he collapsed over me, our heartbeats hammering in unison.

Even if I wanted to, my body wouldn't have been capable of moving. My bones were gelatinous. My muscles may well have not existed.

But what was more important, I think, was the fact that there was no desire to.

To get up, to get dressed, to get gone.

That was how it used to be.

My heartbeat couldn't even slow before I needed to flee.

Everything within me, though, wanted to stay. Stay as long as I possibly could. Until this warm feeling became a part of me again, settled down, took root.

"Let me up," Vance demanded softly, making me realize I had wrapped him up with all limbs, had my face planted in his neck.

Realizing just how needy that was, just how new this was, I released him as though he burned me. I should have known he would notice the change, would call me on it.

"Don't do that," he demanded. "Just give me a minute."

"Take as long as you need. I, ah, I need to get back to my room. We shouldn't have done this here," I added.

"Yeah, probably not," he agreed. "And you are going to have to go back to your room. But not just yet. We still got that talk," he reminded me, giving me a pointed look before disappearing into the bathroom.

Alone, I pressed a hand to my heart, wondering if its frantic pace was still from the sex—the amazing, world-tilting sex—or the prospect of the upcoming conversation.

Both, maybe.

"Was I fast enough that you haven't started overthinking yet?" he asked, emerging barely a minute later, still perfectly naked and breathlessly unfazed by it.

"I can't really think much at all right now," I admitted, finding my brain slow. "And I'm not prone to overthinking."

"Yeah, okay," he said, rolling his eyes as he reached for an old beer on his nightstand, taking a swig, holding it out to me. "Once overheard you and Iggs debate what it meant when that girl in class called your outfit for the school dance 'daring' for *eight* days."

I felt my lips curve up at that.

We'd spent so much time worrying about the thoughts and opinions of people who didn't matter, who never mattered, whose names I couldn't even remember after all these years.

What a waste.

"Alright, well, I am not an over-thinker anymore," I corrected, moving over to make room for him to drop down. Which he did. Then threw an arm around me, curling me onto his chest. A part of me said I should pull away, get some clothes on, go back to my room. The other part—arguably a larger part—wanted to stay, never wanting to know what it might be like not to feel his arms around me, his fingers gliding down my arm.

"Good. Then you won't be a pain in the ass about this."

"About what?" I asked. "What is 'this?'"

"It's... something."

"'Something' isn't really a good explanation."

"No," he agreed, nodding, finger tracing over a particularly ugly scar just above my hip. I'd taken a pocketknife there, and yanked away, causing a jagged cut that hadn't healed clean, leaving a feather-like scar in its wake. "But it is more than saying it's nothing. We both know it's not nothing. It's never been nothing."

"No, I guess it hasn't," I agreed. "But things are different. We're different."

"It's a good thing you plan on sticking around for a while then," he said, plugging on quickly so I couldn't interject and remind him that I hadn't made any promises about how long I would be staying around.

"We aren't going to be public with this, are we?"

"Worried about your dad?"

"I think you're the one who should be worried about my dad," I reminded him.

"Probably right," he agreed, fingers moving up to trace up the short sides of my hair. "What made you buzz your head?"

"Practicality," I told him, giving him enough of the truth but not all of it. "I recently grew the top longer."

"It suits you. Always liked your long hair, but think this suits your personality."

"You don't really know my personality. Not anymore."

"I'm learning. And I am liking it. If you stop being such a pain in the ass, I could learn more."

"I'm not being a pain in the ass. I'm being cautious."

"You know what I think, Ace?"

"What?"

"Think you maybe need someone you can talk to."

"I can't talk to anyone."

"Babe, the fuck we going to be able to start if you won't talk to me?"

"I do talk to you."

"About the other shit."

"I can't talk to you about the other shit."

"Yes, you can."

"No, I can't," I objected, pushing up, looking down at him.

"You're going to have to."

"I don't *have* to do anything."

"Alright, let's not do this right now," he suggested, holding up a hand.

"You're right. Let's not do this," I agreed, moving over him, standing off the side of the bed.

"You know that's not what I meant." He sighed, reaching out, but I was already pulling on my panties, my tank.

"Look," I said, taking a deep breath, reminding myself that normal people who lived normal lives opened up, shared. Even if there was shame. Even if there was insecurity. The problem was, I was not a normal person and I didn't live a normal life. And the things I had done were things that normal people couldn't handle. Vance might have been an outlaw biker, but there wasn't blood on his hands. There weren't nightmares that kept him awake. I couldn't open up to him. But I also couldn't exactly be mad at him for not understanding why I couldn't. "If you want something here, you need to understand that there is some shit about me that you can't know about, that I can't tell you."

"And if I can't accept that?" he asked, those piercing eyes of his almost sad.

"Then I guess this stops before it really starts."

Ten

Vance - Present Day

She was a stubborn ass.

Still.

I couldn't decide if I was relieved by that fact or annoyed.

Or maybe both.

Probably both, I decided as I dragged myself into the shower a little before seven in the morning, knowing Summer was already up, had already been up for hours, excitedly cleaning the clubhouse, likely jotting down a long list of things to make one of us grab from the store.

I knew she'd been up because I'd been up.

I'd been up because it was proving impossible to sleep after Ferryn left.

I'd tossed for hours before I finally gave up.

I didn't know what Ferryn had been up to over the years, but judging by the map of scars on her body, she hadn't exactly been knitting sweaters and eating BonBons.

Whatever she'd been doing, she found herself bleeding more than a few times. The weird scar on her hip, dozens up her arms, four on the stomach and rib area, one particularly gruesome one near her throat that had some serious fucking implications it made my stomach twist to think about.

Her life had clearly been hard and dark and cold and ugly for a long time.

It was hard for her to even understand light and warm and comforting. Let alone to accept it as something she could have.

I knew I needed to understand that.

I knew she would need time.

I could give her that.

She'd consumed almost nine fucking years of my life already. I'd been searching for her in every bar and grocery store in every state I had been in for nearly a decade.

I could give her more time.

The question was if she would give it to me.

Clearly, I had no fucking idea what her life was about since she left Navesink Bank, but it was still an active part of her life. It still made her run when her phone rang. And that meant I would never know how much time I had with her before she would up and run off. For who knew how long.

She was a known flight risk.

I didn't want to clip her wings.

I just wanted her to know I could fly too.

Or I could hang back and wait for her to return.

So long as she returned.

Which was what I had to convince her to keep doing.

But slowly. Over time. Because I knew that she was easy to spook right now. She'd handled her parents, siblings, and aunt and uncle well. Even Fallon's refusal to spend any time with her. Today would be a bigger test. It would be overwhelming handling everyone's happiness and relief mixed with some definite anger and resentment at once.

So I wasn't going to go at her again this morning, knowing she had enough on her plate. But we damn sure weren't done talking.

She'd walked into my room while I had that new song floating through my head. For the first time in years. And that song? Yeah, that song was about her. Like all the rest had been since she left.

It had been starting to really come together, words cascading into my head, begging to be put in the right order so it could all finally become something.

I'd all but given up hope on having that part of myself back again.

All I needed was her.

Not to say she was my muse. That was a cheap and ugly thing to call a person who existed to do more than help you write music, but I think maybe being able to complete the story I had started to albums ago was what was calling to me. Her return was the completion of one thing.

And the beginning of something new, something unexpected.

I always wanted her to come home. But I never expected it to be for personal reasons, that there could be something between us.

I wanted her to come home because around every holiday and every club gathering, Summer could be found with a far-off, sad look in her eye. I wanted her home because Iggy still couldn't have an outing with me without mentioning Ferryn and wondering where she was and if she was okay.

I wanted her to come home because it bothered me that one event had so wholly changed the entire course of her life.

And, yeah, I wanted her to come home because I felt a little guilt in it all, I wondered if everyone looked at me as though me acting faster or refusing to take the girls to that shopping center in the first place could have prevented all of this.

I had a hand in all that happened.

I wanted to know she was okay and living a good life so that some of that guilt could go away.

I didn't want her to come back expecting that a crush she had eight years ago might be something she still carried with her and now that she was legal, I could act upon.

But here we were.

In so many ways, everything had changed. Yet in others, there was so much that was still the same.

We still fell into conversation easily. We still debated things with a lot of passion. We still enjoyed each other's company.

She was changed, yes, but I don't think quite as much as *she* thought she was changed. I was pretty sure that under a few deep levels of hard that a rough life had piled on her, she was still the same girl. The one who liked baking Christmas cookies with her mom. The one who fretted about her library books being late because her Aunt Reese was the local librarian. The girl who soaked up all the life lessons casually tossed at her from her uncles who had all led pretty colorful lives. The girl who had a connection with my sister like nothing I had ever known until I was a much older adult, until I had become part of a brotherhood.

Those were all still parts of her. And, for some reason, I felt like *she* was choosing not to see them. Maybe it made it easier for her. Maybe whatever life she had been living couldn't allow those things into it. Maybe those parts of her were seen as soft and weak in a place where she had to be hard and strong just to survive.

She had likely been so steeped in that world that she forgot that she deserved more than to simply survive.

I was so lost in my own thoughts that I missed that someone else was in my room until they spoke.

"I know my brother had some words with you last night," Cash started, making me jolt back, finding him standing just inside my doorway. "But I just wanted to come in here and tell you that if you ever fucking lie to my face again, you will be out of this fucking club, you get me?"

Cash was generally not the brass. Reign, always groomed from boyhood to eventually take over the club, was the harder one, the one who cracked down, the one who made it clear that you would pay for fucking up.

Cash, well, Cash was generally known for fucking up. Under his older brother's shadow, Cash was given a longer leash and he used it to screw around, break rules, have fun. It made him a more laid-back person. He wasn't known for cracking down or doling out threats.

So the fact that he was doing so now said a hell of a lot.

"I get you," I agreed, nodding.

"Good," he agreed, tension leaving his body. "Now on the other hand, thank you for keeping an eye on Ferryn. I get wanting to keep the surprise. I'm glad she had one of us to take her in when she needed it."

"If you think your niece *needs* anyone else to get by, we must not be talking about the same woman."

"Christ," Cash sighed, running a hand through his hair. "Woman. That is a hard one to swallow, y'know? Especially because she was still firmly in kid territory when she left."

"Yeah, she's done a lot of growing up," I agreed.

"Yeah. She's still passed out, but some of the girls are filing in. And I'm being sent out to grab eggs. My advice is to stay out of the kitchen or they'll have you running out too," he added, moving off into the hallway.

"Whoa," I said, nearly slamming into Peyton—the mermaid-haired, fully tatted, pierced woman of one of my brothers—standing in the middle of the hall, holding up two pairs of pants.

"Oh, hey, good. Which pair do you think she'd like better?"

"She being Ferryn?" I asked.

"Yeah. Summer asked me to pick up something for her to wear."

"Are those pussy flowers on the pink pair?" I asked, raising a brow.

"I know. She'd probably like the cock ones better, but they were sold out."

"I think Ferryn would prefer pants without genitalia on them."

"Really?" she asked, brows pinched like this information made no sense. "Alright. I guess the black and white plaid will have to do."

"Much more her style," I agreed, nodding.

"Not allowed in the kitchen, huh?"

"Not after the baby shower thing," she agreed, nodding.

The Baby Shower Thing was when the others put her in charge of cake decorating since she tended to have a good hand with it. And then she went ahead and did an anatomically accurate close-up depiction of a baby coming out of a woman.

The children were scarred for life.

I was scarred for life.

"Well, Ferryn is in Finn's room. She might still be sleeping. I think she was up late."

"I heard she looks like some badass *GI Jane* type person."

"She does," I agree. "Really works on her."

"You've been looking, huh?"

"She's an old friend."

"Mmm-hmm," she agreed, sending me a knowing look as she let herself right into Ferryn's room without knocking.

Christ.

Was I being that obvious, or were all the women just basing this off of Ferryn's old crush on me back in the day?

Pretty soon, there were too many voices in the space—those who had known Ferryn and those who had joined the ranks after her departure alike. Even if I had any of my own thoughts, they would have been drowned out by all of those voices around us.

For the most part, Ferryn seemed to relax after the first hour, though a case could be made for the very liberally poured mimosas for her level of calm.

Brunch turned into lunch which turned into dinner before everyone seemed to get their fill. Or simply needed to get home to get their kids to bed.

Everyone filed out.

And after a long day of cooking and cleaning, Summer headed to bed.

Which left me, Ferryn, West, and Reign in the living room.

I wondered if Ferryn sensed it before it came. I sure as fuck did. But I had been around Reign a lot more over the past few years than she had. Maybe tapping into his very subtle mood shifts was not something she knew how to do anymore.

She seemed comfortable enough with the company, switching to the whiskey West supplied her with, after tossing the first one back at him because she knew he had fucked with it, trying to get back at her for her fools' errand the night before.

Reign, though—Reign was ticking.

I wasn't sure what he was waiting for until he finally turned to his daughter and started speaking.

"Didn't want to do this in front of your mother, kid, so had to wait for her to pass out."

I couldn't help but wonder if he had some sixth sense about her being asleep already or if he simply knew she'd had an exciting few days and likely was drained from it all.

"Get into what?" Ferryn said, jaw suddenly tight, a trait she inherited from her father, making it clear she had missed his tension before.

"I know your mom doesn't want me to start any shit or rock any boats. She's happy for you to be home and she doesn't want me fucking with that."

"Okay..."

"For the record, I'm happy you're home too. But I think we both know I am not someone to let shit pass."

"You let a lot of shit pass that mom wouldn't have let pass," Ferryn reminded him, trying to lighten the mood, sending him a little smirk, making me wonder what she had gotten away with that I didn't know about.

"Yeah, stupid teenage rebellion shit. This, kid, this is not some shit I am going to let slide."

"I'm not a kid anymore, Dad," she reminded him.

"I know that."

"I don't have to answer to anyone."

"See, now, that is where you're wrong," he informed her, leaning forward, resting his forearms on his thighs. Somehow, it was more intimidating than if he rose to full height. Menacing, that was the best way I could think to describe it. "You come back into *my* house, you upset *my* family, that is when you fucking answer to me."

One glance at Ferryn let me know something very interesting.

While she had dealt with Reign, the father her whole life, she had clearly never dealt with Reign, the outlaw biker president.

"I'm not back in your house."

"This is my house," he declared, waving an arm out.

"And I didn't upset your family. And, for the record, they're my family too."

"Yeah?" he asked, giving her eye-contact that made *me* fucking squirm in my seat and it wasn't even directed at me. "I don't know what the fuck kind of warped ideas you got in your head about family, Ferryn. But family doesn't run away and leave everyone else behind. Family doesn't make everyone else worry. Family doesn't waltz back in here and expect for everything to be okay without giving so much as a simple explanation for where they've been and what they've been doing. That's not what family does."

Really, she had no comeback to that.

There *was* no comeback to that.

"You don't want an explanation."

"I'm sitting here, aren't I?"

"You don't want to know what I've been doing, what I've become."

"Look, kid, I get you wanting to protect your mom from ugly realities. I even appreciate that. But this is me. You don't have to protect me from shit. I doubt you've done shit that I haven't done in my life."

That was true enough.

I hadn't been around in his early days or during the street wars that shook the club and decimated its numbers a long while ago, but I had heard the stories. I knew how much blood was on Reign's hands.

"You haven't been chained up in a basement wondering if it was going to be you who was raped next, Dad," she told him, giving him the same eye-contact he'd given her.

Reign shocked back at that a little, maybe not expecting quite so much bluntness from her. "No, that I haven't."

"And you didn't have to worry that those same men who trapped you in that basement would use another girl's rape against you either."

Chris.

She was talking about Chris.

The other girl in the basement. The one who hadn't been able to escape predatory hands. The one who she managed to save. The one who was adopted by her Aunt Lo and Uncle Cash when they brought her back to Navesink Bank to heal.

"No," he agreed.

"You don't know how that fucks with your head, Dad. Like I know you think you can imagine, but trust me, you can't imagine."

"You're right. But I know you got out. You were free."

To that, there was a small scoff.

"I wasn't free. There's no way to be free of that. It's a part of you. It fucks with your head."

"And that is what getting help is for."

"I didn't want help. I wanted to make it stop."

"Make it stop?" he repeated.

"I wanted to make sure that bastards like the ones who had me would never be able to sleep soundly again. I wanted them to sit up at night worrying about people like *me* coming for them."

"That's what you've been doing then?" he asked. "You've been hunting them down."

"I've been taking them out," she corrected.

And suddenly, oh, suddenly it all made sense, didn't it?

The coldness. The distance. That reaction to me grabbing her arm once. The random disappearance right after she'd just arrived.

She'd been dealing with the scum of the Earth since she left. No wonder she thought any softness was a weakness. In a world like that, it was.

"Taking them out," Reign repeated, rolling the words around, likely trying to imagine the little girl she'd once been doing anything even related to murder.

"Yes."

"How?"

"Are you asking how I tracked them down, what skills I acquired, or what method of murder I utilized?"

"Yes," Reign answered, sitting back.

"Working at Hailstorm, I got to know some of the case files, some of the people Aunt Lo couldn't get to join her ranks. I tracked one down."

"And he was willing to train you?"

"Yes. He believed in my mission. I tracked the traffickers down on the dark web." Like several of her aunts knew how to do. "And I couldn't use guns because the cops couldn't be alerted."

"Up close and personal," Reign murmured, clearly mentally tallying the repercussions such acts could inflict on a person mentally, emotionally.

"Yes."

"Someone almost cut your throat," he added, voice a little rougher than usual, betraying a bit of his fatherly concern for the first time.

"Yes."

"You go to the hospital?"

"Not for that one. Not for most of them. Just two."

"Which two?" That one came from me. Me, who had personal knowledge of all of them. Me, who maybe just exposed that he had personal knowledge of all of them.

"Had a through-and-through above my knee that needed to be looked at. And a punctured lung."

"Broken rib?" West asked, regarding her with an oddly blank look.

"Yeah. That one was... close," she admitted, giving her father a careful look.

"Choking on your blood sucks balls," he added, making her lips curve up ever so slightly.

"Yeah."

"If we stuck you in an X-ray, how many breaks would we find?" West demanded.

"More than you could count."

"How many of them healed clean?"

"Not many," she snorted. "I am going to be a wreck when I'm fifty."

"You two done commiserating about your reckless pasts?" Reign demanded, shooting West a look that said he better drop it.

"It's not my past," Ferryn told him, voice just a tad softer than was normal. Tentative. Like she didn't want to break what she thought of as bad news to her father.

"Say that again?"

"I'm not done."

"Yeah, you fucking are."

"No, I'm fucking not," she countered. And if I wasn't mistaken, Reign's lips twitched just the slightest. In the past, they always did when she got smart or pushed some boundary.

You had to figure that a man who ran an arms dealing MC did appreciate a little bad behavior now and again.

"You gave it nearly nine years. That's enough."

"It's not enough."

"When will it be enough, then?"

"When there are no more bastards selling women against their will for sex."

"You and I both know that's never going to happen."

"Then you understand why I can never stop."

"There are other people who do this sort of thing."

"You're not seriously trying to tell me to leave it to the cops, are you? You, of all people?"

Oh, I couldn't imagine it felt great to be called a hypocrite by your own child.

"They have task forces and means."

"They have red tape and you know it. They answer for every bullet that leaves that gun. Even if they were putting down animals like these traffickers. You know as well as..." she trailed off as her phone dinged in her pocket.

I felt myself shift straighter in my seat. Because as far as I could tell, only two people had that phone number. Me. And whoever messaged her about a job. Otherwise, it was completely, unusually silent.

Judging by the tension in her jaw, I was right about it.

Her hand moved into her pocket, pulling out the phone, scrolling through.

I knew she was gone the second she shifted her legs off the arm of the chair and placed them on the floor, her body still curled over her phone, finger moving up then down again. Like she was trying to confirm that she read what she thought she'd read.

"We're not done here," Reign declared. And it was the most fatherly thing I think I had ever heard from him.

"We seemed to cover it all, I think," she objected, tucking her phone into her pocket. "My mind got fucked up in that basement. I decided I have a mission in life. I trained for it.

I paid my dues. And now I take down human traffickers. I might be back, but I am not retiring. That, I think, covers it."

"How the fuck am I supposed to let you just run off when I know you're almost getting your throat slit and collapsing a lung when you go?"

"I'm good at what I do, Daddy. I know you don't like this. But I have to remind you that you were the one who demanded to know. If you couldn't handle the truth, you shouldn't have asked it of me."

With that, she moved away from us, heading toward the door.

"West," Reign demanded, a silent command that West had no problem hearing.

He hopped up, rushing across the room, getting to the door just a blink before Ferryn did.

"Move."

"Got orders."

"West, move," Ferryn demanded, voice damn near as authoritative as her father's.

"Can't do that, Prez..." he started, cutting off when Ferryn whipped a hand into and out of her pocket, holding a curved blade to his throat before he could even know what was happening, let alone react.

"I'm not scared of you, Sweeney Todd," he told her, smirking even as the blade cut in enough to make blood prickle up on his skin.

In another move almost too fast to even see the individual steps, her arm pushed, her leg kicked, and West was on the ground.

"You should be fucking scared of me."

With that and nothing else, not even a glance at her father, she was outside.

"Not trying to tell you how to parent, Daddy Reign," West said, getting off the floor, swiping the blood from his neck casually, not seeming the least bit fazed by the whole ordeal, "but I am pretty sure that girl should have her allowance docked for a week or two," he added, laughing as he got himself a shot, jabbing his finger into the liquid, then running it over the cut.

"You," Reign said, ignoring West, pinning me instead.

"Yeah?"

"You and my girl, you always got along well."

"Ah, yeah."

"And you've been keeping an eye on her since she showed up."

"Breakfast, lunch, dinner, and late night snacks," West declared, making it clear I *did* have to worry about him and what he might say.

Reign, thankfully, seemed too worried about his little girl to pay West any mind. "I think she's going off on a job."

"I think so too," I agreed.

"I don't want her to go alone," he told me. "And I got a feeling she isn't about to let me tag along."

He wanted *me* to follow her into the home or workplace of a human trafficker and help her murder people?

"You know, Prez," West cut in, either seeing my thoughts on my face, or simply thinking them himself since he knew me better than most, "think maybe that is more my forte than his."

"Yeah, 'cause that's what I want: two reckless kids on the same job."

I didn't bother to remind him that both West and I were the same age. "Besides, you barely know her. Vance cares about her. Got a history there. He'd be the one to make sure she got out without a scratch."

"He's not exactly had the kind of..." West tried again. Not because he wanted to show off, to get on Reign's good side. But because he genuinely didn't know if I had what it took to kill people in that sort of situation.

To be fair, I wasn't sure I did either.

But I did know one thing.

Reign was right.

I would do anything to keep Ferryn safe.

"I'll do it," I agreed, nodding, already getting to my feet.

"Yo," West called, reaching into his boot, coming back with a pretty deadly looking hunting knife. "She won't let you use a gun. You're going to have to settle for this."

"Thanks, man," I told him, clapping a hand on his shoulder, taking the knife, slipping it into my pocket.

"Take off the cut. And don't take your eyes off my girl," Reign demanded.

I slipped off my cut, took a deep breath, and made my way outside.

I could certainly follow those instructions.

I didn't want to take my eyes off her anyway.

Eleven

Ferryn - Present Day

"No," I called, already hearing his footsteps behind me.

It could have been my father. Or West. But, somehow, I knew it was him.

"No, what?"

"No, you're not going to talk me out of it," I told him, reaching for my helmet.

"I'm not going to try to talk you out of it," he assured me, but there was something in his voice that told me I shouldn't trust him. But I couldn't quite put my finger on it. Especially because I had never known Vance to be anything other than trustworthy. He wasn't a liar. It wasn't his way. He always told you the truth. Even if it was ugly.

"Well... good," I said, watching as he moved two bikes over, reaching for his own helmet.

"Well, where are we headed?"

We?

"*We* aren't heading anywhere. I am heading somewhere. You are staying here."

"Afraid not, Ace," he told me, shaking his head.

"You're not coming with me."

"Actually, I kind of am."

"No, you're not. Go back inside. Are you out of your mind?"

"Well, see. I have to come."

"My father is making you, isn't he?" I asked, eyes getting small.

A part of me, the newer part of me, the part of me that felt like she could handle everything on her own and didn't need anybody or anything, wanted to be annoyed about it. The other part, though, the part that was raised by a loving and often lenient father who not only tolerated, but enjoyed my often rebellious ways, couldn't find any anger about it.

Of course he wanted me safe.

Especially now that he knew what I had been up to all these years.

I should have known it was coming. My mother may have been the sort to let things slide so as not to create conflict. My father, though, was not the same way. He wanted answers. And what he wanted, he got.

There was no way he was going to let it slide that I had been gone for nearly nine years, I was covered in scars, and I was colder and more guarded.

I guess I had a false sense of security because literally no one else asked. I wasn't sure if it was because they were happy to see me and wanted to fill me in on the goings-on in their lives, or if my mother had reached out to them and told them to mind their P's and Q's. But no one had asked, let alone demanded, my story.

I guess my father had always been pretty damn good at playing his cards close to his vest.

And, honestly, of all people, I was worried about telling him the least. Well, him and some of my uncles. Wolf, Pagan,

Edison, and Adler in particular likely wouldn't even raise a brow to the information. They'd all led such colorful lives, had seen and done some terrible things. And I guess you could say the same for my father.

He had always been careful when telling us war stories, not wanting to get too gory on the details. But everyone else talked. And Iggy and I had a tendency to eavesdrop when we had sleepovers at the clubhouse.

There was the war, of course, and an untold number of bodies in the wake there.

There had been the time he saved my mom.

More bodies.

There was a story I caught bits and pieces of about there being a rat in his club and how he had handled it out in the back shed before the shed blew up one day, taking all the evidence of the bloodshed with it.

He had lived a very different life than most people. He was in charge of a ton of men who had lived similarly colorful lives. He didn't regard it the same way my mom and some of my aunts and even a few of my uncles would.

That didn't mean, though, that he had to like it.

Because no matter what, I was his little girl. Even if I had been on my own since I was sixteen.

So of course he wasn't going to let me go off on a job on my own. Not when he knew that was where I was going. Not when he had twenty or so men at his beck and call, ready to lay down their lives if he asked it of them.

That said, why would he send Vance? When West was clearly more likely handle such a unique situation? I didn't know his history per se, but it sounded like he had known his fair share of knock-down-drag-outs.

Vance was a biker. I was sure he did drops. He might have even dealt with some sticky situations, but things were relatively calm with the MC. There were no bodies hitting the ground. Vance was the last person who should have been coming with me.

Especially on this particular job.

This one—this was going to get bad.

Blood was going to paint the walls, make a river of the halls.

That is if I had anything to say about it.

This was the big one. The one I had been trying to pin down almost from the beginning. These men were the worst of the worst.

This would be ugly.

It was going to make *me* ugly.

Because I wasn't just doing a job, exacting a cold sort of revenge.

Oh, no.

I was going to enjoy this.

I was going to fucking *love* this.

I was going to take actual physical pleasure in pressing my blade into their throats, hearing them beg for mercy, then sinking that blade in, slowly, so fucking slowly, refusing them any fucking mercy.

They didn't deserve it.

I didn't want anyone to be a part of that.

But most especially, I didn't want Vance to be a part of that. To see me like that. To know just how dark I could get, how much joy I could gain from doing something so unimaginable.

I knew that Vance was still seeing the old Ferryn when he looked at me. And maybe there was more of her still hanging around than I realized, but this was a surefire way to show him just how much I wasn't like that anymore.

A part of me hated the idea that he would see the real me. And therefore, never be able to look at me again. At least not like he had looked at me the night before in bed. With sweetness. With tenderness. Like I was someone that could easily be loved, someone who could accept that kind of softness.

"He asked me because he knows I care about you. But I would want to come regardless."

"I don't want you to come."

"I'm afraid that is not going to be a factor."

"You don't know where I'm going. I could lose you—What?" I asked when he smirked.

"On that?" he asked, waving to my bike. "I mean, maybe you could lose me in some nondescript black sedan. But not on a bike."

"Vance, listen, this is going to be bad."

"All the more reason for me to be there. I'll have your back."

I won't lie, someone having my back on this one wouldn't be terrible. But that someone being Holden, who knew already how brutal I could be, how I could turn into a wild animal. Someone who turned into one himself so he didn't judge me for my claws and teeth.

Short of that, I would rather take my chances alone.

"You don't understand," I hissed, feeling a completely humiliating sting at the backs of my eyes. Like I was going to friggen *cry*. I never cried.

"Hey, help me understand then," he demanded softly, snagging my chin, forcing me to face him.

I swallowed hard, something that forced the lump out of my throat, letting all the words tumble out unbidden, unfiltered, raw and real.

"I don't want you to see me like that!"

"Like what?" he asked, brows furrowing, thumb moving distractingly up my jaw for a second.

"Ugly," I admitted.

"Ace, you could never be ugly."

"Not like *that*," I snapped, yanking away. "A different kind of ugly. Soul ugly."

"I think I know a thing or two about your soul by now, Ferryn. It's not ugly."

"It can be."

"Everyone's can be. We're all capable of angry and ugly and bitter."

"This is different. Most people's angry and ugly and bitter doesn't include blood splatter and screams for mercy."

"No. But I know that going in, Ace. And I know why you do it. And I'm fine with it."

"Fine with it," I scoffed, shaking my head. "Fine with it. You are fine with me grabbing a knife and slicing someone's throat right in front of your eyes? Even if he is unarmed? Even if you don't know what he did?"

"I do know what he did, though."

He didn't know about these guys in particular though. Some part of me actually wanted to protect him from it. The worst part of the world. The ugliest part of humanity.

"Vance..."

"Ferryn..." he mimicked, making a small laugh/snort hybrid escape me.

"We're getting close."

"Getting close to what?" I asked.

"To the real truth. If your stubborn ass wasn't so fucking guarded, we'd have gotten there already and we could be on our way."

My gaze fell from his, studying the tips of my shoes, scuffed from endless wears. The marks made it hard to get the blood out all the way. I should have gotten a new pair ages ago. But I had a hard time letting go, I guess.

Story of my fucking life.

"You're going to look at me differently after this. And I... I don't think I could take that," I admitted.

Then, too chickenshit to face the aftermath of my words, jumped on my bike, turned it over, and peeled off.

There was only a short moment before I heard him following behind me.

It was a long drive.

I hoped that by the end of it, I could pull myself together, bank down the burning thoughts, focus on the task before me.

Rough intel said four traffickers, but a likelihood of security.

And, yeah, that made sense.

Alone, the plan would be to take out the first couple as silently as possible moving through to get the others. If they ganged up all at once, I knew I was in over my head.

With backup, I could handle more. Providing I wasn't distracted by trying to look out for Vance.

It wasn't that I didn't think he could take care of himself. I was sure he'd been to the gym, had gotten into the ring with some of the guys, had maybe even taken some mixed martial arts classes with some of the teachers there. That, combined with pure survival instinct, meant that he could likely hold his own well enough.

But there would be a part of me that felt responsible for his well-being since the only reason he would be there was because I was there, because my father made him follow me.

I wasn't sure I could forgive myself if something happened to him.

No.

I couldn't think like that.

I couldn't let the doubts in, water them, watch them take root. Once they started growing out of control, it was impossible to see through them.

I had to focus.

I had to see him as an asset.

Because this was too important.

This was the most important job in my, erm, career.

"Alright," Vance said a few hours later at the second gas stop since we got on the road. "You're going to have to give me something," he told me, leaning back against the pump nearest mine.

He was right.

He couldn't go in blind.

"I don't have an exact number. But I am expecting five or six," I told him, figuring blunt was the best method. There was no sugar coating something like this. He would need to steel himself for what was to come.

"And we both know you've trained enough to take on four of them by yourself," he told me, giving me those dancing eyes of his. If there was any hesitance in him, he didn't show it.

"There shouldn't be any victims there. Not this time. This is more of like the traffickers' headquarters. They don't bring clients there. It... it makes things easier."

"I imagine so," he agreed, nodding.

"No one is innocent when you go in there."

"Got it."

"This is going to be inside an abandoned coffee place."

"Traffickers squat in abandoned buildings?"

"When they can get away with it. It's always better when nothing traces back to them. Abandoned buildings, foreclosed houses the bank hasn't put back on the market yet. They move around a lot, so places that don't require contracts work best for them."

They also really liked the sleep-and-fuck style motels that let paperwork slide if enough money passed hands. These guys, in particular, liked motels. Which was why it had been so hard to pin them down. I couldn't do what I needed to do in a motel. First, because of the obvious risk of being overheard. But also because of cameras and the likelihood of being seen by others in the vicinity.

When I was on a job where there were no victims to alert the police, it sometimes took weeks or months for the bodies to be found. Usually by then, the remains were horribly degraded, evidence swept or rained or hauled away by scavengers looking for a meal.

Which, well, was good for me.

I was careful. But modern advances meant that even careful people could get caught by a stray hair or drop of blood.

"What happens after the guys are taken care of?"

"Do you mean do I bury bodies?" I asked, watching as he shrugged. "I clean up any obvious signs of my being there.

Which is hopefully not a whole hell of a lot. I wear gloves. My hair is relatively short. I try to avoid bleeding all over the place. So I just open a door or window and leave."

"Open a door or window?"

"To let scavengers in, to let the wind in."

"Wouldn't it be better to leave them closed so things don't start to smell?"

"Ever smell a decaying body?"

"Can't say I have."

"They smell for like a mile. You know when you are in the vicinity of one. Even if the windows are closed. Air escapes eventually. If the house is in a relatively congested area or something, I might forego the window or door. It really depends on how worried I am about evidence."

"Meaning how much blood you left behind?"

"You'd be surprised. Even with the odds against me, sometimes I manage to get away with just some bruises. These kinds of guys are generally more used to using guns, not hand-to-hand combat."

"Well, let's hope for that this time."

"No promises. You want to follow me in there, it could get dicey. You might be sporting some new scars when we get back to Navesink Bank."

"Lucky I got myself a girl who seems to dig scars, huh?" he asked, climbing on his bike, turning it over, cutting off any objections I might have had about him calling me his.

Because, well, I wasn't.

One sex session did not a relationship make.

And I wasn't exactly a relationship kind of girl anyway.

There was no denying, though, as I got on my bike and led us out of the parking lot, that there was a part of me that was buzzing with the idea of him claiming me. Even if the other part of me knew it couldn't happen, that he would revoke his feelings as soon as this job was done, that he was a good man and I couldn't subject him to being in a relationship with someone like me.

"Where is the coffee place?" Vance asked when we finally reached the town we needed, but I had driven us right up to a patch of dense woods.

"Through the woods. We're hiding the bikes in here so no one sees them," I told him, climbing off mine, leading it into the woods a of couple yards, flipping up the seat to dig around in the storage compartment. "Here," I told him, handing him a pair of gloves I hoped would fit him. "And here," I added, giving him one of my spare knives.

"West gave me this," he told me, showing me the hunting knife.

"Nice." It had a good blade. Thick enough to withstand multiple stabs if need be, not likely to break off in the bone. "But take the backup too. I always have a few even though I prefer my karambit. You never know what might happen in a fight."

"Got it," he agreed, slipping the extra knife into his boot which was a decent place for it. I kept one there as well. "So this is it? We walk through the woods, we sneak into the building, and we get to work?"

"Pretty much," I agreed, rolling a crick out of my neck, trying to take a few breaths in, chasing away the familiar surge of adrenaline. It could be useful in the right amount. It made your reflexes faster. It made you sharper. But too much could make you lightheaded, could make your heart race, could convince you that you were having a goddamn heart attack. "You need a couple minutes to prepare yourself?"

"I've had hours for that," he told me. "I think I'm good."

He wasn't.

And I hated that he might never truly be good again.

Because of me.

Because he felt the need to protect me.

Because my father made sure he did.

It was too late for regrets, though. This was going to happen. We would have to deal with the fallout after.

A few minutes later, we stood at the other end of the woods, looking at a building that had seen better days—white siding splattered with green, chinks taken out in more places than you could count, the back screen blowing around in the wind, creating an eerie clapping noise every few seconds. It would made good sound cover.

There looked to be a light on in a back room facing us, away from the road where someone might see it and report it.

"Ready?" I asked, feeling the fire start to burn through my veins. Strong. Familiar. Effortless.

The planning, the waiting—I sucked at that. And maybe an argument could be made for me sucking at the aftermath sometimes as well.

But this?

This, I was good at.

This was why I had worked so hard to turn myself into a weapon.

"Yes." There was certainty in his voice, something I found comfort in.

"Hey Vance?" I called, looking at his lovely profile for a moment, not wanting to feel anything, but getting a stab of need so hard it nearly brought me to my knees.

"Yeah, Ace?" he asked, looking over at me.

"These guys?" I started, jerking my chin toward the building. "They aren't just normal traffickers."

"No?" he asked, brow furrowing. "Do they have a specialty or something?"

"Yeah," I agreed, jaw so tight it was hard to even get the words out. "Toddlers."

As soon as the shock on his face faded to rage, I knew it was time. I knew he was at my level. I knew he could do it.

Finding the back door locked, I slit the screen, crouching in the open space to work on the lock while Vance clapped the metal against the building so no one suspected anything was amiss.

Feeling the lock disengage, I tucked the kit away, giving Vance a nod.

He pushed the door hard against the other side of the building as I pulled the handle.

And just like that, we were in.

Vance moved in at my six, both of us holding our chosen weapons, glancing around the darkened space.

My footsteps—this time, our footsteps—always sounded like thunderclaps when I was tip-toeing through an abandoned, nearly silent space.

There were voices coming from the back where we'd seen the light.

From the sound of things, a poker game. If you took a deep breath, you could smell the cigars, the cheap vodka.

A door opening right between me and Vance nearly made gasp erupt from me.

"H..." the guy started, jerking back at seeing us in the shadows.

I went to move, but Vance proved faster, clamping a hand over the man's mouth, jerking him back against his chest, holding his head arched backward by the top of his hair.

Then he did it.

He gave me a nod.

He gave me *permission* to bleed a life out right there on his chest.

Not much of a life, one that lured children out of cars, pulled them right out of grocery carts when their parents looked away, and then sold them to the highest bidder to endure hell until their bodies gave out. But a life. Something Vance likely held as more valuable than I did.

There was a moment's hesitation before I saw him go to reach for his own blade.

But I couldn't let that happen.

It was my kill.

If he thought he could handle all my ugly, I had to show him, to prove him right or wrong.

It doesn't take long to bleed out.

Longer than the movies, of course.

It wasn't a slice and instant death.

If you are good at what you do—and I am—you sever the trachea below the larynx, something that prevents the initial shocked screaming. But the killer was making sure you got that carotid and jugular, preventing new oxygenated blood from reaching the brain, and making the blood flow easily from the brain until there was unconsciousness and then death.

If you are standing there watching it happen like we were, it felt like hours passed as you waited for the body to slump, for the life to leave the eyes.

I usually didn't wait.

I trusted my ability to accomplish the task, then went ahead and lowered them to the ground, leaving them to die there alone like the beasts they were as I went in search for more prey.

But there was simply no way to communicate in the darkness with Vance, so he held the body until it went heavy, life leaving it, then he slowly lowered it down to the ground, not even paying any mind to the blood soaking through his shirt.

Standing, he gave me another nod, jerking his chin toward the end of the hall.

There was no more time to think, to analyze, to make a mental plan.

Because a man was pulling the back room—an old storage space, metal racks and all—open, moving into the doorway, casting us in light.

"What the fu—"

My arms went up, grabbing the back of his neck, jerking it violently down as I slammed my knee upward, landing my mark to his nose with relative ease, sending pain shooting through his system, distracting him.

I shoved him to the side, leaving him to Vance, as I charged into the room as men started to gain their feet, cards and chips flying.

From there, it was all instinct.

Uppercut to a chin, sending a body of a smaller man flying backward.

Punch to the liver, incapacitating another while I made my way toward the one I had been tracking for years.

The leader.

A man so vile I wasn't sure hell would even accept him. But I was going to send him there just to be sure.

He wasn't a good fighter, per se. He was just big. Big and strong and angry.

I took a punch to the stomach and one to the jaw before I could scuttle back far enough to use my arm, to slice my blade through his hand as he raised it.

Deep.

That was fucking deep.

If I could have been just an inch closer, I might have been damn near able to sever the fucking thing.

But it was enough.

To take him down for a moment just as uppercut guy came up behind me, arms encircling my upper chest and neck, pulling me clear off the floor, my legs peddling in the air for a second before I could get enough momentum to jerk my body downward. Feet planting, I pushed off, propelling myself upward, loosening the hold on me, so that when my feet would have touched down again, I fell to my knees instead, bowing him down with me, breaking his hold completely, allowing me to slam my blade upward into his throat.

It wasn't a slice.

A slice was clean and easy and quickly fatal. Like the guy back out in the hall.

This was a stab.

A stab to the neck that seemed to jab a hole in his throat, judging by the horrific, rasping sound coming from him.

The following slice wasn't mercy. Not in the least. It just took one thing off my plate.

His body didn't slump to the ground, it crashed, slamming headfirst into one of the metal racks as I spun around, a deafening sound.

Turning, I sought liver-guy, noticing Vance engaged with someone else, some guy who must have come running from somewhere else in the building because he hadn't been in the room when we'd surged inward.

Liver guy put up a pretty decent fight given the pain he had to have been in. A shot to the liver was one of the injuries I hated the most. I'd take a broken bone over a liver shot any damn day.

In the end, my jaw was hurting, my eye would be black, there was a trio of deep claw marks in my arm, and there was another body at my feet.

I was just about to gain my feet when I felt a hand grab me at the wrist, yanking hard and fast, nearly dislocating my shoulder before I found myself tossed onto the makeshift pool table, an ashtray jabbing me in the lower back as money fluttered into the air around me.

It was a bad angle. On your back with no easy escape. A giant, angry man towering over you.

He had giant hands, one making its way around my throat, crushing so hard I was sure he could manage to break my neck before he actually strangled me.

I was just grabbing the sides of the table to try to toss my body off the side when I saw two bloodied hands raise, one grabbing the hair to angle the head back, the other slicing across the entire man's meaty throat.

The blood spilled downward, gruesome as the life slowly left a man I had been hunting for ages.

It wasn't my kill.

There should have been a sense of defeat in that.

But as the body was tossed to the side, leaving Vance there towering over me, chest heaving, arms and shirt bathed in blood, eyes burning bright with the fight and what I could only call a sort of... protectiveness, well, I couldn't seem to muster any sense of disappointment about it.

The man was dead.

His operation would die with him.

Only for a short time, of course, before someone else stepped into his place, but it would save an untold number of children in the meantime.

"Are you hurt?" he asked when I continued to lay there, staring up at him, feeling a sort of squeezing sensation in my chest that should have been off-putting, but it was almost, I don't know, comforting. "Ace?" he demanded when I couldn't seem to muster words. The knife fell from his hands onto the table, his fingers grabbing at my clothes, dragging my shirt up, looking for the gaping hole, the flowing blood.

"I... I'm fine," I managed, swallowing hard. "It's all surface," I added when the worry didn't immediately leave his eyes. "Are you hurt?"

"Just a graze on my arm," he said, giving me his hand, helping me fold up on the table. "The water isn't off."

"What?"

"The water isn't off. That other guy, he came from the bathroom. I heard the water running. We can clean up," he added as I started up at him a little dumbly. Not because I didn't grasp his meaning, but because I hadn't heard the water. Why hadn't I heard the water?

"They're all dead?" I asked, glancing around at the scene scattered around us. Blood. A lot of blood. There always was. But this seemed like more than usual.

"Yep."

"You checked?" I demanded.

"No one's chest is raising, Ace," he told me, but I had to check myself. "Satisfied?" he asked, rolling his eyes at me.

"We did a good thing here," I told him, feeling the need to reassure him as we moved back into the hall, as I shouldered in the door to the bathroom.

"Yeah," he agreed, both of us moving in at each sink, flicking on the water, scrubbing. "Your shirt," I mumbled, glancing over at him, making sure he got all the visible blood off his body.

"I got another one in the bike. I can change when we get back," he told me, cutting off the water, moving over toward me.

I watched in the mirror as he came up behind me, as his gaze held mine.

"What?" I asked, not sure what the look was in his eyes. It was deep, though, almost blazing, even.

Anger? Was he angry at me for involving him?

His hips pressed forward then, jabbing his cock into the flesh of my ass, making a gasp escape me.

Not anger.

Heat.

He was turned on.

Maybe to someone else, that would be insane, would have been revolting to know that he was hard after a fight and murder.

Me, though—I got it.

The adrenaline, the fear, the uncertainty.

It was still all there after the fight was over.

It raced through your system, making your skin feel electric, making your belly swirl.

It needed an outlet.

And you sometimes needed an affirmation-of-life fuck.

It was stupid and reckless, but then again, so was I, but I planted my hands on the sink, angling my ass out toward him, an invitation if I had ever seen one.

Vance didn't need more than that, either.

His hands moved around me, grabbing my pants and panties in hungry hands, yanking them down so hard I heard a rip, but couldn't bring myself to care as I felt them gather down below my knees.

Vance wasted no time reaching around me, pressing his fingers between my thighs, rubbing his thumb over my clit, sinking his first two fingers into me with a barely-contained violence, something that made my walls tighten, that made my ass angle out further.

His other hand worked his button and zip free.

A low whimper escaped me just as something flew into the sink in front of me.

His wallet.

I understood that silent demand.

My hand fumbled with it, finding the condom, handing it back to him as I finally felt his bare cock glide against my pussy, making a shiver rack my system.

A rumble moved through Vance's chest, as he pulled back, focusing on protecting us for a second before his gaze found mine in the mirror, eyes molten, making my sex clench hard, enticed by the dark promise he was showing me.

"Vance," His name rushed out of me, airy, needy.

Whatever control he'd had snapped at the sound, one hand sinking into my hip, holding me still as he slammed inside me.

Hard.

Rough.

An aching, brutal sort of pleasure gripped me, making a strange whimpering moan escape me as my gaze held his in the mirror.

His free hand reached for one of mine, pressing it between my thighs, guiding it over my clit until I took over fully, then moved upward, closed over my hand braced on the wall, holding on as he started to fuck me.

There was no other way to describe it.

This wasn't slow and sweet and explorative.

This was hard and fast and dirty.

Each thrust jammed my hips forward into the unyielding sink, guaranteeing bruises when we were finished.

It didn't take long.

His cock, my fingers, the tension buried deep inside.

"Come, Ace," he demanded, eyes on mine in the mirror as he thrust deep.

And I fucking shattered.

If it wasn't for his arm going around my center, I was pretty sure I would have collapsed to the floor. My legs lost any semblance of structural integrity. I wouldn't have been surprised if I looked down and didn't even see them there as the orgasm crashed endlessly through my system, stealing my breath, wiping my brain of any thoughts.

"Fuck," Vance hissed, his body curving over mine, forehead pressing into the back of my neck.

Sucking in a deep breath, I forced some strength back into my legs, pushed myself upright as Vance slid away from me.

"We have to go," I said, leaning down to pull my panties and pants back into place.

"Yeah," He agreed, dropping the condom into the trash, then taking the bag with him.

It was probably weird that I found myself turned on by his forethought, but there was no denying I was.

"Wait," I said, stiffening.

"What?" he asked, tensing too. "Is someone here?"

"Do you smell that?" I asked, moving toward the door.

Something was burning.

"No," Vance growled when I went to reach for the door, slamming his hand down on it, keeping it closed. "Look," he told me, nodding down to the bottom of the door where a small bit of smoke was wafting in. "Window," he said, jerking his head over toward it. "Here," he called, slamming it open, holding his hands down for me to step onto.

I didn't need to be told twice.

I hauled myself up and out the window, waiting for Vance on the other side.

"Should we do something?" he asked, reaching for the bag he had thrown out ahead of him.

"Let it burn," I decided, reaching for his hand, and hauling ass back into the woods.

Both seeming to sense the urgency of getting as far away as fast as possible, we didn't speak, didn't plan on anything. We just got on our bikes and drove blindly away.

Sirens wailed, but none followed as we got one town away, two, five, over an hour outside of the area.

"We have to stop for the night," Vance told me after we fueled up the bikes again.

"Yeah," I agreed, taking my first real deep breath since before we'd gone into the building.

"I tossed the gloves in this dumpster when I went in to pay," he told me, nodding over toward them. "We will get rid of the garbage at the hotel."

"We need clothes too. And to get rid of these clothes."

"And call your father," he told me, brow raising, daring me to object.

"Okay," I agreed.

"Are we heading back tomorrow? Or do you need time?"

"Me?" I asked, feeling a smile pull at my lips. "I think you're the one who would need time."

"Maybe I would have. If you hadn't told me what they specialized in. Could have taken them down by a thousand cuts my fucking self."

"Is my black eye coming in?" I asked, knowing it was only a matter of time.

His hand reached out, fingers nagging my chin, lifting and turning it to the side to inspect me.

"It's getting there. Has a bit to go still."

"What am I going to tell my mother?" I asked, then felt a hysterical little laugh bubble up inside me.

"What?"

"I just... I haven't thought that in so long. Like I missed curfew or something."

"Think you can count yourself lucky that you have parents like them, Ace. You really lucked out in that department."

I was not prone to displays of affection. Not even before I went away. I always accepted them from those I loved, but I rarely initiated unless someone was upset or something like that.

But I felt myself moving toward Vance, sliding my hands around his side, circling his back, resting my forehead against his chest.

"I'm sorry your parents kinda suck, Vance."

There wasn't a moment of hesitation in Vance's arms going around me. He was someone who hugged pretty readily. I think it was something he did because his parents never showed them any sort of affection, so as the bigger brother, he felt the need to compensate, giving Iggy hugs on bad days or when she had done something he was proud of.

He used to give me one-arm hugs when I showed up somewhere. Casual. Friendly.

This was not a casual or friendly hug.

This was long and tight and perfect.

"It's okay. I get to kind of have yours here and there."

"Think they might have preferred another daughter, but..." I said, smiling into his chest when he slapped my ass.

"What? With the royal pain in the ass you chose to be? They'd welcome a dozen sons."

I was smiling still when I pulled away. Vance's finger traced over my lower lip.

"Missed that smile, Ace."

I was finding I had missed a lot of things about him that I didn't even realize I missed.

"And there it goes," he said, shaking his head, but shrugging it off. "Come on. Let's go find some clothes and a room."

"And *food*."

"Yep," he agreed, chuckling. "And food. Grilled chicken and steamed sweet potatoes?" he suggested, making me small eye him. "Sicilian pizza and a side of garlic knots?"

"That's more like it," I agreed, hopping onto my bike.

"What happened to you two?" the nosy cashier who had already critiqued every single item we had purchased, making me desperately wish we had gotten a value pack of condoms and a big old tub of lube, asked as she bagged out items.

"Bar fight," I grumbled at her, taking the bags as Vance reached for cash.

"The lady next to us looked at me," Vance went on, shaking his head.

"No one looks at my man."

"She was eighty if she was a day."

"Did I stutter? You look, you pay," I told him, having to press my lips into a firm line when the cashier ducked her head, carefully avoiding any chance she might glance at Vance.

"You're mean," Vance informed me as we walked out, leaning over to sink his teeth into my shoulder.

"Hey, she's the one who had to imply that I was going to get fat if I kept eating Devil Dogs."

"Had it coming, huh?" he asked, then glanced at me from the side of his bike.

"What?"

"Do you get jealous?" he asked.

I wasn't going to pretend I didn't know what he meant. Or that he'd called me his. Or that I had just called him mine.

"You remember all those girls at all those shows when we were younger?"

"Vaguely," he admitted, having the good sense to look chagrined at the sheer number of them.

"I wanted to claw their faces off."

"Well," he said, grinning. "It's a good thing you didn't find your killer instinct until later in life."

"So many lives saved," I agreed.

"You ready?" he asked, jerking his head in the direction of the hotel. We'd already checked in before we headed to the store. We'd ordered our food to be delivered to. I think we both knew that once we got in that room, once we cleaned up, once we refueled, we were going to pass the hell out and not wake up for a solid twelve hours.

"What?" Vance asked a couple hours later, our bellies full, our bodies cleaned, our clothes changed, our evidence-filled clothing tossed, my father called, everything handled.

I pressed my lips together, looking over at him in the bed, not sure how real I wanted to get with him right then.

"Come on, Ace. Give me something without making me pry it out of you," he suggested, lying flat, placing a hand behind his head.

That was fair. Especially after the night he'd just had because of me.

"I've never slept with a guy before. In the literal sense," I clarified, since it was clear I was no virgin when we'd hit the sheets.

"Really?" he asked, eyes going soft.

"Really," I agreed, nodding. "Men, ah, you know... things were always casual. For obvious reasons."

"I know a thing or two about casual too," Vance agreed, clearly trying to remove some of my discomfort in the admission. "But you know what?" he asked, waiting for me to answer.

"No, what?"

At that, he knifed up, grabbing me, pulling me down onto his chest, anchoring me with his arm as though I had any intentions of moving.

"I like this infinitely more. And don't try to tell me there is no *this*. Because we both know there is. And you can't say I only want it because I don't know what you've been up to, or because I haven't seen it with my own two eyes. Because I know. I've seen. And guess what, Ace?"

"What?" I asked when he waited again for my answer.

"I still fucking want you."

My heart and belly skipped and fluttered at that, those words I had wanted so badly to hear for so many years.

"I've *always* wanted you," I admitted, voice small.

"Well, you got me now. Like it or not."

I liked it.

God, I liked it.

I maybe even kind of, well, loved it.

Twelve

Vance - Present Day

I didn't want to go back to Navesink Bank.

And, what's more, I didn't think Ferryn wanted to either.

We seemed perfectly content to stay in bed late, only taking a short break to go down to the dining room to grab the complimentary breakfast, taking it back to our room to eat in bed while watching *Saved by the Bell* reruns.

Eventually, I climbed up to grab a shower. Which she joined.

And it all just felt right.

Her and me.

Without any outside influence.

But this was an illusion—a vacation from what was going to be our real life.

It didn't escape me, either, that our real life would mean that we were going to have to break this news to everyone.

To be perfectly honest, I think Summer and even Lo already suspected something. And who knew what stories West had been telling them since we took off.

But I would have to tell Reign.

And all the guys in the club. Who I thought of as brothers. But whose loyalty to her as their niece could mean that some serious fucking talking-tos were in my future.

I'd do it all. Take it all. If that's what was necessary for us to go public with this, to not have to hide it.

A part of me was worried that Ferryn preferred it this way. A dirty little secret. Something that maybe felt more temporary to her.

It didn't escape me that she was struggling to let herself put down roots. That she wasn't sure how to make her mission and her *life* work together. A part of her was maybe even convinced that it wasn't possible to marry those two things together, that they were too opposite, that one couldn't exist alongside the other.

And for any normal relationship or any normal family dynamic, that was probably true. But there was nothing normal about her family full of bikers and bomb makers and paramilitary leaders.

There wasn't a single person in that group—and I was even counting the sweet, soft souls like Rey—that wouldn't openly embrace her mission if they knew what it was, why she was doing it, what kind of rabid dogs she was putting down for good so they couldn't keep going along hurting innocent people.

To be fair, at first, I hadn't been sure how I truly felt about it. I didn't know how I could rationalize it, even knowing she was serving a greater good.

There had been a knot in my stomach as we drove out of Navesink Bank, as a certain coldness overtook Ferryn.

I genuinely wasn't sure I could see her brutally murder people and still see her the same way.

I didn't have anything to worry about.

See, when you thought of traffickers, if you were a decent human being, your stomach turned, your saliva went bitter. But you imagined woman snatched off streets. Maybe even young women.

But because it was so fucking impossible even to imagine, you didn't immediately think of children lured away from their parents or snatched off of playgrounds. You couldn't fathom someone sexualizing a toddler, let alone some scumbag trading them around to perverts.

It wasn't a reality most of us could wrap our heads around. It was an ugliness we simply didn't let into our minds.

But Ferryn did.

Ferryn had to.

The second those words were out of her mouth, I understood with one-hundred percent fucking clarity that what she did was needed, was necessary, was the only thing tipping the scales more toward good than evil

I thought I knew myself pretty well, had experienced most of the highs and lows of life.

I couldn't have been more wrong. Because I had never felt anger like the kind that burned through my system as we moved into that building.

I wanted blood.

I wanted to paint the fucking world with the blood of those men.

I didn't even pause in making that a reality, either.

Though I did pause for a moment to admire the way Ferryn tore into that room. With confidence. With righteous vengeance. With the ease of true purpose.

See, if it weren't for Ferryn, those men would be alive. Those men would be *free* to continue to traffic *babies*.

How could you not embrace her lifestyle when she saved countless families from untold heartbreak, children from torture?

I didn't have to like the idea that she was putting herself in dangerous situations, that she often did it alone.

I did have to accept it as part of her reality, though, if I wanted to have her.

And I did.

It really was that simple.

But also that complicated.

"Does it look any better?" she asked, coming out of the bathroom in her underwear and a nearly see-through tank—something I damn sure wasn't complaining about—waving the concealer tube at her face. We'd picked up one that claimed it covered tattoos the night before and she had been layering it on for a few minutes already, mumbling about how she didn't know why she used to actually *enjoy* putting on makeup when she was younger.

"I think in the right light, you can see a bit of a shadow still, but they will probably write it off as sleeplessness."

"It will have to do," she said, shrugging, reaching for the nondescript black sweatshirt she'd picked out of the teen girls' section the night before because all the adult shit would hang off her body. "At least I won't have to explain these," she said, waving her hands toward the blue marks on her hips. From where I had apparently slammed her into the sink. I knew I was supposed to feel bad for marking her, but I couldn't find one damn shred of apology in me for those ones. "Pretty proud of yourself, huh?" she asked, responding to the smirk I didn't even try to hide.

"Yeah, pretty much," I agreed, nodding, finally dragging on my clothes too. "How long is the drive back from here?" I asked, knowing she was the one with all the plans. Which was funny considering she was the girl who never had any plans, always kind of just flew by the seat of her pants.

"About four and a half," she grumbled. "As if I'm not sore enough."

"At least we'll be back for dinner."

Her mom was cooking. Of course, she was. She was looking for any excuse to do motherly things for the girl she'd lost for so long.

"This is true. And she's making her famous banana bread too. I haven't been able to think of anything since else since she texted you that."

"Think you might want to consider getting yourself a phone that everyone else can text too, Ace," I reminded her, stepping into my shoes. "They're all going to want access to you. It's gonna get weird going through me all the time."

"Speaking of you," she said, gathering up the takeaway containers from the night before, stuffing them into the trash.

"I'm telling Reign tonight," I told her, watching as her eyes went wary. "I figure if everyone else knows, your chickenshit ass won't try to back out of this for no good reason."

"Chickenshit," she mused, giving me a strange smile. "That... that is a new one."

"Yet fitting. You ready?"

"I, ah, yeah, I guess so."

About five hours later, we were back at the compound, nursing our sore thighs and asses with a few drinks as Ferryn's aunts and a few of her uncles rushed around getting food ready.

"My girl has a black eye," Reign told me, moving in at my side, jerking his chin toward his daughter who was catching up with one of her cousins.

"Yeah," I agreed, nodding.

"Caught the news about an old coffeeshop getting burned down and finding bodies inside."

"Imagine that."

She hurt anywhere else?"

"Just a couple bruises. She handles herself well, Prez."

"She always did. But I'm glad you were there for her."

With that, he went to walk away, making me realize it was now or never. "Hey, Prez?" I called, making him turn back, a brow raised over his green eyes.

"Yeah?"

"Plan to be there for her a lot in the future."

Reign was not a man of many words, so he didn't exactly need it all spelled out for him. He knew exactly what I meant.

"Yeah? So that's the way of it?"

"That's the way of it," I agreed, nodding.

A deep breath strained his chest as he looked at Ferryn, then back at me, eyes unreadable as they often were.

"Guess that makes sense."

And that was it.

In a way, that was his approval.

Reign didn't need to issue threats. He knew his existence was threat enough. If I hurt Ferryn, I knew my body would never be found. That was the way of it. And that was alright by me. Because I didn't have any plans on hurting her. Occasional bruises from extracurricular activities aside, of course.

Everything was going well.

Ferryn seemed to be thawing out, warming up, smiling more, losing that tension that tightened her shoulders around seeing her family again.

And then the door opened.

And shit got real.

Thirteen

Ferryn - Present Day

I don't know who I had been expecting when the door opened. Another aunt, another uncle.

Not her.

"Why the hell didn't you tell me you were coming back to Navesink Bank?" Chris demanded loudly, making all conversation silent immediately.

Because the secret was out.

"Excuse me?" Aunt Lo demanded, voice deceptively calm. A woman who made her life's work the way she did, she wasn't quick to outward emotions, knowing that for a woman in a position of power, she had to be ten times colder than men in similar positions just to be taken half as seriously.

So calm, in this situation, was not a good thing.

"Aunt Lo," I started, trying to reason with her, trying to take some of the focus away from Chris.

Though, to be honest, that was where my focus was as well.

The last time I had seen Chris, she'd still been in that dingy t-shirt she'd lived in for months. She was greasy-haired and malnourished. Her mind and body half-broken from months of rape and torture.

I had gotten her out of that basement with me.

I had made sure that when I left, she would be taken care of.

From what Vance told me, my Uncle Cash and Aunt Lo had taken her in, had adopted her, had helped her heal—body and mind.

And healed she looked. From the outside. Of course, I had no idea what her head was like. But where she'd been this frail, breakable girl in that basement, good food and freedom and lack of fear had thickened her up. Not overweight, but thick—rounded in the thighs, hips, ass, bust. Her blonde hair was clean and waving around her face that had always been a bit hauntingly beautiful.

She looked amazing.

A part of me felt bad for always viewing her as I last remembered her instead of this much stronger, much more vibrant woman before me.

"No no," Aunt Lo said, holding a finger up to me. "We will get to you. Chris, I am going to need you to repeat that. Did you just ask her why she didn't *tell you* she was coming back? Like she's been in contact with you before she got back here?"

To her credit, even with Aunt Lo being at peak boss-bitch, Chris's chin lifted and her gaze was unwavering, not intimidated. "Because she has been."

"For how long?" Lo demanded as my mother cast devastated looks in her adopted niece's direction.

Which was exactly why I had told Chris this needed to be something we kept to ourselves, that no good would come from this particular truth coming out.

"Six years," Chris told her, making my stomach drop.

"Six. Years. You've been in contact with Ferryn for six years without telling me?"

"Yes."

That was it. No explanations. No defense. Just the blunt truth.

Damn.

She was going to take over Hailstorm one day. She'd been working there for years, of course. And it maybe even seemed like Aunt Lo would like a protege to groom to eventually take her place so that she could retire. But I had never been able to *see* it before right at that moment.

She would be a fearsome leader.

"How did you get in contact with her?" Lo insisted.

"Ferryn's been... busy," Chris decided, choosing to be careful about this truth, likely knowing I would kill her if she slapped my mother upside the head with the truth like that. "And I've been looking. Luckily, she's just as cocky as you guys all told me she was," she added, giving me a smirk. "She left some traces of herself around just itching to be found."

"And?" Aunt Lo demanded, wanting the whole truth.

"And I found it. And I tracked her down. And I got in touch."

"Without telling me?"

"Yes," Chris agreed again, nodding.

"Why? Why wouldn't you tell me?"

"Because I didn't want her to," I cut in, drawing attention back to me. And, well, I simply couldn't look at my mother right then, I couldn't stand the hurt and the confusion I would likely find there.

"Yeah, well, that shouldn't have mattered," Aunt Lo declared, turning back to Chris. "Since you answer to *me*, not her."

"That would be so if you hadn't given me control, told me to handle operations that I found that I was passionate about. You gave me full control. You told me to show you what I was made of. You can't have it both ways, Ma."

"You know the hell we were going through not knowing where she was, if she was okay."

"You knew she was okay. She wrote every week."

"But none of us had contact with *her*. How could you keep this from us? From me?"

"Because you would have made her stop," Chris told her, sticking with the truth even though she was clearly losing a little bit of her cool.

"You don't know..."

"That first time, when she was in surgery for a punctured lung, yeah, I do know. I know. You would have gone there en force and made her come home. You never would have let her out of your sight until you were sure she was done, that she decided it wasn't worth it."

Out of the corner of my eye, I could see my Aunt Rey shuffling the young kids out the back door, likely knowing that where this was going was not something they needed to be part of.

"Decided that what wasn't worth it?" Aunt Lo demanded, voice steel.

"Lo, let this drop," my father cut in, giving her a heavy look, having a silent conversation.

Sometimes, my father forgot that he couldn't get anything past my mother.

The look she gave my father didn't need any interpreting. It said *I know you have been keeping something from me, and you are going to answer for it later.*

"Chris," my mom said, giving her the *Mom Look*, the one that said you better not lie to my face, no matter how uncomfortable the truth might be. "What has Ferryn been up to that you thought was worthy enough of a cause to keep all this from us?"

Chris's gaze slid to me, seeking permission even though we both knew it had to come out now. All of it. To everyone.

I gave her the nod she was looking for.

"She's been hunting down human traffickers. Specifically, sex traffickers."

There was a crushing silence following the words, everyone in the room trying to process this new information, this uncomfortable truth.

See, no one could object to it, could they?

After what Chris had been through especially.

When she found out what I was up to, of course she had wanted to help in any way that she could.

Help she did, too.

If not for Chris, I was sure I would have been dead years ago. I definitely wouldn't have been able to get out from underneath the crushing medical care debts.

She did the research for me, having the resources available to her up at Hailstorm where hackers and dark web trackers were a dime a dozen. She found the guys; she found where they were staying; she gave me all the information I needed so I didn't go in blind. On top of that, she provided funds.

"I don't understand," Aunt Lo said, shaking her head. "You've made a good ROI with the money we have funneled to you for your cases. There is no money in murder."

She said that word casually.

Murder.

It was a word that made most people flinch.

And I think it was telling that not a single person in the room flinched at it.

Not even my mother.

"I only funneled Ferryn five percent of the money you gave me. And I cut down to a minimum crew to make up the difference on the other cases. Really, Ma, you waste a ridiculous amount of money at Hailstorm. You could cut down costs by a third and use that money to fund good causes."

"Like making your cousin a murderer," Aunt Lo said, gaze steely.

"Ferryn was already a murderer," Chris shot back, shocking everyone else into stunned silence even if they all knew it.

It was what they likely all thought was the reason I ran in the first place.

Holding up that gun.

Aiming.

Pulling the trigger.

Shooting my own maternal grandmother.

"That was different and you know it," Aunt Lo insisted. "That was a life or death situation. *Your* life, if you recall."

My grandmother was going to shoot Chris.

That was the tipping point.

That was what turned me from a relatively normal girl into a killer.

And I had never, ever regretted it.

"What are you saying, Ma?" Chris asked, raising her well-shaped brows. "That my life is worth more? That Ferryn's life is worth more? Because you know us? Than the dozens or hundreds of others who we have saved? Before Ferryn saved me, I had nobody. Just like these women and girls have *nobody*," Chris declared, voice raising, hitching ever-so-slightly. She wouldn't break down. I'd known her to have grown a little too hardened for that. At least in public. But she was struggling with holding it together. "They were crammed in ships and in basements and men were holding them down in beds and forcing themselves on them and they had no hope, no one to come for them. You can't stand here and tell me that saving them wasn't worth some dark marks on *our* souls. Wasn't worth a little heartbreak due to the separation. It was worth it. I would do it again a thousand times over. Because not everyone has someone like you. They don't have people like this club. They don't have heroes and heroines to rush in and get them out. So, they have *us*. You don't have to like that. You don't even have to accept that. But that is how it is. We do this for them. And if that means we sacrifice our relationships with you, then that is something we have to live with."

"That's the thing, though, Chris," Aunt Lo said, voice losing its edge, getting softer, shaking her head at her daughter. "We wouldn't have made you choose."

"Yes," Chris corrected, voice softer too, "you would have. You know you would have."

"That's where you were last night," my mother's voice broke into the silence following Chris's words, no one able to contradict her convincingly. "That is why you have a black eye," she added, eyes moving to mine.

"That makeup was a waste of money," I told Vance, shaking my head.

To that, my mother snorted. "Oh, honey. You know what town this is, right? I've seen more black eyes covered with tattoo concealer than you could count over the years. You could have told me," she insisted, then looked at my father, "and you *should* have told me."

"Mom..."

"No. Don't *Mom* me in that condescending 'you wouldn't understand' way, Ferr. Because, in case you don't know this story—and that was my bad for not being more open about it—I was a girl in a basement with men threatening to rape me, beating me, slicing open my back, burning a brand into my skin. I was *that* girl. If there is anyone here aside from you and Chris and your Aunt Janie who understands this reality, it is me. So you don't get to pull that childish 'you don't understand' crap with me. I understand. I get it. So I am going to repeat myself— you could have told me."

Sometimes, my mom was just, well, Mom. It was hard at times to remember that she was more than bedtime stories and late-night chats and baking parties and great dinners.

She was the daughter of a drug dealer and a trafficker. She was the wife of an outlaw biker. She was best friends with killers and enforcers. She'd been through a war with the club. She'd seen her father gunned down right in front of her eyes.

She'd known hell on earth.

Forgetting that, thinking of her only as a mom instead of a person, was a disservice to her.

"I'm sorry," I told her, meaning it, actually feeling tears flood my eyes with the words, making me close them tight, fight them away.

"Good," she told me, voice firm before she wrapped her arms around me, squeezing me tight. "Your father would like to claim all your badassness as coming from him, but I think we both know it is me in there," she added, clearly trying to lighten the mood, trying to defuse a tense situation.

"Definitely you. And Dad. And everyone here," I added, pulling away, knowing I owed my life to every single person in that room who had spent time with me, trained me, educated me, taught me about life. It was their voices in my head in low times. It was them pushing me on when my body and mind and soul were screaming for it all to end.

"And?" Aunt Lo asked, eyes keen, arms crossing over her chest.

"And?" I repeated.

"And who else? Clearly, you've been training. Who with?" she asked, making me wonder if she wanted to know if it was someone she knew, someone she had likely reached out to when I had gone missing to tell them I was out on my own, to call her if they saw me.

"34691." There was no reason not to tell them. They'd already tried to get him. They learned their lesson. He had nothing to fear from them. "Holden."

"Holden Stryker?" she asked, mouth gaping a bit. "But... what... how... no, why?" she decided.

"Why what? Why did I go to him?"

"No, I know why you went to him. He's one of the scariest bastards I've ever come across. Why did he help you?"

"Honestly, I don't know. But he did. He gave me a room. And food. Horrible, horrible, healthy food..." I added, giving Vance a smile. "He then whipped my ass every single day of my life for eight years."

"Until he didn't," my father guessed.

"Until he didn't," I agreed.

"So, what now?" Chris asked, pinning me with cool eyes.

"What do you mean?"

"You come back here. You make amends. You jump into bed with Vance." Oh, sweet Jesus. I could *feel* all the gazes shifting in his direction. I almost felt bad for the shit he was about to get. But I couldn't help but be a little pleased that I had so many people who would even want to give the guy I was seeing shit. "Now what? You're done?"

"I went on the job last night, Chris," I told her, eyes getting small, confused. She had to have seen the news. Aunt Lo had a group of new guys at Hailstorm whose job it was to comb the news from all states, finding anything that might be useful to them. That was how she'd found me in the first place.

"What? Your last hoorah. You finally got the baby dealers, so now you're retired?"

"I never said I was retiring. I just... look, I don't know what is going to happen from here on out," I admitted. Things were getting blurrier by the moment. "But I can't see myself wasting all those years of pain and missing my family by deciding right here and now that I'm done. I won't be able to sleep at night knowing there is a trafficker close by that I could take down and don't. I just... I don't know. I think we need to sit down and figure out a way to make the job work alongside a life. You have a life. I think it is only fair that I have one too. While still removing some evil from the world."

Deflated, she nodded a bit tightly.

"I'll work on it," she told me, giving her mother a shrug, then taking back off.

"She's gonna be a good boss, babe," Uncle Cash told Aunt Lo, pulling her to his side, kissing her temple.

"She deliberately went behind my back."

"Well..."

"Well?" Aunt Lo asked, shooting a hard look at her husband.

"It's not like she disobeyed you. She found a loophole. That's the kind of shit bosses do, don't you think?"

I could tell she was torn. On the one hand, she was still the boss; she didn't tolerate insubordination or backhandedness. On the other, though, she had to have been proud that in just eight years, she had taken a very broken girl and turned her into a very strong woman.

Aunt Lo was good at that.

It had to have given her a warm feeling in her chest to learn that Chris didn't just want to head a criminal empire, but that she wanted to find a way to do good with it as well.

"I'm glad to hear that you are going to try to strike a balance," my mom cut in, giving me a squeeze to the wrist. "I think I might know why," she added, glancing over toward Vance.

"Mom... no," I insisted, a little bit insulted that she thought I would let a man change such fundamental parts of my life.

"Oh, but I think a lot yes," she told me, shrugging. "There's no shame in that, baby. These Henchmen, they have a way of getting in and taking root, don't they?"

With that, her eyes twinkling—likely remembering all the times I had fawned over Vance as a girl, had decided he was my one and only, and thinking fate was a truly wonderful thing if, even after all this shit, we still found our way back to each other—she went over, grabbing my father's arm, and dragging him along with her down the hall to their room.

"I don't envy him that ear lashing he's about to get," Uncle Cash said, grimacing as he led Aunt Lo outside to talk.

"So," my Uncle Adler said, walking over as Vance moved in at my side. "How's the pride feel knowin' she could kick yer arse?" he asked, slapping a hand on Vance's shoulder so hard he made him slam into me.

"Says the man who got beat up by a skip three weeks back," his woman, Lou, told us, chuckling as she moved up next to him.

"The woman was *four-hundred*-pounds."

"She was on an electric scooter," Lou added, pressing her lips together to try to keep from smiling. "She beat him with her cane. Then ran over his arm when he was down. It was fucking hilarious."

This.

This was what I had been missing for so long without even realizing.

A part of me had been convinced that I had become cold because of the life I had led. I was starting to see now, though, that this wasn't the case.

No.

I had turned cold because I was deprived of the warmth of my family, of this town I loved so much, of these connections, these stories, this bottomless source of love and support.

No one was looking at me as though I was some kind of monster.

No one was condemning me for the life I had led.

They were just accepting it as part of me.

And that was the beautiful thing about this place, this town, this club.

They didn't judge you for your past, for all the ugly things you thought were so unlovable. They just welcomed you in with open arms, compared scars with you, let you know that we'd all been broken and lost along our way at some point, that it didn't make us hard to love. It just gave us some really good fucking stories.

"I don't think we have formally met," Lou said, offering me her hand.

From the stories I'd heard, she and Uncle Adler had met right around the time I had been taken.

"I think we are going to get along really well," I told her. "Can you tell me some other times Uncle Adler has made an idiot of himself?" I asked, giving him a sugar-sweet smile as he clutched his chest as if I'd wounded him.

"After all the hours I spent teaching yer ungrateful arse to fight..." he said, shaking his head.

I spent the rest of the night mostly regaling my uncles with my own personal war stories, never before feeling quite so much like I belonged as I did then, hearing them compare mine with theirs, praising me when I told them how I'd gotten out of a dicey situation, watching their eyes get warm when I reminded them that I had learned certain important moves from them.

"Here, Ace," Vance said some time later after most people had headed home. Save for my parents who still hadn't come out of their room and West who was passed out on the couch. "Saved you some of this," he told me, holding out a napkin folded over something rectangular. "That's the biggest slice I could snag. Everyone was like starving fucking animals around that shit," he added, shaking his head as I unwrapped the banana bread slice.

"Thank you."

"Ace?"

"Yeah?"

"They don't fucking care," he told me, making my gaze find his. "They know what you've been up to. And they don't fucking care. You see the crazy amount of love you have here now, right?"

Even just mentioning it made that warm feeling fill me up once more.

"I do."

"Good. Now go get your ass on your bike."

"On my bike?"

"We're going back to the apartment. Can't fuck you with your parents right down the hall now that they know."

"Oh, my virgin ears!" West declared, putting his hands over them, making a chuckle move through Vance.

"Virgin, huh? Then all those girls who have spent the night here..."

"They were my tutors," he told us, smirking.

"Oh yeah? What are they teaching you?"

"Don't ask him *that*," I hissed, shaking my head at the wicked look West had on his face.

"Still haven't mastered that, man?" Vance asked, tsking.

"Hey, what can I say, I like the practice. Though now that you stole my fucking wingman, I will probably be out of commission for a while. Thank fuck I am heading to the new compound this summer."

"Wait... what?" I asked Vance as West disappeared. "The new compound? This place has been in the family for ages."

"New compound. For the new chapter," Vance told me. "In Florida," he added, clearly thinking this would have come up before now. "That was why your parents caught their cruise out of Florida instead of here. Your father wanted to check shit out. West is going to head down there to set shit up. Bit of an info dump on you, huh?" he asked when I couldn't seem to make any single thought stick.

"But... who? Why..."

"Think that is a story for another day, Ace. Let's go home."

"Oh, God," I grumbled.

"What?"

"Don't call that place home," I insisted, face screwing up.

"Fine. Let's go to our clandestine fuck pad."

"That's better," I agreed, smiling.

And fuck we did.

On every surface.

Until the sun damn near came up.

"Hey," Vance said, slapping my ass, making me grumble.

"I'm not moving," I declared, body composed entirely of Jell-O.

"Can I play something for you?" he asked, making my head turn to find him holding a guitar that had been stashed in the back of the closet.

"You wrote something?" I asked, pushing up, too interested to care about the objections of my tired body.

"Wrote you something," he clarified.

And just like that, every single girlhood dream I had of Vance came true.

I got his attention.

His touch.

His affection.

And now he had written a song for me.

He had called it *The Rise*.

Hearing it, well, it filled me up completely, went deep into all my hidden, dark corners, chased out any lingering cold, replacing it with a warmth I had never known before.

Falling in love with Vance the first time had been amazing.

But falling in love with him this time?

It was fucking perfect.

Fourteen

Ferryn - Present Day

"You're leaving?" I asked, hearing an embarrassing hitch of desperation in my voice, a neediness that I didn't like hearing there. Even if he was the only one there to bear witness to it.

Love was love.

But neediness was neediness.

And I would be damned if I was needy.

I could absolutely do this on my own.

That said, I just figured he would be going in with me, would be by my side.

This was, after all, his sister.

"Think you two need some time to catch up. I'll be back later. I'll bring donuts," he added, giving me a quick kiss to the temple before ringing the doorbell then taking off.

Leaving me there alone.

"I don't know how many times I have to tell you that you don't need to ring the bell," Iggy's voice called through the door as she reached for the knob, opening it. "You have a key..." she trailed off, mouth falling open, eyes seemingly confused by my presence, like she was sure she was seeing things. "Ferryn?"

"Hey, Iggs," I said, giving her what felt like a really wobbly smile.

"Oh, my God. Wh.. when..." she trailed off, having trouble putting words together.

"Uncle Vance!" a little voice shrieked, bare feet slapping on the hardwood floor behind Iggy. Then, "Oh." The disappointed sound of a child not getting what they clearly wanted.

Child.

Uncle Vance.

"What... when..." It was my turn to not be able to make my thoughts and tongue work in unison.

Iggy put her hand down on the top of the sandy-blond hair of what seemed to be a five or six-year-old girl with brilliant blue eyes that her mother and uncle shared.

"This is Olive. Ollie. We call her Ollie. Ollie, this is..."

"The girl from the pictures," Ollie declared with confidence.

"Yep. The girl from the pictures. Ferryn. Your aunt..."

"Not really," Ollie objected, rolling her eyes.

"No, not really. Not by blood. But still. You call her Aunt Ferryn."

"Where have you been?" Ollie asked, and I couldn't help but wonder where she got her bluntness from. Iggy had never been so sure of herself, so bold. But maybe that was the point. She was trying to foster things in her daughter that she hadn't always possessed.

Her *daughter*.

God.

"I, ah, I've been learning things."

"Like in school?"

"Sort of."

"Boring," Ollie decided, making a surprised laugh burst out of me as she turned and walked away.

"I have a feeling it was not boring," Iggy declared, opening the door wider. "Come on in."

Iggy's house was the exact polar opposite of the household she herself had grown up in. I always felt uncomfortable walking in her front door where her parents insisted I take off my shoes, where the soft surfaces were always covered, where there was never so much as a speck of dust on any surface, where there were bare walls and not a single knick-knack unless religious memorabilia counted. Everything had been painted in an oppressively drab off-white color, the windows heavily draped.

Iggy's house, though, was a mishmash of unapologetically bright colors.

Red bathroom.

Bright yellow living room.

Periwinkle blue kitchen, where she led me to a small round table with a chalkboard top, little childish pictures of one-legged birds and three-eyed monsters donning the top.

There was art everywhere; huge canvases butting up against one another, photographs on the mantle three deep. Toys positively littered the living room floor. Sneakers were forgotten in the hall.

Not dirty.

Just lived in.

Comfortable.

After years of living in a show house, I imagined Iggy felt like she could really breathe here.

"You're a mom," I declared when she carried the stainless steel coffee carafe over to the table, two mismatched mugs dangling from her fingers.

"I'm a mom," she agreed, nodding.

"She's... five?"

"Six," Iggy corrected, going back for the sugar and cream before sitting down.

"You were..."

"Eighteen when I got pregnant. Nineteen when I had her."

"Your parents..." I started, then suddenly recalled how Vance had said things had finally blown up. I guess now I knew why.

"Oh, yes. As you can imagine, they were just *thrilled* by the news of their unwed teenaged daughter who was supposed to be a virgin until marriage and then only have sex for means of procreation getting knocked up."

"I mean, to be fair, they would have lost their minds if they knew you ate meat on Fridays during Lent."

"That's true," she agreed, nodding.

"What did they do? Demand you get married?"

To that, her lips turned up. It wasn't a smile, but more like a bitter sneer. "They wanted me to 'take care of it,'" she said, using air quotes.

"Take care of it," I repeated, sure I was not interpreting that right. "As in... get an abortion?" I clarified, dropping my voice in case Ollie was nearby.

"Yep."

"You can't be serious. They used to drag you to rallies against abortion."

"Apparently, they are only devout when it involves someone else's daughter. When it is their own, they're hypocrites."

"I can't believe they would come out and ask that of you."

"Demand. They demanded that of me," she explained, shaking her head. "If I wanted to keep living there, if I wanted to keep having them cover my college tuition, then I had to get rid of 'my little mistake,'" she told me, the words coming out thick with distaste.

"Who is the father?" I asked, not seeing a masculine touch to the house. The colors, the art, the fact that there was a box of tampons sitting on the kitchen counter, it all spoke of a very female household.

"Elias Michael Schway."

"Fancy name."

"Fancy guy. Also another person who wanted me to take care of it. Though *he* offered to pay to do so."

"How generous."

"In his defense, it was a one-night thing. I was tired of being known as the only virgin in my dorm. Went to a party. Got it over with. Of course, right at first, I wasn't thrilled either. I was too young. I had just started school. I had no family support. But this baby fought its way through two forms of birth control. I felt like that is just fate right there. I just... I wanted her. I wanted her and I was terrified."

I'd had several moments over the past couple of weeks while reconnecting with my family when I felt shitty. When I met children I hadn't even known were born. When I saw the faces of kids I had known, but didn't recognize thanks to the passing of time. When my mother told me she'd made me a scrapbook for each year I was gone, so that when I came back, I could see what everyone had been up to.

This, though. This might have been the worst gut-punch.

Iggy had been a sister to me, the one person I trusted with all my secrets and hopes and dreams, the person I shared the most inside stories with, the first person I told good or bad news to, my partner in crime, my 'person.'

And the one time when she really, truly would have needed me, I hadn't been there for her. I hadn't even known.

"Iggs... I'm so sorry," I told her, reaching across the table to put my hand over hers. "I should have been here for you through that."

"I wanted you to be, I won't lie." We'd always been honest with each other, even when the truth hurt. I appreciated that she wasn't going to be more reserved with her feelings out of fear of me wanting to rush off again. There was no stepping on eggshells with old friends.

"What did you do?"

"I called Vance. He came back to town for a bit. The band was so pissed. But he came because of course he did. We sat down and figured out how I could make it work. Then, when he was back on the road, he sent me some of his money so I wouldn't worry in those early days."

"What did you guys decide?"

"That I would quit school. There was really no way around that. I couldn't afford it. I didn't really like what I was doing anyway. I figured I could always go back or do something online when Ollie got older. And then the first five months, I worked my ass off while renting a room in someone's spare bedroom. Waitress, dog walker, stocker at the grocery store, a gift wrapper over the holidays. You name it, I did it. And I socked every penny away so that I could take some time off when I had Olive."

"I hate that," I admitted, shaking my head, thinking of an eighteen-year-old Iggy working sixty-hour-plus weeks for the first five months of her pregnancy.

"Honestly, it wasn't as bad as it sounds. I was determined. The harder I worked, the more I saved, the longer I could be home with my baby. It was actually while I was serving tables that someone gave me a brilliant idea."

"What brilliant idea?"

"He said I had a great voice, and should do some voice acting."

"You do have a great voice," I agreed, always having been envious of it. She had a smooth, almost polished voice.

"So I went home and figured I could look into it. I did my first sample recording on my ancient iPhone. But I got offers. And then more offers. And then so many offers that I had to invest in some good recording materials and soundproofing. And, well, it became a business. I am not rolling in it, of course, but we are comfortable enough in our little life. And I can be here for Ollie. You know how school is. Off all summer. Spring break. Winter break. All the friggen teacher conferences and minor holidays. Plus sick days."

"How'd you manage to find quiet time?"

"It wasn't easy at first. Ollie wasn't a very happy baby. Always with the reflux, crying until I was sure I would go half-mad. The only way it worked was when she was sleeping and I had to lay her across my lap like a cat. But it worked. Now, it's easier. She goes to school for six hours which gives me a ton of time to get some work in."

"What kind of books do you narrate for?"

To that, her lips curved up, mischievous and familiar. "Mostly romance. Really smutty romance," she added, grinning.

"Oh, your parents must have hated that."

"They do. I made sure I told them about my new job in a Christmas card. And included a few titles with it. *'The Virgin's Beast,' 'Shared by the Biker Club,' 'Drilled by the Mod Boss'*..."

A laugh bubbled up and burst out at the idea of her ultra-conservative parents opening up a harmless Christmas card to read titles like those, to know the daughter they had pushed away had done the voiceover for them.

"To be a fly on that wall, right?" she asked, smiling. "I send them an updated list every year. I swear I sometimes take a job just because the title is so raunchy that I want to write it down for them."

"I always hoped you would find that rebellious streak I knew was in there somewhere," I told her. "I'm not happy I missed it."

"Oh, it is an ongoing process," she shrugged it off. "Did you notice how I *didn't* make you take off your shoes when you came in the door?" she added, voice grave in an imitation of her mother.

"That was one I never thought you'd break. You took your shoes off at the *clubhouse*."

"We have three dogs. It is idiotic to make humans take off their shoes when dogs run in and put their filthy feet over every surface."

"Wait... dogs?" I asked. "Where?"

"You'd never know, right? Lazy, fat things they are. If we got robbed, they'd snore right through it. They're a trio of bulldog siblings we came across at an adoption fair. Olive insisted that they had to grow up together. So... we got three dogs. They're probably sleeping in my bed right now, drooling all over my pillow. They have the life we all dream of."

"So, what happened to Olive's dad after you decided to keep her?"

"Nothing. He walked away. Got his degree. Is working in some big firm in the city."

"He doesn't want to meet her at least?"

"He probably forgot she exists, to be honest. If he wants to meet her some day, I am open to that, but I am not going to force it. And, quite frankly, I don't want to have to deal with him in court over child support. Me and Ollie, we are perfectly happy with just the two of us. Well, and Vance," she said, eyes going soft.

"He comes over often?" I asked.

"Every weekend. More if he has nothing else going on. I hate that he had to leave his dream behind, but I am not going to lie, I am a bit selfishly glad he settled down in Navesink Bank so we can see him all the time."

"I brought donuts!" Vance's voice boomed into the room, making me jerk back a bit. Because we hadn't gotten to that part yet. I meant to tell her. I just wanted to hear what she had been up to first.

"Uncle Vance!" Olive's voice cheered, feet slapping down the hall once again, this time followed by the tap tap tap of dog feet.

"They heard the word donuts," Iggy told me, nodding. "You think I'm joking," she went on, shaking her head. "You'll see."

Then there was Vance, walking in, trailed by three extremely fat bulldogs with comically hideous overbites and corkscrew tails, sniffing the air, looking up at the box in Vance's hand.

His other hand had his niece snagged around the middle, flipped completely upside down, making her squeal uncontrollably.

I expected the somewhat neurotic Iggy, the girl I used to know, to squeak about dropping her on her head or something. Instead, Iggy gave them a soft smile and reached down to pet the head of the brindle colored bulldog that sat near her feet.

Vance dropped the donuts down, then flipped his niece over his arm and back onto her feet before moving over toward me.

"Oh, yeah, Vance, look," Iggy said, completely in the dark.

"I got your old lady ass one of those stupid sour cream ones you like," Vance told me, pressing a kiss to my temple as he moved past to sit in the other open chair.

"If you warm them up, they taste a lot like funnel cakes," I insisted.

"Yeah, sure, Ace. *I'm* going to eat a coffee roll like a normal human being."

"Oh. My. *God*," Iggy gasped, mouth open, eyes huge, her head shaking a little like she wasn't sure she was actually seeing what she was seeing. "Ohmygod," she added, slapping her hand on the table.

Olive, oblivious to the big reveal moment, steadily ripped a glazed donut into four pieces, handing one to each dog and then herself.

"Yeah," I said, lips curving up tentatively. "I was, ah, going to get to that."

"*Get to that*," she squeaked. "This is the kind of information you use to cut into my monotonous dialogue. Holy *shit*."

Iggy, as a rule, rarely cursed. Vance had told me it was something that *was* still the same about her. So the fact that she was cursing was just proof of her excitement.

"Guess who was at the clubhouse when she finally rolled her ass back into this town?" Vance asked, giving me a smile.

"Okay. Okay. I am going to need this story from the beginning," she decided, reaching for the jelly donut—sugared, not powdered, because she had very strong opinions on such things.

"Ollie, didn't you say you were working on getting those fatties to lose some weight?" Vance asked, nodding down at the dogs she was handing more donut pieces to.

"That's not a nice word," Olive insisted, giving her uncle a firm look.

"No, it's not," Iggy agreed. "But now that they are full of donuts, maybe you can go run them around the backyard for a little bit," she suggested.

Ollie, clearly a wild, outdoors sort of kid, took off full-tilt, the dogs barreling behind their reckless leader.

We waited until we heard the screen door smack against the frame before we went into it.

All of it.

My past.

The homecoming.

The build-up between me and Vance.

Iggy was silent afterward, her jelly donut still in her hand, uneaten.

"So," she said finally after sorting through her thoughts. "What I am hearing is, I get to be a maid of honor in the near future."

"Iggs..." Vance tried.

"What? That's what I heard. And just so you know, if you expect Ollie to be a flower girl, you are going to have to let her dress the dogs up in dresses and walk down with her. That's... just the way it is going to have to be."

"Iggy, things are new," I insisted.

To that, she rolled her eyes.

"New," she scoffed. "I believe you told me you were going to marry Vance when we were all of, what, thirteen years old? This is the oldest of old news, if you ask me. Oh, what did your dad say?" she asked, looking between us.

"He said it made sense," Vance answered.

"It does though. So, what is the color palette for the wedding? And who is in charge of the bachelorette party?"

"God, I missed you," I told her, the words bursting out from somewhere deep.

"I missed you too," she said, reaching across the table to squeeze my hand. "And I kind of wished we knew you were coming..."

"You have something going on?" I asked.

To that, her smile spread, eyes bright. "Krav Maga class for me. Karate for Ollie."

My own smile curved upward at that, my eyes getting just the tiniest bit glassy.

Iggy had been the one to help me shave my head, to feed me after I escaped the basement, to give me what precious few valuable possessions she had so I could hock them for bus and food money while I ran off to find my new path in life. And my parting wish had been to beg her to join a self-defense class, to make sure she could handle herself in a fight, to make it so no one could ever snatch her up off the street.

She took that to heart.

And she hadn't just gone for a couple weeks after I left out of respect for my request.

No.

She was still going nearly nine years later. She was bringing her daughter too.

"Your aunt Lo is still giving us both free classes. In exchange for advance copies of the audiobooks I narrate."

Some things never changed.

Aunt Lo and her deeply rooted love of all things romance.

The unshakable bonds of true friendship even when life tears you apart for a long span of time.

And the mushy-heart feel of your first true love, I added to myself as Vance's hand squeezed my thigh under the table.

I had been so terrified to come home, so uncertain of what I might come back to.

As it turned out, it was exactly what I had left behind.

Family.

Friends.

Love.

"Good timing, actually," Vance said, swiping through a text with his free hand. "Chris wants to talk to us," he said, glancing at me. "She's at our place."

"Do you hear that, Ferryn? *Your* place," Iggy said, placing a hand over her heart, faux swooning. "It's all our girlhood dreams coming true."

"Rein it in a little Iggs," Vance demanded, but was smiling as he did it.

"Go go, be in love. I will start picking out bridal magazines. Good timing, Ollie," she said as her daughter came rushing in. "We have to get ready for class. Say goodbye to Uncle Vance and Aunt Ferryn. They have to go and nest."

"Nest? Like birds?"

"Something like that," Iggy agreed.

"Are they going to have babies?"

"Not yet," Iggy said, shooing her daughter up the stairs to go change. "Okay. All teasing aside, I love this. I love the both of you. And I expect to see the both of you here for Taco Tuesdays."

"Have you met her?" Vance asked, wrapping an arm around my hips, pulling me to the door. "She never passes up a meal. We'll bring the dessert," he added, moving outside, closing the door behind us.

"We just became Taco Tuesday people," I said, a little dumbfounded as we stood there watching the slow trickle of traffic pass us by.

"You love it," he countered.

"I kinda do," I agreed, smiling when he hauled me closer to his side, pressing a kiss to the top of my head. "What did Chris want?"

"She said she solved the problem," he told me, leading me over to his bike, climbing on, then waiting for me to slide on behind him. And because it was him, because I knew he wouldn't judge me for being just the slightest bit clingy, I wrapped my arms around him tight, resting my head against the cut on his back.

"Let's see what she has to say," I said before he drove off.

When we got there, Chris was standing in the open doorway, not touching even the doorjamb.

"This place is, ah, kinda gross," she told us, nose scrunching up.

"She's not wrong," I agreed, climbing off, moving over toward her.

"There are like, two-hundred places in this town you could be staying instead. Just... give that some thought. The water in your tap is gray."

"Great?" I repeated, confused.

"No. Not great. *Gray*. It's gray. Please tell me you aren't drinking that."

I didn't know Chris.

Not like I knew Iggy, like I knew Vance, like I knew half the people up at Hailstorm where she worked.

We'd spent time together in that basement, but the vast majority of it, she had been lost inside her own mind, trying to escape the horrible reality she faced daily.

I didn't know what to expect from her as a person when I returned. And I wasn't entirely sure if who she was now was the same as she had been before she had been dragged down in that basement and brutalized.

Apparently, though, who she was now was a tad bit uptight and controlling with a bit of a mom-vibe. Which, well, I was kind of digging.

"I will compile a list for you," She went on, reaching for her phone, tapping at it for a second before tucking it away.

"You said you had an answer to our problem. What problem?" I asked, moving inside, watching as she cast wary eyes around the room, deciding against trying to sit down anywhere, crossing her arms over her chest like she was afraid she might accidentally brush against the wall or the couch.

"Right. The problem. The 'you're here now and won't be as active on the missions' problem."

"Chris, I said it won't be a problem."

"Yeah. But it will. I prefer being proactive."

"I'm starting to get that," I agreed, nodding. "So, what did you come up with?"

"So, I looked for some men and women."

"Men and women who... do what I do?" I clarified.

"I figured you could show them the ropes. Take them on a few missions. Get them used to it. I mean these are men and women who have killed before anyway. I drew up a psych eval to give candidates to figure out who would be the best fit."

"You created a psych evaluation?" I repeated, not sure if I was impressed or a little intimidated by her productivity. Or both.

"Yeah. I mean my mom has a bunch of different ones. I kind of just meshed some, took out other questions that were irrelevant. It wasn't that big of a deal."

"And Aunt Lo is okay with this?"

"She is coming to terms with it. So long as I come up with the funding, she is going to let me run with it."

"And how are you going to come up with the funding? I mean my medical bills alone were astronomical. And the more people you put on these jobs, the more those numbers are going to rack up. Plus hotels. Plus food. Gas. Weapons. All that shit."

"This is the fun part," she declared, giving us a strange little smile, moving toward the door. "Come with me," she demanded, moving outside, waiting for us to follow. Which we did, brows furrowed, unsure what she had up her sleeve.

"What are you doing?" I hissed when she moved next door, reaching for the door to Finch's apartment, and throwing the door open, moving inside without a word.

"Jesus," I gasped, moving inside, already reaching for my knife.

Inside, we found Chris standing there, smiling, victorious. While Finch leaned back in his chair, a gun pointed at her.

And every square fucking inch of his apartment was stacked with money.

"Holy shit," I said, mouth gaping, not quite ready to accept what I was seeing as reality.

Sure, Finch was a criminal.

Clearly.

He had the prison tats to prove it.

But I hadn't exactly pegged him as someone who was rolling in it.

"Ferryn. Ferryn's fuck buddy," Finch greeted us, more curious than concerned, despite what looked like millions of dollars surrounding him. "And this ravishing creature I don't believe I've met," he said, giving Chris a smoldering look.

"Yeah, no," Chris said, rolling her eyes.

"You're breaking my heart, beautiful," he declared, putting his gun hand over his heart.

"Something tells me you'll survive. *Anyway*," she said, looking over at us, waving her arms out. "Meet the mission's bank."

"Alright, sweetheart, you might have the face of a fucking angel, but I'm not giving you money."

"It's not money!" Chris declared to us, face triumphant, positively beaming.

"Alright, Chris, um, you kind of have crazy eyes right now," I said, looking between the parties in the room, trying to figure out what the hell was going on. "What do you mean it's not money?"

"Oh, right," she said, shaking her head. "I forgot you guys are a couple steps behind me."

"I'm pretty sure the whole world is a couple steps behind you," I told her. "But go on."

"Right, so. This is Finch McAwley. And he is possibly the world's best counterfeiter."

"Not going to complain about you knowing my name, dollface, but I can't be having you spread my business around like that."

Suddenly, things I had missed when we'd first walked in were clearer to me now.

Like the fact that he had covered the kitchen surfaces in computers and scanners and printers. The massive piles of some sort of specialty paper. The ink. The dryer that the units didn't come with, plugged into an outlet.

"Anyway," Chris went on as though Finch hadn't spoken. "Let's just say that Finch's counterfeit money can pretty much fool anyone."

"Then how do you know who he is?"

"Oh, please. I know who everyone is," she said, shaking her head. And, well, there was probably a lot of truth in that. "Anyway. Finchy here has absolutely perfected five and ten dollar bills. He sells them for two and five dollars respectively, leaving him with a nice little profit. I mean the ink and paper and such cost very little."

"The paper is linen, and imported from Poland. It's not that cheap."

"In the grand scheme of things, it's cheap," Chris told us, ignoring him. "Don't let his shabby little office fool you, he's rolling in it. And he is going to help fund us."

"See now, here is the part where I need to interject. Dollface, I never said I was going to fund shit," Finch insisted, placing the gun down on the table.

"Oh, but you will say it," Chris insisted, smirking. "And do you want to know *why* you will say it?"

"Is it just me, or is she terrifyingly creepy when she makes veiled threats like that?" Vance whispered to me. And, well, I couldn't disagree. Her intensity, her knowledge, and her utter self-assurance mixed with the fact that she clearly had a lot of power in this town, well, it was scary and impressive and hard to look away from.

"Yeah, angel, I'd like to know why I would say something like that," Finch agreed, not as intimidated as Vance and I seemed to be.

"Because if you don't agree to fund our little mission, then I am going to have to make a little call," she said, leaning forward slightly like a mother about to tell a child the repercussions of their bad behavior. "Do you know who I have the number for, Finchy?"

"No, doll, can't say that I do."

"Does the name Ewan O'Neil ring a bell?"

Finch was pale in general.

He went ghostly right about then.

"I thought that it might," she said, nodding. "Anywho. You've done a pretty good job of avoiding him thus far. It would be a real shame if he learned where you are hanging up your cap these days."

"That would be a shame," Finch agreed, giving Chris some unnerving eye-contact that didn't dull her almost bubbly mood. In the end, he was the one to break it, looking over at me and Vance before glancing back at Chris. "And what mission do you want help funding?"

"How do you feel about human trafficking, Finchy?"

"Look," Finch said, holding up a hand. "I might not be the most moral of men, but I draw the line at that fucking shit. I'm not getting involved with trafficking. Not even for you, dollface."

"We don't traffick people," Chris snapped. "We take down traffickers."

To that, Finch let out a low chuckle, his gaze moving to me, piercing, penetrating. "That makes a lot of sense. Well," he said, taking a breath as he got to his feet, unfolding much like a cat. "It is important to be altruistic. Think we have a deal, Chris, was it?" he asked, extending his hand.

Chris's gaze moved downward, looking at the tattooed hand like it might jump out and bite her.

It was right then that I saw the girl I had shared a basement with. She'd come so far, she'd healed so much, but there was still some damage there, some remnants of the abuse she had endured.

Maybe she managed it in part by the fact that all the men at Hailstorm were technically beneath her in terms of power and that all the men in our very extended family would never hurt her, could be trusted wholly.

But men like Finch, strange men, men who didn't have to answer to her per se, there was still hesitation there, fear there.

It felt like forever that her gaze stayed there. Eventually, it seemed like Finch picked up on something being wrong, curling his hand into a fist, and bumping it into hers.

"We got a deal."

Chris shook her head, knocking the lingering thoughts loose. "Perfect. I am going to need a number to reach you at."

"You want my number, angel?" Finch asked, eyes dancing.

Again, Chris ignored this obvious attempt at charm. "We are going to need to do something about your security here. I mean, I don't want our money just walking off if the local delivery guy spots all this cash lying around. And, really, smoking?" she asked, picking up a pack of cigarettes on the table. "Are you literally trying to burn up all this money? I will write you up a PDF about all the changes that need to be made," Chris prattled on, picking up Finch's phone, swiping through it, seeming to find the number, typing it into her phone. "And I expect the changes to be implemented immediately upon receipt of said PDF."

"Yes, ma'am," Finch said to Chris's retreating form. Her hands were already typing away at her phone, likely working on that form she promised him.

"Told you I had it all worked out," she said on her way out.

"Like your friends there, babe," Finch said, looking a little whiplashed by the whole ordeal. And I couldn't exactly blame him.

"She's my cousin," I corrected.

"Think I might like getting bossed around by your cousin, babe," he said, smirking.

"Well, that works out. Because she's really good at bossing people around."

"Oh, little hint," Finch said as we inched closer to the door. "If you guys don't want me to hear you fucking, you might want to do it in the shower for a change."

With that, we went back to our shitty apartment.

Had some shower sex that still likely managed to be overheard by all the neighbors.

Then we sat on the couch eating leftover Chinese while looking over the apartment options Chris had sent over with records playing in the background.

It was simple.

And sweet.

And completely freaking perfect.

"Hey, Ace?"

"Yeah?" I asked, finding it hard to keep my eyes open.

"I'm really fucking glad you decided to come home."

And, well, so was I.

Fifteen

- Journal Entry - 24th Birthday -

I had a dream last night.

I don't dream often.

At least, I don't have pleasant dreams often.

Nightmares and me, we have become fast and steady friends over the years.

But actual dreams?

I thought they were something I had left in my old life.

I was standing in a flower-blanketed yard. Irises and peonies and snapdragons and amaranth and zinnias were in full bloom, their happy faces reaching up toward the beaming yellow sun, just warm enough for the comfort of bare arms without too much heat.

I looked downward, seeing my arm there, fingers tracing silky petals as I walked through the seemingly endless paths of beds.

To what destination, I had no idea until I found myself there. Standing in front of a massive gilded mirror propped up between two swaying weeping willows.

My reflection was shaded until I got right up to it, the sun beaming through the branches to show me myself.

And there I was, my hair a little longer on top, my face a little fuller, my eyes not quite so haunted.

In a flowing white dress, lace-trimmed, impossibly elegant. The kind of dress that spoke of special days and special words and promises you wanted to keep. Until death do you part.

Just as my mind was reconciling the meaning of the dress, another figure moved in behind me. Dressed in black. The fancy kind of dressed.

His head pressed to the side of mine, his hands sliding around me, one hand reaching down to grab my left one, the sun catching the flat face of my diamond ring. There was another one settled before it, too. Plain, but solid, full of meaning.

Confused, my gaze lifted from our linked hands, searching for the man who had slid those rings there in the first place.

Vance.

I woke up gasping, heart hammering in my chest, eyes stinging.

Never before had I wanted a dream to be reality so badly.

Epilogue

Vance - 3 weeks later

He was gone.

After working out the minute details with Ferryn, Chris, Lo, and the small team of Hailstorm men and women who decided this was a cause they were happy to pursue, Chris approached Ferryn with an idea.

Approach 34691.

See if Holden would be interested in being in charge of re-training the new team members. He'd done such a good job of working with Ferryn. And these Hailstorm men and women had made their lives of martial arts training, of working in the military, so they didn't need to be worked on like Ferryn had needed to be worked on, hardening her, making sure she was capable of taking lives.

Ferryn had been pretty sure that he wouldn't be interested, not even if he got to train these people at his place without any pressure. But Chris had been just insistent about asking him.

I was a little surprised to hear that Ferryn had no way to get in contact with Holden, that in all the years they had been working side-by-side that they never so much as exchanged cell phone numbers.

I couldn't begin, in fact, to understand the strange disconnect the two seemed to share. Almost nine years together and she didn't have any stories about him to share outside of training stories and war stories.

I'd asked Ferryn about it, and she'd seemed confused by what I meant. Like they were just distant work colleagues, not people who shared a life for the better part of a decade.

I'd suggested going to see him mainly out of curiosity. I mean how could you not feel almost fatherly toward a young runaway girl who depended on you to keep her alive? I wanted to see how they interacted so I could better understand the kind of relationship they shared.

So we had borrowed one of Hailstorm's SUVs, packed it down, and hit the road.

It was almost jarring as I rode passenger to realize that she had been so damn close the whole time she was away. I guess, in my mind, I had pictured her on the other side of the country, up in Canada, or somewhere else that was not so easily reached by just a simple road trip.

I wondered if her parents felt a swelling of resentment at that when they'd found out. To know that, had she been in the right headspace, she could have visited from time to time, could have let them see her face, let them know she was alright.

I knew that, as time was going on and they knew Ferryn was planning on sticking around, Summer was losing that fear she'd been carrying around that made her hesitant to be anything other than Mom Of The Year toward Ferryn. I'd even overheard her make a few cutting comments about selfishness and the importance of family that Ferryn took in stride because she was starting to understand what had happened to her after the basement ordeal.

Chris had started making her do therapy with one of Hailstorm's former shrinks. Because Chris was convinced—rightly so, we were all beginning to realize—that there was more trauma in Ferryn than we all realized. That she got away with it because she covered her hurt with hard, and that shell was hard to break through. But it was there. The more time any of us spent with her, the more we saw it.

The way she struggled with being grabbed, even when it was just one of the little kids.

The way she couldn't make herself go into the laundry room at her parents' house because it was in the basement.

The way she tossed and turned, cried out in her sleep.

It was there. And it was buried under years and years of trying to deny it, or trying to use it to fuel her to complete her missions.

The missions themselves had left damage she wasn't ready to admit to. The way she scrubbed at her skin until it was raw. The way she sat out in the rain for hours on end.

I was secretly glad that Chris had come up with the solution she had. I was sure it would do Ferryn some good not having to do everything on her own, to not have to be completely alone in the world.

I had no doubt she would continue to go on missions, that it would still be important to her. I would have to learn to not let that worry me. Or convince Reign to let me follow her whenever she went on one, so someone would always have her back.

"What?" Ferryn asked, turning back to me with drawn-together brows.

"Nothing. Just trying to picture you here," I said as we stood in the living room of Holden's house.

It was very masculine. All dark woods, dark old leather sofas, no curtains, no pictures on the walls, no carpets or toss pillows on the couches.

There was, however, an insane collection of hand-carved figurines. Scattered across the coffee table, over the mantle, on the windowsills, stacked five-deep on shelves.

"I didn't live here," Ferryn told me, making me turn back from where I had been examining an amazing goldfish carving.

"What do you mean you didn't live here?"

"I have never stepped foot in here before," she told me, running a finger over the shell of a carved turtle.

"You lived with Holden for almost nine years and you were never in this house?"

"We had separate spaces."

"Will you show me where your space is?" I asked, watching as she slipped the turtle into her pocket.

"Yeah."

"We should package them up," I suggested when she looked enviously at an intricately carved sunflower. "If you don't think he is coming back. It would be a crime to leave all this here."

"Maybe," she agreed, torn. She wanted the collection, but wasn't sure if she would be overstepping by taking them. Especially seeing as they had such a distant relationship. "Come on," she said, leading me back outside into the gloomy woods.

It was strange. The area in general they lived in was a bit overcast, a bit moody. But as soon as we got closer to Holden's place, it seemed to get darker, gloomier, the rain spitting even though the main town just a few minutes away didn't have even a hint of rain.

"You lived in a garage?" I asked as Ferryn led me there, plugging in a code, making the door chug up, the sound almost off-putting in such a quiet place.

"I trained in the garage. I lived in a room behind it," she clarified.

And, sure enough, we stepped into a gym/ training center. Still fully loaded despite Holden's absence.

"Training facility, obviously. I can't tell you how much blood I have lost here. Or how many bones I broke," she said, eyes a little far away, lost in those memories. "My room is back here," she said, and I chose not to mention that she said it in the present tense.

With that, she opened the door.

I tried not to judge people on the conditions they lived in. Sometimes, it was all they knew. Sometimes, it was all they could have. And no one deserved to feel shame about that.

But this?

This was fucking depressing.

Because she'd been raised with so much more. Because she could have so much more.

Then again, most people could. More than a mattress on the ground and a toilet and sink combination.

She'd spent nearly nine years in this room. With no creature comforts.

Christ, there wasn't even air or a way to get heat. She must have sweated and froze every summer and winter.

"What's that?" I asked as she moved inward, going over toward a moving box in the corner.

"I have no idea. It's not mine," she said, going over to it, ripping the clear packing tape off the seam, pulling the flaps open.

"What is it?" I asked as she sifted through what almost seemed to be paperwork.

"He left me the house," she said, voice far away, disbelieving.

"He left you this whole property?"

"I... ah... yeah."

"Where did he go?"

"He didn't say. He just has all the paperwork here. And a note to 'sign this shit.'"

"You alright?" I asked when she just continued to kneel there.

"I... I guess I always thought I would see him again."

"Maybe you will, Ace. You have the powers of Hailstorm behind you now. And I am convinced that there isn't a fucking thing in this world that Chris can't figure out if she sets her mind to it."

"That's true," she agreed. "But I don't think he wants to be found."

"Pretty sure he didn't want to be found the first time either. You still found him. And I'm thinking that if he left all of this to you, that he gave a shit about you. Even if you had a distant sort of relationship."

"Yeah," she agreed, taking a few deep breaths. She gained her feet a few moments later, looking around. "I can't live here," she declared, making the tension I hadn't been aware of leave my jaw.

"No?"

"No. But... I... I can't get rid of it either. There is too much of me here."

"I get that, babe. You know... we know a lot of fucking people. I'm sure some of them would like a little woodsy retreat. At least it won't be empty all the time then. And we can come up here too."

"That's true," she agreed, nodding. "I want to take all the carvings out, though. I know they will probably be too much for the apartment, but maybe we can disperse them out over the holidays. I think Aunt Rey will kill for those cockatoo and macaw ones."

"We can load them up with us. If we have to, we can stick them in a storage unit until we find homes for them. And take all this paperwork. I don't think you have to worry about anyone robbing the place. If you didn't know it was here, you wouldn't be able to find it. But just in case, y'know, you get a roof leak or some shit, you want to make sure you have all the stuff you care about out of here since you wouldn't know."

"Sounds like a good plan," she agreed, hauling the box up, leading me out of the room, out of the garage, out into the moody woods.

"Are you going to miss it here?"

"I don't know," she admitted. "I spent a lot of time here. And while I wasn't miserable, I can't say there were particularly happy times either. And, God, I still don't feel like I have dried out from the constant wetness here. Plus, I used to have to bathe with a garden hose. I don't think I will miss that."

"Hot showers aren't overrated," I agreed. "And pretty soon, we will be in a place that doesn't have gray water."

"And an actual bed," she agreed, swooning a bit at the idea since we'd spent the last few weeks on the couch and floor.

"We'll have to break that in," I added, watching as she shot me a smoldering look over her shoulder.

"I was thinking we have a whole new house we have to break in," She told me, jerking her chin toward it.

Yeah, we didn't waste any time getting to that.

Ferryn - Six weeks later

It felt strange to have a place in the world.

It shouldn't have, of course. I had grown up with a place, with a family home, with a bedroom to call my own.

But I had lived in a room off of a garage for so long. And then had come home to crash in an apartment that wasn't mine either.

It was a small thing, a thing most people had managed to do by the time they got to my age. But for me, it was monumental. To move into my first ever apartment.

It was humbling, too, to watch my entire family show up in force, even Fallon—though he scowled the whole time—helping us haul furniture up the stairs, slapping paint on the walls, hanging shelves, putting together complicated Swedish furniture, bringing dishes to fill our refrigerator.

"What's this?" I asked when my Aunt Rey moved inside, carrying a box that was not one of ours. "We said no gifts," I added. Mostly because I wanted to take our time in picking things out, not just filling the space quickly with characterless items just so everyone could contribute an item.

"Prepare yourself," Aunt Lou declared, shaking her head. "Rey has a habit of providing something living and breathing and requiring cleaning up after as house warming presents."

"A house isn't a home without an animal to share it with," Rey insisted. "I also brought some homemade first aid essentials and cold and flu teas."

"Also?" Vance repeated, looking bemused as he tried to glance in the box.

"We can't have dogs here, Aunt Rey," I reminded her, even if I had been a little bitter about that fact. I hadn't been dog crazy per se, but spending time with all the four-legged companions in my family had definitely given me a little bit of puppy fever.

"I know. I think that is a crime but I'm not breaking any rules," she insisted, putting the box down on the coffee table, pulling it open, producing a wheeking, squiggling, cowlick-haired guinea pig. "Don't worry!" She rushed to say, eyes wide. "I brought two."

"I, ah, okay?" I said, brows furrowed.

"You can't have a single guinea pig. It's cruel. They actually forbid it in certain countries. They need to be with a buddy. So, this is an Abyssinian, and this little love muffin is a Teddy Bear," she declared, reaching for the second one as the first one chewed at the edge of her hair. "They're a relatively low maintenance pet but they have loads of personality. If you can't have a dog to run up with a wiggly butt to greet you when you come home, at least you can have them squeaking when they hear you come in. Reeve is going to be here in a couple minutes with everything you will need to set them up. As soon as my garden gets going, I will drop by to give you some fresh greens for them too," she added as I reached for the cow-licked one, pulling it to my chest, rubbing its butt with my other hand, feeling it purr and shiver at the touch.

"Got any names picked out?" Vance asked, reaching for the other one, and I was pretty sure I had never seen something quite as heartwarming as a big, strong, intimidating gun-running biker gently holding a tiny little rodent like it was something precious.

He would make a great dad someday.

I honestly hadn't given children a thought since I was pretty much still one myself. My life since didn't allow me to be anything even vaguely resembling motherly. I had been worried about coming back and trying to connect with all the club kids. I didn't know if I had the softness and silliness kids needed to like being around you.

As it turned out, having really cools cars and a boyish haircut was interesting enough for them. Plus, no one could climb a tree like I could, and they were all-too-happy to learn that particular skill even if their parents would maybe have preferred I didn't show them how to scale things they could easily fall out of and break things.

Vance, though, kids flocked to him. His niece especially. Ollie thought he was who made the sun rise in the morning. And he lit up whenever she was around.

We hadn't had the kid conversation. And things were new. We were new. There was time.

But seeing him coo over the tailless rat with the cute squeak, yeah, it was doing weird little squeezy things to my ovaries.

"Think they'll be good practice," Vance said much later that night after we configured and then reconfigured their 'cage,' which was really just a guinea pig maze that stretched half of our living room full of playhouses, with things to climb on, places to do their business, and food. A lot of food stations. Guinea pigs might not have actually been related to pigs, but they sure ate like them.

"For what?" I asked, holding out a romaine leaf to them.

"Raising something," he said. A casual toss out, but there was a little tension behind the words, like he was uncomfortable bringing up, but wanted to regardless.

"I think I might like raising things. I mean, you know, later in life."

"Yeah?"

"I think Ollie would like some cousins," I added, reaching down to rub a butt, getting the purr I was looking for, smiling.

"I'm pretty sure Holden would resent you naming something after him that purrs when you rub its butt."

"Hey, maybe Holden purrs when you rub his butt too. You don't know his life," I shot back, making a chuckle more through him.

"You sure you want to let Olive name the other one? She's heavy into *Doctor Who* right now. She is probably going to give it some pretentious British name like Basil or Digby, or Aldrich."

"I'm trying to gain her favor back. I really lost some serious points when I told her I haven't seen a single superhero movie."

"She looked at you like you'd sprouted another head when you asked what Shazam! was."

"Kind of hard to tell a little kid you've been living in the woods without electricity for longer than she's been alive."

"True. But I think you're gonna win her over when you sub as her karate teacher next month," he told me.

I was still not sure how I had gotten roped into that one. A bunch of my aunts were talking about how the current sensei was taking an early maternity leave. And not five minutes later, I was somehow signed up for the task of teaching a group of six-and-seven-year-olds how to defend themselves.

"I think it makes sense with your mission in life, "Chris said when I had told her about the whole situation. "You want to make sure girls don't end up in basements like we were. What better way to do that than to teach little girls how to defend themselves, how to stand up to anyone who might push them around?

Really, I couldn't argue with that.

And I needed a paying job.

Sure, there was still the potential to do my mission, to take out bad guys, and to have those expenses covered, but I wasn't living in the woods off the good graces of someone else. I needed to have an income. I needed to pull my weight in the world.

Vance was perfectly comfortable covering things. He'd been infinitely clear about that. And I had been just as clear about not having been raised to be dependent on anyone.

No, my mom didn't work in the traditional sense. But that was after she met my father. That was because it was a decision based on the fact that she had babies to raise and he made more than enough for the two of them.

I knew Vance made good money. All the guys at the club did. But we were new still. And bearing the financial weight of the entire cost of living could easily weigh on someone.

So I was going to teach self-defense to little girls. And I maybe bought myself a new car and half of the rent thanks to the stack of fake money Finch had dropped at my door.

Sure, I was almost positive he did so not out of genuine affection for me, but in some half-assed effort to get on my good side so I would bring Chris around more, but whatever the reason, it was a good sum of fake money that I washed to make real, and then used to start this new life.

It was strange and scary and unfamiliar, but also exciting and fun and comforting. To have a life again. To have family and friends and the opportunity to do things again.

Catch up on superhero movies.

Buy new clothes.

Go out to eat.

Make a dent on the giant pile of books my Aunt Reese had been building for me over the years anytime she came across something she thought was amazing.

Raising guinea pigs.

Decorating an apartment.

Teaching classes.

And building solid foundations with Vance, the guy who had been my dream before my life veered off its original course.

He was still my dream.

Except I actually got to have him now.

It was every bit as perfect as I had imagined.

More.

"Alright," Vance said, hopping up, back in decorating mode. "So, which ones of these are going on the shelves in here?" he asked, pulling some of Holden's carvings out of a box.

Seeing him turn that first little wooden bear around in his hand gave me the strangest sense of rightness.

My past and my present, all in one place.

Yeah, I could really get used to this.

Vance - 6 months later

A somewhat childish part of me hoped this day wouldn't come.

The rational part of me, of course, knew that it would. There was no way around it.

Ferryn was Ferryn after all.

And she hadn't dedicated nearly nine years of her life to something just to toss it to the side when it became a lot less convenient.

There had been jobs since Ferryn had settled in Navesink Bank with me in a more permanent way. But Chris had set it up so that the new team members took care of it. She claimed that she did that so they could get their feet wet, so they could get the thrill of doing some good in the world. I suspected, though, that Chris was trying to give Ferryn a little time to put down roots.

Sure, she had initially given Ferryn a hard time about giving up the mission now that she was home, but I think some time with her therapists, her mom, her aunts, had softened her to Ferryn's very unique situation.

Chris had, after all, been afforded every bit of help that money and love could buy her. She'd been nurtured and guided. She'd been allowed to heal in her own time.

Ferryn needed a chance to do that as well.

And Chris, someone who seemed to value rationality almost above all else, had been persuaded to understand that, had jumped on the bandwagon to help Ferryn readjust to normal life.

So she kept her away from the missions for as long as possible.

But not even her stubborn ass cousin could keep Ferryn on the bench forever.

The flu had torn through her karate class, making work no longer an obstacle to overcome.

So she was slipping into an all-black outfit, sticking a knife into her boot, tucking her karambit into her pocket, a hard shell came down over her body, blanking out her eyes.

"Ferryn, come on," I reasoned, trying not to be too pushy, knowing that was a surefire way to make her freeze up, freeze you out.

"You're not changing my mind. I want to do this alone."

Pointing out that she wouldn't be alone, that her team would be there, was definitely not the route I needed to take right then.

"I was helpful last time."

"You just want to have affirmation-of-life sex afterward," she told me, a little bit of light teasing in her eyes once again.

"I won't lie, that is a major perk," I agreed.

"You told me you won't get in the way of me doing this for as long as I still wanted to do it."

"I know," I agreed, nodding, maybe selfishly wishing the me who said that had just shut his fucking mouth.

"It is literally three hours from here. I will be home right after you finish your shift at the clubhouse."

I still suspected that she had asked Chris to schedule the mission for the day Colson had asked to switch shifts with me so he could go to Jelly's dance recital, knowing I would never back out on him when he needed me to be here.

That said, in a pinch, I would con someone else into taking my shift.

"I want to be there to have your back."

"And I really appreciate that. You have no idea how much I used to dream of knowing you would want to be there for me. But I need you to understand that I can take care of myself too."

"Seeing as you whipped my fucking ass in class last week," I started, referencing the time she decided it would be fun to teach her girls self-defensive moves by practicing them on me, "I think we have established that I know you can handle yourself, Ace."

"Is your ego feeling a little better about that?" she asked, giving me a smirk in the mirror.

"Not a bit," I admitted. "It is hard to get over a class full of eight-year-olds laughing at you. That shit sticks with you."

She smiled at that, but it slipped quickly away as she stared at her own eyes in the mirror for a long time before her gaze found mine again. "Would it help you if I told you that this is going to be my last mission for a while? Maybe forever?"

"You're serious?" I asked, brows furrowing.

"I'm serious," she agreed with a nod.

"It won't change how anxious I am about this particular mission," I admitted. "But I might be able to deal with it better if I know it is the end for you."

"So you will stop arguing with me and let me go?"

"I, ah, yeah, I guess I can do that."

"Okay good. I'll be back around eleven. Have Chinese here. And some electrolyte drinks for you. You're going to need them."

My lips curved up at that. "I can do that."

"Okay. Good. I will see you later," she said, pressing a quick kiss to my lips before rushing out like she was worried I might change my mind and try to stop her.

I still worried.

Even knowing she had a team of five with her.

And there were only four targets.

I couldn't focus on my rounds at the clubhouse. We could have been invaded by a troop of humanoid raccoons bearing AK-47s and I wouldn't have even noticed.

I went home, fed the guinea pigs their lettuce, ordered Chinese.

Waited.

And waited.

And waited.

It was after two a.m. and I had just started dozing when I felt Ferryn's body climb on top of mine on the couch.

She'd stopped somewhere to shower, to change. Her short hair was still wet, and she was dressed in a white tee and gray yoga pants instead of the all-black she'd left home in.

My gaze shot all over her, looking for any injuries, but finding nothing. Not even a light bruise.

"I took a pregnancy test four days ago," she declared suddenly, making me jerk back at the information.

"You..." I started, blinking rapidly a few times, trying to make some thoughts make sense. "Are you..." I tried again.

"No," she said, shaking her head, giving me a small smile that didn't quite reach her eyes. "I just thought I was. We haven't exactly been careful lately," she added, making me think of the shower sex the week before and the training room floor sex a few days before that. We'd definitely gotten lax in the protection department.

"Are you upset about that?" I asked.

"No. And yes, I guess. I mean... when I thought I might be, I guess I got a little excited about it. And when it turned out I wasn't, there was maybe a little disappointment."

"Okay," I said, putting my hands on her hips, waiting, knowing there was more to this.

"And I just... my first thought when I was thinking I might be was that I needed to be done. I needed to retire. That there were other ways of putting good back into the world other than killing bad guys. Like raising good men of our own or strong women. You know, whichever. And I just... all a sudden, all the rage was gone. It's always been there. It's been more buried since I came back to Navesink Bank. But it was still there. I always felt it. But at the idea of starting a family, it was gone. Just completely. So I knew I was done. Even though I'm not pregnant."

"Tell you what," I said, reaching into the nightstand. "I've been waiting for the right time for this. And I don't think it could get better than this," I said, pulling out the box, flipping open the lid. "Thinking maybe we should do it in the proper order. First, I marry you. Then we have those boys. Or those girls. Whichever," I added, giving her words back to her as her gaze went to the ring. "What's the matter? Too soon?" I asked, feeling my gut twist at the strange look in her eyes.

"No. No. Not too soon at all. I... I mean... you know I have wanted this since I was a kid still. I just... this ring looks so familiar and I don't know why."

"I maybe had Iggy try to gauge your taste in rings over the last few weeks. Maybe that's why."

"Maybe," she agreed, but didn't sound convinced. But, realizing this wasn't the moment for that, she shook her head, knocking those thoughts free. "Anyway. Back to your proposal," she said, giving me a wobbly smile.

"Right. Well... marry me, Ace."

"One condition," she said as I slipped the ring out of the box.

"What's that?"

Her lips pressed together for a long second before she blurted it out. "You write our wedding song."

Seeing as I had been full of music since she walked back into my life, I didn't think that would be a problem.

"I think I can manage that," I agreed, sliding the ring onto her finger. "Love you, Ace."

"I love you too. In fact, I've loved you longer," she declared with a nod of her head.

"Not everything is a competition, Ace."

"Ah, yeah it is," she countered, rolling her eyes. "You're just saying that because you're clearly losing."

"Dunno. I got the girl. I think I am winning in this situation."

And I so was.

She might have loved me the longest.

But I was going to dedicate my life to loving her the hardest.

Vance - 1 year later

I'd had Chris working on a secret project for me for months. A little surprise for Ferryn for her one year homecoming anniversary.

It had taken longer than either of us had anticipated. When I'd told Chris my idea, she'd shrugged her shoulders and said to give her a week or two. Which was great. It gave me a few months to work on it.

As it turned out, I only had three weeks to make it work after Chris had finally gotten me the information I needed.

I'd needed to include pretty much everyone in our lives on the secret since I had needed to leave town for a few days. We'd told her I had to go on a drop. Which meant a few of her uncles had to get lost for a few days as well since Reign would never send me alone on a job.

Even when I had left, I wasn't sure I had accomplished my goal.

Until the middle of the dinner party when the door opened.

And the surprised walked in.

Holden.

See, Ferryn would never outwardly say she missed the man, that she was worried about him, that she wanted to know what he was up to. But every time we went to his old place, when someone else said they were heading there for a little get away, every time she would dust all the wooden carved figures, she would get this faraway look in her eyes that stayed there sometimes for hours.

I wanted to fix that.

He'd been a tough man to track down, settling deep in the mountains of Vermont, existing without most basic necessities because he didn't want to be on the map.

How Chris eventually even found him was completely beyond me. And how I had convinced him to come was an even bigger mystery. When I'd left his place, he'd been giving me a steely stare, one that said he didn't give a shit about me or my surprise to my woman. Even if that woman was a girl he'd helped raise in a way.

Hell, I was pretty sure I was just as surprised as Ferryn when he dwarfed that entire doorway, when he looked around the room, spotting Ferryn sitting on the back of the couch, talking to one of her cousins.

"Kid."

Really, he hadn't even yelled, but his voice was the sort that boomed, that made all conversations around him grind to a halt.

Ferryn's lips fell open, her eyes went wide.

I didn't know what to expect when she turned finally to face her mentor.

I understood their relationship to be an odd one. No personal connections. She didn't know his life story. He didn't know much of hers. They didn't seem to have warm and fuzzies toward each other.

So when she hopped off that couch and made her way to Holden, we all sort of tensed.

When she got in front of him and threw her arms around him, *he* fucking tensed. His arms never went around her, clearly even more damaged than Ferryn had been when she'd returned to us a year ago, being away from his own warm and soft life for much longer than she had been away from hers. But one arm raised and awkwardly patted her back.

"That's enough of that," he rumbled out, making her pull back, giving him a smile that he seemed confused by.

"What... how..." she started, not sure which question she wanted to ask first.

"You got a persistent fuckin' cousin. And a dedicated fuckin' man," Holden told her, making her look toward Chris, then me, eyes a little dumbfounded.

"I, ah, yeah," she agreed, giving him a wobbly smile.

"You deserve 'em. Heard you're gettin' married," Holden said, gaze moving to her hand.

"Yeah. I mean... we don't have a date or anything yet. But yeah. Eventually."

To that, he made a grunting noise, reaching into his back pocket, producing a box, handing it to her.

"Wedding present," he said, shifting his feet, clearly uncomfortable with the large company gathered around, gawking at him. "Your people know where to find me if you need me," he added, already starting to make his exit. "You look happy," he said, turning back to Ferryn.

"I, ah, yeah. I am."

"Good," he said, giving her a firm nod. "That's good."

With that, he was gone.

She didn't try to go after him, get him to stay. She knew he needed to go. And she respected him too much to try to convince him otherwise.

"I can't believe he came," she said, coming over toward me, cradling the box like a bird with a broken wing. And, well, that was a perfect analogy for Holden, wasn't it?

"Honestly, me either," I agreed. "He might now know how to show it, Ace, but he loves you."

"I guess he does," she admitted, giving me a sad smile. "I love him too, but I don't think he would be okay with me saying that."

"He knows," I assured her, giving her a squeeze. "Are you going to wait to open that?" I asked as she ran her finger over the top of the box.

"Oh, please," Summer said, rolling her eyes, and we shared a smile because we both know Ferryn had absolutely no patience and was known for desperately trying to find presents she knew you'd gotten her.

Ignoring us, Ferryn clawed at the box, tossing the top to the floor along with the little sheet of tissue paper.

"What is it?" I asked when her eyes went soft, almost swimmy. She still wasn't much of a crier, but she got misty when she was feeling really emotional. Like now.

"Two doves," she said, holding up the intricately carved figurines.

"Doves are a symbol of love and fidelity," Lo declared, being the expert on all things love related. "They mate for life," she added.

That was fitting.

Since she was going to be mine for life.

If I ever got her to agree on a fucking date.

Ferryn - 1.5 years later

This was the place.

This was the place from the dream.

When I walked into the hall, nothing had clicked. It was just as nice as the fifteen other halls—yes, literally—my mom and aunts had dragged Vance and me to thus far. And we were quite a sight, me the upcoming bride and groom who seemed wholly uninterested in the giant fairytale extravaganza my twenty or something aunts were determined to give us.

It had a sort of rustic feel that I knew Vance was loving—reclaimed wooden floors, mismatched wooden chairs, high, beamed ceilings, understated shiplap on the walls—and I liked that there were a ton of windows so that it wouldn't feel too crowded with all our loved ones gathered there. Because there were a lot of them. And no one was going to miss it.

The first wedding of one of the Navesink Bank kids.

It was a big deal.

And Vance had convinced me to let them run with it since I had no head for such things and they were so excited.

We would have happily had a little courthouse ceremony.

But it was nice to see my mother so happy.

Feeling a little dizzy from all the voices in the hall, I decided to take a walk out back since the owner had mentioned it being a nice place for pictures.

It was then that it clicked.

This was the place from my dream.

It was ridiculous to think that, of course.

It was just a fancy garden.

But there was this niggling feeling of having seen it before, despite never having visited.

Sure, there were the irises and peonies and snapdragons and amaranth and zinnias. But those were all common flowers, weren't they? Nothing to feel such a feeling of deja vu about.

I ran my hand over the silky flowers, seeing my hand, my ring, getting that sort of tightening in my belly again, that weird, unshakable feeling.

And then I saw it.

The gilded mirror between two weeping willows.

I didn't really believe in premonitions, in dreams being a window into your future. But there was no way to deny that I had dreamed this place, that I had seen myself in a white dress with Vance behind me in a tux standing in *that* mirror.

"Hey," I said, going back in the doors, voice raised to be heard above all the other people talking. "This is the one," I declared, watching as a few faces deflated, clearly set on other venues, but my mom gave me a warm smile. And Vance, well, Vance looked like the weight of the world had just been lifted off of his shoulders.

"You heard her," my Aunt Lo declared. "This is the one. Now to figure out what to do about this awful alter."

Yes, they could figure that all out.

Me?

I moved back outside, taking a deep breath, smelling the flowers, basking in the warm sun, hearing Vance follow me out, draping an arm around my lower back, curling me into his chest.

I felt it right then.

The deeply rooted certainty in my soul.
Me.
Vance.
Our family.
And happily ever after.

Don't Forget!

Also by Jessica Gadziala

The Savages
Monster
Killer
Savior

Mallick Brothers
For A Good Time, Call
Shane
Ryan
Mark
Eli
Charlie & Helen: Back to the Beginning

Investigators
367 Days
14 Weeks
4 Months

Dark
Dark Mysteries
Dark Secrets
Dark Horse

Professionals
The Fixer
The Ghost
The Messenger
The General
The Babysitter
The Middle Man

Rivers Brothers
Lift You Up

STANDALONES WITHIN NAVESINK BANK:
Vigilante
Grudge Match

OTHER SERIES AND STANDALONES:

Stars Landing
What The Heart Needs
What The Heart Wants
What The Heart Finds
What The Heart Knows
The Stars Landing Deviant
What The Heart Learns

Surrogate
The Sex Surrogate
Dr. Chase Hudson

The Green Series
Into the Green
Escape from the Green

DEBT
Dissent
Stuffed: A Thanksgiving Romance
Unwrapped
Peace, Love, & Macarons
A Navesink Bank Christmas
Don't Come
Fix It Up
N.Y.E.
faire l'amour

Revenge
There Better Be Pie

About the Author

Jessica Gadziala is a full-time writer, parrot enthusiast, and coffee drinker from New Jersey. She enjoys short rides to the book store, sad songs, and cold weather.

She is very active on Goodreads, Facebook, as well as her personal groups on those sites. Join in. She's friendly.

Stalk Her!

Connect with Jessica:

Facebook: https://www.facebook.com/JessicaGadziala/
Facebook Group:
https://www.facebook.com/groups/314540025563403/

Goodreads:
https://www.goodreads.com/author/show/13800950.Jessica_Gadziala
Goodreads Group:
https://www.goodreads.com/group/show/177944-jessica-gadziala-books-and-bullsh

Twitter: @JessicaGadziala

JessicaGadziala.com

<3/ Jessica

<<<<>>>>